HE OFFER

STAN PICKERING MEETS THE WORLD

ARTHUR L. FORD

To

Penny, Peg, Jean

Meegan, Lauren, Ryan, Michael, Aaron, Samantha

Author's Note

Travelogues are a drag. And so I decided not to write one. I did want, however, for my children and grandchildren to know something of what my travels were like, or more accurately, what our travels were like, since Mary Ellen went along on many of them, most of them in fact. And so I decided to write a novel and to make the places we had visited the characters of the book. The protagonist — not me — is an excuse to introduce my characters, these places, to my readers. Most of the events here actually happened to me, or to us, but not all of them. Some I just invented in order to more fully display some amazing places. I leave it to the reader to determine what really happened and what did not. What is the real truth of life, and what is the truer truth of fiction? At any rate, this is my gift to my children and my grandchildren and to anyone else who reads these words.

I grew up in Columbia, Pennsylvania, just a few houses from the Lincoln Highway, the original Route 30 that crossed the continent before the interstate system was developed. One of my most satisfying memories is sitting on a large rock by the side of that road and watching the cars and trucks go by, noting which ones were out of state, and thinking some day I'm going to take this road, all the way to California, maybe even beyond. I did that.

But as I did that I also taught at Lebanon Valley College and traveled. At first in the early 70's I traveled to England on a sabbatical with Mary Ellen and our three children, living in Cambridge for a year. Then as the children went off to college and the rest of their lives, we lived for a year each in Damascus, Syria, and in Nanjing, China, where I taught as a Fulbright lecturer. That was in the 80's. Then as my career began to wind down in the 90's, I had the good fortune of working with two LVC men, President John Synodinos and Dean Bill McGill, who understood the importance of international experiences for our undergraduates. They allowed me, even encouraged me, to travel the world recruiting international students and setting up study abroad centers. Mary Ellen often went along, enjoying the travel as much as I did. I remember waking up in Penang, Malaysia one morning, stepping out onto my balcony eighteen floors above the Straits of Penang, and thinking, "They actually pay me to be here." What a deal!

And then, with the arc of a good piece of fiction, Mary Ellen and I returned to England, this time London in the fall of 2000, for a semester as teacher and companion to twenty-one Lebanon Valley College students, who were themselves just beginning to experience the joys of living in a different culture, English but still different. We told them then they will never be the same. We had earned the right to tell them that.

This book then is a fictionalized autobiography of sorts, a novel of travel. I hope you enjoy the trip.

PART ONE OHIO

CHAPTER ONE

Now the offer. Out of the blue. Why can't life be simple, the way it has always been?

What Stan knows about life he has learned from the books he has read and taught. He learned about heroism from <u>The Iliad</u>. He learned about living from <u>Walden</u>. He learned about friendship from <u>Huckleberry Finn</u>. He learned about love from <u>Pride and Prejudice</u>. What else is there to know? And he learned that life could be as simple as books. Books, at least the ones he assigns, have a beginning, a middle, and an end, as they should, as Aristotle had said of Greek tragedies. Stan never could understand those books written after 1950, those books with no coherent form, with no suitable ending, leaving the reader with a confusing and even infuriating lack of resolution.

Stan often said, to himself, that the only thing he is good at is his teaching. He's not flashy like some of his colleagues, the ones that always get the teacher of the year award, those popularity contests that Stan dismisses, and he never published much, just enough to get tenure early on. But he can teach. He knows he has a knack for organizing classes, with a beginning, a middle, and an ending . His students appreciate the clarity of that organization and even the predictability of it all. Stan also has just enough enthusiasm to bring his students along with him as they explore the literature of various lands, from England to the Middle East to the Far East, and although he can get himself and his students caught up in Jane Austen or the Sufi poets or Li Po, he never actually goes to those countries. He never goes anywhere. He agrees with his hero, Thoreau, who said he had traveled much in Concord, and that's good enough for him, living and working quietly in Carlow, Ohio, along the banks of the Ohio River. If he wants exoticism, he goes to Cleveland. His life is settled, and he enjoys it, at least until recently, and now as he's about to leave the college, he realizes even more how much he has enjoyed being there. Then the offer. Everything is too complicated.

Stan looks younger than his fifty-five years, perhaps ten years younger. His sandy hair is thin but in no real danger of falling out completely, and he does work out occasionally and walks almost everywhere. He has to admit, however, that his trimness is probably the result of a genetic inheritance. He had barely

known his father — he had left when Stan was five years old — but he remembers
him as slender. He never saw him again. His mother had been fit right up until
her death when Stan was sixteen. Most of the women at the college think Stan
is simply skinny. All he needs, they insist, is a good meal several times a week,
perhaps prepared by a wife. They don't know that Stan is a good cook, or at
least a conscientious one, one who buys most of his groceries at the health food
store in Bering, the county seat about twenty miles up Bering Road. The women
in fact don't know anything at all about Stan. Except perhaps one woman, and
that only recently.

The past year had been difficult for Stan. It began when the college hired
a new chair of the English Department. Stan knew he was possibly in line for
the position, but he also knew he wouldn't get it; in fact, he didn't want the
headaches and uncertainties that came with the position. The academic dean,
Sydney Deane, (Stan as others was amused by having a colleague by the name of
Dean Deane.) was hired to upgrade the faculty, which meant they would have
to publish more. Dean Deane (Most people simply called him Sydney — never
Sid.) decided early on that the English Department needed a high-powered
outsider as chair, someone with a publication record, quantity at least, quality
if possible, and so he conducted an outside search. After the usual winnowing
through hundreds of applications by the search committee, which Stan had not
been invited to serve on, they narrowed the search to five candidates, and finally
hired one. Dr. Priscilla Kinsella, or Dr. Kinsella as she preferred to be called,
was a Queer Studies specialist, and quite beautiful Stan thought, although he
was not able to determine her sexual orientation. In fact, he decided shortly
after her arrival that he didn't care about her sexual orientation. Dr. Kinsella had
several books to her credit and numerous articles and reviews. As is usual with
new chairs, one of her first acts upon arriving on campus was to meet individu-
ally and in-depth with each member of the seven member department.

"I'm so glad to have this chance to discuss the department and its future
with you, Dr. Pickering," she said.

Stan asked that he be called Stan. She said, "Certainly, Dr. Pickering."

She then asked about his background (B.A. Carlow, Ph.D. Nebraska), his
current interests (the novels of Chinua Achebe and the stories of Lu Xun). His
plans for the future (more reading in Chinese fiction, especially the pre-Cultural
Revolution writers).

"And what theory are you currently pursuing?" she asked. Dr. Kinsella was
sitting upright behind her desk, her reading glasses down her nose, her gaze,
above her glasses, fixed on Stan.

"Theory?" Stan said, "I'm not sure I know what you mean. I teach literature, not theory. We do have a theorist in the department. Have you met Tim Osgood?" He tried unsuccessfully not to squirm.

Dr. Kinsella said she certainly had and had been very impressed with Dr. Osgood, but she wondered what theoretical point of view informed Stan's current teaching of literature. Was he currently a post-colonialist, especially with his interest in African and Asian literature? Stan said no, he didn't come at literature from that particular point of view, although he certainly was aware of the recent upsurge in post-colonialist studies. He neglected to mention that he had no idea what post-colonialist studies entailed.

"Don't you find that approach useful in discussing your sort of fiction with your students?" she asked.

Stan hesitated. "No, well, yes, I suppose so. What do you mean my sort of fiction?"

"You know. The kind of fiction resulting from western colonialist practices. Exploitation. Subjugation. Destruction of sovereign identity. That sort of thing."

Stan was not enlightened. He thought for a moment and then decided to tell as best he could what he actually did in class. "I just concentrate on the text itself. You know, the kind of language used, the metaphors, the ironies."

Dr. Kinsella's face brightened; she leaned forward. "Oh, the New Criticism. You're of the old school. You were probably in grad school about the time that was all the rage."

"Well, I suppose so," Stan said, straightening his tie and sitting up straight, "I focus on a close reading of the text; I try to teach students how to read, as it were." Stan did not know why he added "as it were." He never used phrases like that. Was he becoming a department chair?

"A noble endeavor," Dr. Kinsella said, "and I'm aware of how close reading as a legacy of the New Criticism has been important, especially to the development of much post-modern literary theory, and not just post-structuralism."

"Post-structuralism?" Stan said before he could muster a knowing smile.

"Yes. Derrida. Foucault. All that slippery stuff about language. No one can really know what a text means."

"They can't?" Again Stan let it slip without thinking. He knew this didn't look good, but he couldn't for the life of him understand why. The signs were ominous.

Dr. Kinsella then brought up the subject of publications. She noted Stan's rather meager publication record, a few notes and a number of book reviews for a library journal, and those years ago. "Be that as it may," she said, shuffling some papers on her desk, "it's never too late to get started with serious criticism."

Despite Dr. Kinsella's concerns about Stan's scholarship, or lack thereof, she seemed even more interested in his critical stance vis-à-vis his teaching. She actually said "vis-à-vis" before addressing the issue of how Stan approached a class. "I don't believe the New Criticism alone can provide the theoretical basis for any current serious scholarship," she said, adding in a studiously casual way, "Surely, you must be aware of the importance of locating one's studies in a particular school of criticism, and besides," she remarked snidely, "how can something fifty years old be called new?"

"I don't know," Stan said. And he really didn't know.

"So pick one.

"One?"

"A school of criticism. There are certainly enough of them around these days," she said, laughing to herself and nodding her head knowingly.

Just as Stan was about to collapse in gibberish, he looked at Dr. Kinsella. She's so beautiful, he thought, regardless of her sexual orientation. Priscilla. He once had a student named Priscilla. Also beautiful. Also dark. Also trim. Also intelligent. At least he assumes Dr. Kinsella is intelligent, since he can't understand anything she's saying. This Priscilla, Priscilla Kinsella, does not look directly at him. The other Priscilla did. Too directly perhaps. This Priscilla barely acknowledges his existence. The other Priscilla gazed from the front row. He found both equally disconcerting.

At that moment the English Department secretary knocked on the door and told Dr. Kinsella her next appointment was waiting.

"That must be Dr. Sweeney, our Medievalist," she said. Stan stood, not knowing what to do next. "Nice to chat with you, Dr. Pickering," Dr. Kinsella said, holding out a limp hand. Stan wondered as he left the room how Priscilla had so easily become Dr. Kinsella again.

Stan passed Rodney Sweeney on his way out, but stopped just outside the door and turned back to Dr. Kinsella, "Stan," he said.

"Who?" Dr. Kinsella closed the door.

As the academic year went on, Dr. Kinsella seemed to select two or three department members for criticism, muted and low-keyed but criticism nonetheless. Stan was her favorite. He received constant questions about publication plans, an unusually high number of classroom visitations during which she sat in the back and scribbled notes relentlessly, and telephone calls about committee assignments, visiting lecturers, the department newsletter which Stan edited. Stan considered her actions tantamount to harassment, but he didn't say a word to her or to anyone else. Finally, she called Stan in her office to discuss his salary for the next year.

"I know it's still early," she said, "but it looks as though I'm not going to be able to recommend you for a raise next year. There's just not much to justify it. You seem to do the minimal amount of work here and spend most of your time on your teaching." She admitted that his teaching was acceptable, perhaps even better than that — his student evaluations were in fact excellent — but his professional performance was woeful. "If you could just give a paper at a regional or a state professional meeting, that would help," she said," maybe even at the local library, but there's nothing, nothing at all. I'm telling you this now so you have time to work on your professional development."

Stan took the news badly. He always thought that teaching is what teachers were supposed to do. Maybe the times are just passing me by, he thought. Although he didn't need the raise, he did feel he was being insulted. She's got it all backwards, he said to himself but to no one else.

One day, halfway through the semester Stan was in the library, looking up some things on post-modern literary theory and finding them essentially incomprehensible. He banged his head against the stacks and muttered in frustration, "Goddamit, Goddamit, Goddamit." Normally he did not swear.

From the other side of the stacks he heard a woman say, "Hi there. What's the problem?"

Stan looked around, embarrassed, and then saw, through an opening in the stacks, a woman he recognized as the new librarian. He peered through at her. "I know the feeling," she said. Stan apologized.

"Bad day?" She had the hint of a smile.

"Bad semester." Stan did not have the hint of a smile.

"Anything I can do?"

"No, but thanks. I'll be fine."

"Okay," she said and then added, "By the way I'm Maria. Nice to meet you." She stuck her hand through the stacks to shake Stan's hand and then disappeared before Stan could tell her who he was.

Stan went into the reading room and picked up a copy of the <u>Times</u>. He sat there not reading it, thinking over the mess he was in. She's a witch, he decided, and then told himself that's too simple. Dr. Kinsella is just doing her job, changing the focus of the department from teaching to publications in order to give it a more professional veneer. He realized it's a cheap and quick way to raise the department's stature in the eyes of peers at other, nearby institutions. He also feared that the students might be the losers in all this.

Later that week while working in the library on an upcoming class and wondering how he could fit post-colonialism into his discussion of "The True Story of Ah Q," especially since China was never a colony of the United States, Stan heard a woman's voice behind him ask how he was doing now.

He looked up. "Oh, better, I think." It was Maria and he didn't know what else to say.

"You look better, at least calmer." She laughed lightly.

"Yeah, I suppose so. By the way I'm Stan Pickering. You disappeared before I had a chance to tell you that."

"I know," she said, and Stan didn't know if she were referring to her sudden disappearance or to his name.

Now Stan remembered. He had met Maria and her husband at one of the opening parties of the semester, one of several new additions to the college staff. Maria Delaney. She seemed pleasant, friendly, and then he promptly forgot about her, as he did most people. Normally he would come to the library only occasionally, preferring to work in the familiar surroundings of his office. This semester, however, he was spending a good deal more time in the library, primarily to get away from Dr. Kinsella. His office, even loaded with books, was no longer attractive to him.

Maria sat beside him at the reading table. "Look," she said, "It's none of my business, but if I can help —"

Maria was earnest. Stan was embarrassed. He said no, that's all right. Thanks. It's just a professional thing. Maria said she knows how that goes. Stan wondered how she knew that.

Stan looked at Maria. Her long brown hair reminded him of some of his students back in the late sixties when he had started teaching. One particular student with hair hanging straight to her waist said she ironed it every morning. Maria's hair, not nearly as long, looked like it might have been ironed. She was short and a bit overweight Stan was embarrassed to notice. Middle forties? Her face was easily her most attractive feature. It was open, Stan thought. Her eyes were brown and large, and she tucked her hair behind her ears, constantly it seemed to Stan. (Look – tuck – It's none of my business – tuck – but if I can help – tuck). She also smiled easily. Open, Stan thought, that was it. He liked the openness.

They chatted. Maria said she was still trying to find her way around the college, meeting people. She also said she noticed that not many of the faculty come into the library. Stan admitted that he was here only because he was trying to stay out of a colleague's way. That's too bad, Maria said, adding that she thought people at a small school like this would get along. Stan grunted something and leaned back toward his work. Maria took the hint and stood up. "I guess I should get back to work," she said. "Yeah, me too," Stan said. Maria smiled and excused herself. Stan liked her smile.

Later that day Stan was back in his office. He had just finished a conference with one of his students about a paper she was working on: "Sin and Redemption in Crime and Punishment." It must have been the fifteenth paper on that topic he had received since he had started teaching. The main thing about these papers, he noticed, is that the sin is always much more interesting than the redemption. He made himself a cup of tea and had just squeezed the bag when Tim Osgood, the theorist, stuck his head in the door.

"Your door was open," Tim said. Stan grunted and told him to come in. As he came in, Tim added, "Must have been a female student here." Tim was going somewhere with this, but Stan wasn't quite sure where. He never could follow most of what Tim talked about. "Theory. "Lawsuits," Tim said. Stan continued to stare blankly. "Harassment. Sexual harassment. You know. Keep your door open when you're with female students. The whole ball of wax." Stan caught on, but Tim continued, "You remember the old days when you didn't have to worry about things like that." Stan thought of Priscilla, the other Priscilla. Was that harassment back then? And who was harassing who? Or is it whom? Another kind of theory. Tim confessed to him one time that he really didn't like reading literature. He did, however, like the philosophical challenge of reading about literature. Stan didn't see the difference.

Tim sat down in the only other chair in Stan's small office, the one reserved for students during conferences. Stan offered tea; Tim said thanks, he had just had a cup of coffee in the Student Center.

"I was just wondering how you're doing," he said. "I know that Priscilla has been coming down hard on you."

"You mean Dr. Kinsella," Stan said.

"Yeah, she's pretty pompous, I'll admit, but she's doing some good things for the department. Maybe you should give her a chance."

"A chance for what?" Stan said, "She's pretty much decided there's no place around here for me. I don't want to spend my time writing articles I don't like for people who don't read them."

"I guess that's just part of teaching these days, even at a school like this."

"It has nothing to do with teaching," Stan said, "To me it just gets in the way, takes time away from my students. That's what I always liked about this school. I could spend as much time with my students as I wanted to." Stan didn't add that he really had nothing else to do anyway.

Tim tried to point out how research, the proper kind of research, the kind that's consistent with the subject being taught, can actually enhance the teaching by broadening the students' critical apparatus and giving them a point of view for approaching literature. Critical research and teaching can complement each other.

"Maybe," Stan said, unconvinced. Tim plodded on, pointing out that perhaps Stan didn't really have a choice. It was clear, at least to Tim, that Dr. Kinsella – Priscilla Tim kept calling her – was not going to change her mind, and that she can be adamant on the subject of publications. "Maybe you better work up a couple of articles," Tim said, "It's not too late." Stan wondered why Tim called her Priscilla.

Stan swung his chair around to face Tim directly and asked him if "Priscilla" had sent him to give this warning. Tim insisted that was not the case, that he was just trying to help a friend.

At last, or so it seemed to Stan, Tim said he really had to go and stood up. As he was leaving, he turned around to Stan and said, "But she really is a looker, isn't she?" Stan wondered what theory Tim was working on now.

When Tim had gone, Stan began to think seriously about this trap he was in. He could stay at the school and be miserable or he could leave the school and be miserable. What would he do? What could he do? Maybe he could pick up some part-time work at the community college up in Bering. At a fraction of his current salary. It didn't matter. Thanks to a small inheritance from his grandfather, he had enough money to be secure, just not enough to do much of anything except live where he was now living and perhaps spend a week or two at the Jersey shore each summer. He liked Carlow. He hated the Jersey shore.

CHAPTER TWO

The one bright spot in Stan's life was his developing friendship with Maria. She usually stopped to talk with him at the library, which he was frequenting more and more lately. He wished she weren't married. The story of my life, he thought, and then he realized it was anything but the story of his life.

"Let's have lunch today."

"Huh?" Stan was startled out of a Reader-Response text he had been staring at.

"Lunch. You do eat, don't you?" Maria was standing over him in the library. She tucked her hair behind both ears. Apparently, it had fallen because she was looking down at Stan. "You look like you could use someone to talk to, and besides I'm bored with eating my salad from a Tupperware bowl every lunch time. I want a cheeseburger and maybe even a beer. You know any place nearby that can provide that? I can drive."

Stan was coming out of his numbed Reader-Response state and about to enter a new numbed state. He mumbled something about being hungry too since he could think of nothing else to say.

"Good. So, where can we go to have lunch? Someplace out of town maybe. Any ideas?"

Stan thought and finally remembered a bar out on the Bering Road. Well, just off the road actually. He had never been there but he assumed they served cheeseburgers. And beer. Lots of places serve cheeseburgers but to get a beer you have to go to a bar.

"Well, there is Grady's a few miles up towards Bering," he said.

Maria said that would do. "It would give us a chance to talk," she said.

"About what?" Stan asked, genuinely puzzled.

"I don't know. You just look like you need to talk. You've looked that way for quite a while now, and I thought it might do some good."

"What do you mean? What kind of good?"

Maria laughed, embarrassed. "Look, let's just forget it. Maybe I made a mistake. Misread. You know. I don't suppose —"

"No, no." Stan was not sure what was happening here, but he did want to talk with Maria. "I'm just a little confused. It's this damn literary theory I'm trying to read. I guess I just zone out and forget where I am. It takes me a while to get back."

Maria asked why he was reading something that didn't appeal to him.

As Stan began to explain about the problem with his chair and the new direction the department was taking and how he didn't fit in with that direction, Maria interrupted him. "I think you need a cheeseburger and a beer even more than you need to talk." Stan explained that he was mainly a vegetarian, certainly not a cheeseburger eater. Maria held up her hand and interrupted him. She picked up his coat, gave it to him, and said, "Most cheeseburgers have almost no meat in them anyway. Let's go."

Soon they were sitting at Grady's.

"I'm not usually that forward," Maria said, "It's just that you looked kind of forlorn, and I needed a break from the library — they really talk a lot about books in there, you know."

"Isn't that what librarians do?"

"Not all the time. At least I don't think they should. I'm sure the people there have other interests."

Maria went on to describe what other interests she thought the other librarians had, or should have, while Stan relaxed into his own observations. It's a nice bar, he thought, and then he realized he had stolen the line from Hemingway, one of the few twentieth century American authors he taught. Clean. Maybe. Well-lighted. No, not really. But pleasant. He liked the old dark polished bar, and the cherry paneling, and the few old photos on the walls, pictures of the open pit mines that operated nearby years ago. He even liked the small windows with their dark red curtains. Smudged but nice. Papa's kind of place, he thought and smiled.

Maria stopped talking and asked Stan why he was smiling.

"Oh, sorry," he said.

"No. Really. Did I say something funny? I didn't mean to."

"No. I was just thinking of Papa Hemingway and his favorite bar down in the Keys." Stan had never been there.

"Oh," Maria said, straightening her silverware, "Then you weren't really listening to what I was saying."

Stan sat up straight, straighter, in his chair. "No. Yes. I mean I was listening. I just —

"So, what was I talking about?"

"Well. It was about the library. Something about the library. Librarians?"

Maria interrupted and laughed. "That's okay," she said, "I guess it's true that men are all alike. My husband does the same thing. Wanders off to the sports section or something, and then insists he's been listening." Maria patted Stan on the hand. "That's okay. After all, we did come out here to talk about you and your problems."

Stan raised his beer and said, "And to have a beer."

"And to have a beer." Maria clanked her glass against Stan's and added, "And a cheeseburger."

Stan looked at his cheeseburger and remembered how the bartender had laughed when he had ordered a vegeburger with cheese.

The lunch went well. Maria had a way of getting Stan to open up about Priscilla and supported his contention that a school like Carlow should be driven by teaching.

"As a librarian," she said by way of encouragement, "I think I can say we already have too many books, or at least too many bad books. Not that any books you would write would be bad, it's just that I understand your point about scholarship and how it's irrelevant to – "

Stan interrupted. "It's okay. I appreciate your support. And understanding. You're right. It does help to talk about it. To get it out. I really don't have anyone in the department to talk with anymore."

"Friends?"

"No, not really. I mean there are people I talk to, but not with. Know what I mean?"

Maria nodded. "That's what's so nice about this place, this bar. I feel comfortable here, talking. Maybe it's the place. It's kind of homey. I like it."

Stan nodded. It is kind of homey, he thought.

And so over the next few months Stan and Maria had lunch together at Grady's, once a week, and Stan looked forward to it. And so, gradually but quickly, Maria was becoming important to him. Maria listened to him, encouraged him, got him through what he now realized was a depression, mild but still a depression. One time toward the end of the second semester, he told her he had decided to make this his last semester at Carlow. She seemed surprised.

"I knew you weren't happy, but I thought we had worked all that out. I mean you had worked it out." Maria looked at Stan, who was looking down at his hands resting on his knees, palms down. "What are you going to do?" she asked.

Stan said he didn't know, that he might try to get a job at the community college, part-time probably, but that he would probably stay here in Carlow.

"It's just too much," Maria said. "I understand." She then added, "But you must have some other plans. What do you really want to do?"

Stan thought about that for a moment and then folded his napkin neatly and placed it on the table. "I think," he said, looking up at Maria, "I might travel."

"That's wonderful," Maria said, "I know I love to travel."

Stan thought that might be a sign of her interest. They had never talked about themselves, about the two of them, and Stan wasn't sure how she felt about him. She seemed genuinely excited about the travel. He didn't know. He said nothing.

"Stan," Maria said, "What's wrong? Why did you stop?"

Stan turned in his chair, slightly away from her, and adjusted his plate. "Nothing," he said.

"Something's wrong," she said, "I think the travel idea is great. Why did you stop talking about it."

"No, it's okay. Never mind."

"I want to know. Will you do it or not?"

Stan could feel his face begin to heat up. He was afraid to say anything, afraid his voice would quiver. Finally, he said in a small quiet voice, "Would you like to do it?"

Maria sat there puzzled, and then said, "Do it? Travel you mean? Sure. I would travel, if I could, but you know I have this job and – ." She stopped.

Stan said nothing. He just looked at his plate.

Maria sat back in her chair. "Oh, Stan," she said, "I'm sorry. I'm so sorry. I didn't know you were thinking . . . along those lines. I mean, I love my husband. I can't – You're a friend, a good friend. Did I do anything to give you the idea –"

Stan sat up and looked out the window. "No, of course not. Forget it. I was just joking. Well, I don't mean joking, but I wasn't really serious. Just forget it." He began to get up. Maria reached over and held his arm, but he knew he had to leave. "We should be getting back," he said. They drove back to campus in silence. As she got out of the car, Maria turned back to Stan and said, "I'm really sorry. It's my fault. I should have been more . . . I don't know. Something." Stan looked at the steering wheel. "Will you be okay?" she said. Stan nodded.

But he wasn't okay. He knew his feelings about Maria were wrong, but he couldn't do anything about it. He also knew he had to stop seeing her, even for an innocent lunch, which caused his depression to return.

And then the offer came. Out of the blue was the way Stan kept putting it. One day, just a week before exams began, Stan got a phone call in his office. A secretary informed him that she was calling from the law firm of Tenafly and Robey. Lincoln, Nebraska. Mr. Robey would like to talk with him. Please hold. While Stan listened to the canned music, he wondered what this was all about. A lawyer. It can't be good, he thought. Maybe an ex-student was suing him. For a low grade, probably. Harassment? But Nebraska. He didn't remember ever having had a student from Nebraska. Oh well, he would soon be out of Carlow, and at that moment he was even happier about his decision to leave the school.

"Mr. Pickering?" The man on the other end of the line sounded official. "Charles Robey here. Our firm had a client who died just recently. I think you might have known him." Stan did not reply. "Mr. Pickering, you there?" Stan said he was. Robey asked if Stan had ever heard of Andrew Schumer. Stan thought. Andrew Schumer. Andrew Schumer. "That must be Dr. Schumer," he said. "He was my dissertation advisor at Nebraska. You say he died? I'm sorry to hear that. He was a great guy, pretty young then, a bit strange but he helped me a lot with my dissertation. He knew a lot, but he was strange. I remember – ."

Robey interrupted. " Mr. Pickering. Dr. Pickering. You might have thought him strange then, but wait till I tell you what he did." Robey went on to explain that Dr. Schumer never married and had retired a few years ago from teaching. During his years at Nebraska he traveled extensively; in fact, he traveled whenever he wasn't in class, all over the world.

"That's interesting," Stan said, "but what's that got to do with me? I never even saw him again after I left Nebraska. We corresponded for a while and then stopped. He tried to get my dissertation published, but it never worked out. I haven't thought about him in years."

"Well," Robey explained, "I don't know how much he ever thought of you, but he left you an interesting inheritance."

"Inheritance? You mean money? Why would he do that?"

"In a way, money, but in another way not. Damndest thing. I don't ever remember anything like it."

Stan was getting interested, or at least curious. "What? What is it? What did he do?"

"I said he liked to travel. I'll send you a copy of his will, and some other things with it, but for now I can tell you that he wants you to do something for him." Stan asked why him, since he didn't think he was anything special to

Dr. Schumer. "Did you know you were Dr. Schumer's first doctoral student?" Robey asked. Stan said he didn't know that. "Well," Robey continued, "he said you were, so that must be why you got the request."

"You mean bequest?" Stan said.

"No, the proper term is request." Robey went on to explain that Dr. Schumer had arranged for his body to be cremated and that the ashes be forwarded to Stan in a simple wooden box.

"His ashes? What am I supposed to do with his ashes?"

"Scatter them."

"Scatter them? Where?"

"All over."

"All over what"

"The world," Robey said, "all over the world." Stan could not speak. "Dr. Pickering, are you there? Dr. Pickering?"

Stan muttered, "Where in the world —."

Robey said, "Don't worry. I have your itinerary."

"My itinerary?"

"Yes, and money to pay your expenses, including the couple months or so you'll need to take off to do all of this. Dr. Schumer died a wealthy man. It appears he bought lots of IBM stock over the years. He tried to spend it all on his travels, but he just couldn't do it. Lucky for you, I guess. All you need do is go to these places and scatter a few of his ashes there. These were apparently all the places he really liked for whatever reasons."

Stan stood holding the phone, almost at attention. Priscilla stepped into the office. Stan waved her away.

"No need to come out to Nebraska," Robey said. "We'll just send you everything to sign, plus the itinerary, some instructions, and the check. And, of course, the ashes. I'm afraid the check will only cover economy class."

Stan could only utter thank you.

"That's okay, Dr. Pickering. You have a nice day." He hung up.

And that was the offer. Stan stood there and stared at the wall. Dr. Schumer always was strange he said aloud, to no one in particular.

"Dr. Pickering?" It was Priscilla, back in the doorway. "Dr. Pickering." Stan turned and stared at her. Priscilla looked at him, puzzled. "Are you all right?" she asked. He assured her he was. Priscilla went on to explain that she stopped in to see if he had any plans for the future. She was concerned about him, what with his sudden resignation and all. "Do you have any plans?" she asked.

"Oh, yes," Stan said, a smile slowly crossing his face. "Oh, yes."

Stan spent the summer getting his affairs in order, especially his travel plans. Dr. Schumer's instructions included the countries he should visit and the cities, although he didn't specify exactly where his remains should be deposited in each city. In his instructions Dr. Schumer said he expected Stan would know where to deposit the remains of an old English teacher.

Stan decided to wait until classes began at Carlow in September before leaving. He wasn't sure why, but he wanted to see the college open one more time, without him. The summer went by in a blur of anticipation and anxiety. He told no one, not even Maria, of the strange offer. And so in the second week of September Stan Pickering, who never went anywhere, left for England where his first stop was the storied city of Cambridge, the Mecca for any English teacher.

PART TWO ENGLAND

CHAPTER THREE

And so after a dreary flight and an early morning arrival at Heathrow airport, Stan settled into the coach taking him to Cambridge, his first repository, or perhaps depository he thought. Coals to Newcastle. Ashes to Cambridge, Same thing. The one thing that Cambridge doesn't need is more ashes. Stan thought about the great writers moldering in their Cambridge graves. Well, maybe not the really great ones. The really great ones are in Poet's Corner at Westminster. Others, even some of the really great ones, are scattered around England — Wordsworth in Grasmere. Hardy, or at least his heart, at Dorset. Or even beyond England — Byron in Italy, Brooke in Greece. Okay, so Brooke may not have been one of the great ones, but Stan liked him anyway, liked the manliness of his dying during the Great War, liked his sentimentality over Cambridge. All serious critics dismissed him, of course, but Stan liked his simple verse nevertheless. Brooke is buried somewhere on one of the islands. Stan did not know exactly where, but he did know he would have to be there one of these days. To scatter a few more ashes. Dr. Schumer must have loved that island. Stan wondered if he could now call him Andrew. Perhaps the time will come, in the next few months, when he can actually refer to him as Andy, although he knew of no one who had ever called him that back in graduate school, except in derision. Handy Andy. He really was a bit too formal, Stan thought, especially when every other faculty member insisted on being called by his or her first name and insisted on joining students for a joint or two. Born Dr. Andrew Schumer, Stan remembered the joke. Schumer — Andrew — not yet Andy — stayed mostly alone in his office, except when he was off on one of his overseas excursions, gathering more information for his next book. At least that's what Stan thought, and he had no reason now to think otherwise.

Stan let his mind wander and then dozed off as the English countryside, or what's left of it along the outer circular road, the M25, slid by. He woke briefly when the coach stopped at Luton airport and then again at Stansted airport, but he was exhausted from the overnight flight — he did not sleep at all on the plane — and from the effects of jet lag, something he had never experienced before, and so each time he awoke he slid back into the warm comfort of the coach seat and dozed.

He woke once more as the coach entered the outskirts of Cambridge, past the modern buildings of England's silicon valley, strangely out of place to Stan's imagined view of Cambridge, that medieval village where the second great British university was founded sometime in the 12th century, he thought, maybe later As the coach glided down Trumpington Road and turned onto Pembroke, which mysteriously changed its name to Downing Street, before arriving, finally, at the station parking area next to Christ's Pieces, Stan sensed some of the Cambridge he had expected, although he had yet to see the river Cam or the bridge that gave it its name. He also had not seen any of the famous colleges – King's. St. John's. Trinity. The coach did, however, pass something called Emmanuel College. There's plenty of time for that, he thought.

Stan had made trans-Atlantic arrangements to stay at a bed and breakfast on Jesus Lane. Sounds pretty safe, he thought. Across the street was the wide expanse of Jesus College, Coleridge's old school. It was still late summer and warm when Stan had left Carlow, but here in England it felt like late fall. He pulled his coat from his luggage, took a taxi the short distance to Jesus Lane, and rang the bell at 112. Mrs. Barton answered and immediately invited him in. "Yes," she said, "I've been expecting you. It's very good indeed to meet you. I hope you'll enjoy your stay here in Cambridge. Holiday, is it? I hope the weather holds up for you. Been dreary lately, don't you know, but we're due for a good spell. Can't get any worse, can it? Bring your things in, Luv. I'll show you your room. Toilet and bath just down the hall. All nice and clean."

Stan picked up the one large suitcase he had brought, one that he could pull on rollers behind him, and walked up the three steps onto the first floor, other steps leading down to the basement. Mrs. Barton saw Stan looking down the steps and informed him that he would be having breakfast there the next morning. "Would you like some tea and biscuits," she said, not waiting for a reply, "Dreadful day for September." Stan had thought the weather about right for Ohio – in early March.

Stan's room was small, clean, and tidy, exactly what he had wished for. The single bed had a white quilt on it with each square containing a blue flower of indeterminate species. There was a plain wooden desk and chair, a three-drawer bureau and a narrow closet. Three framed pictures of old Cambridge, Stan guessed, hung on the wall over the bed. As he settled on the bed, expecting to be asleep in no time, Mrs. Barton knocked on the door. Stan went over to the door and opened it slightly. "I hope you can join me for that tea and those biscuits," she said. "Plenty of time to sleep. Come down to the sitting room as soon as you can." She then closed the door before Stan could object.

The sitting room was comfortable with two overstuffed sofas, one tan and the other grey. Stan chose to sit on one of three upholstered chairs, tan, grey, and dull green. In front of one of the sofas, the one against the front wall, the wall facing Jesus College, stood a low table with two cups and a tea pot covered with a flowered tea cosy. Beside the pot was a tin of biscuits.

"Do you take sugar?" she asked.

"Please," Stan said.

"One or two?"

"One, thank you."

"You do take it white, don't you? Not all Americans do. Never could understand that."

"Yes, thank you. White will be fine." Stan assumed, correctly, white meant with cream.

"Okay then, here you go, Luv."

Stan felt at ease here, despite Mrs. Baron's overbearing enthusiasm and slyly prying questions.

"So what brings you to Cambridge?"

"Sort of business," Stan said.

"Sort of business? Now that's an interesting phrase. Does that mean you're sort of selling something?"

"No, I'm not really selling anything."

"Buying?"

"No, not that either. I'm sort of delivering something."

"Anything I would recognize, Mrs. Barton said.

"No, I don't think so," Stan said. "It's a little bit unusual." Stan immediately realized he should not have said that. Now Mrs. Barton would never stop her questions.

"Kind of private," he said.

"Oh," she said, "secrets. I like that. You Americans always have your secrets, don't you know now."

Mrs. Barton then began to tell Stan about an American who had stayed there years ago. Many years ago, she said. She told how he seemed very mysterious, going out late at night and coming back hours later.

"Yes," Stan said, "that would certainly be mysterious." He stirred his tea, the cup poised dangerously on his knee.

"Well," said Mrs. Barton, "it turns out that he was spending his time over at Christ's College, sitting under a mulberry tree there and trying to communicate with John Milton, something about a poem that Mr. Milton had written for a friend who had been drowned at sea. He wrote the poem, Mr. Milton did, sitting under that tree, and this gentleman, this American gentleman, thought he might be able to get more information about the friend who drowned. You know, by being there. Communicating with the dead. Sort of from the horse's mouth, don't you know. Writing a book or something. Don't know how he got over the fence into Christ's College. Wasn't a young man, he wasn't. Don't know if he ever got his information, but doubt it. Must be an easier way. You're not planning something like that, are you?"

Stan assured her his task was much less mysterious and could be done in full daylight. "Well," she said, "I hope so. Never can tell what will happen when you go out in the dead of night."

Tea time over, Stan returned to his room and began to think of where he might deposit Dr. Schumer's ashes. He thought he could probably deposit them almost anywhere in Cambridge University and be safe, but he wanted someplace special, someplace out of the ordinary, maybe something to have to do with Byron. Stan remembered Dr. Schumer talking a lot about Byron but not so much about his poetry. He remembered instead something about Byron keeping a pet bear chained to the fountain in the Great Court of Trinity. Maybe that's the place. Then he remembered Dr. Schumer's story about Byron liking to swim naked in something called Byron's Pool; however, he couldn't remember anything about the pool or even where it's located. He determined to do some research on Byron's Pool the next day, but now it was time for his much-needed sleep. He changed into his pajamas and slipped beneath the quilt.

The next morning Stan had the breakfast part of his bed and breakfast: two eggs, several small sausages, two strips of bacon, hash brown potatoes, half a stewed tomato, and cold buttered toast. He enjoyed sitting in the half basement, the sun streaming through the windows along the top of the wall facing Jesus College. He enjoyed his second cup of coffee, stronger than he was used to but delicious nevertheless. He also enjoyed watching the father and mother at a table back in the corner of the room, sitting with their young boy, perhaps six years old, and a younger daughter. They were English and very concerned with the good behavior of their children, making sure they sit up at the table — no slouching — and making certain they keep their napkins on their laps. When the mother noticed Stan watching them, she smiled. Stan nodded to her and smiled in return. Meanwhile, Mrs. Barton busied herself with duties in the kitchen, stopping by Stan's table once to see if he needed anything.

"No," Stan said, "everything's fine."

"Lovely," she said. "I try to keep the place tidy, but it's not easy ever since my husband left me."

"Oh," Stan said, "I'm sorry to hear that. Some men are thoughtless that way."

"Yes," she said, "but it was an easy passing. Just never woke up. I thank the Lord it was easy. Hope I go that way. Couldn't ask for more, could you?"

"No," Stan said, "I suppose not." Actually Stan had never thought of the nature of his own passing. Or even the inevitability of it. Perhaps it's time, he thought, and then dismissed the idea as excessively morbid. Besides, the sun was shining – in England – something he had been told was unheard of. And he had work to do.

But first he wanted to see Cambridge, the storied land of those few courses in English literature he was forced to teach early in his career. He walked into the bright sunshine and down Jesus Lane, on to Sidney Street and the center of town. My God, he said under his breath, there really is a Lloyd's of London Bank. He crossed the market, already at 8:30 in the morning, bustling with vegetable stalls, fish stands, rows of coats, slacks, sweaters, shirts, blouses, shoes, with fresh meat hanging from hooks, rows and rows of books, CDs, magazines. And people everywhere, doing their shopping for the day, carrying already bulging string bags. He walked through a narrow alley, past G. David's Used Book Store, and promised himself a return visit sometime soon. Then suddenly, almost magically, he was on King's Parade, with King's College before him and the chapel blooming to his right, gleaming white as the sun reflected off its stone surface. Magnificent he thought and promised himself a return visit here as well. His stroll down King's Parade soon turned into a stroll down Trinity Street and then down St. John's Street as Stan discovered the English disconcerting practice of changing street names right in the middle of streets. He then discovered the reason, King's College followed by Trinity College followed by St. John's College.

Stan spent the rest of the morning exploring the shops, nooks and crannies of Cambridge, discovering as generations of Americans before him had, the joys of the smaller colleges – Magdalene where Samuel Pepys's diaries are housed in a library built especially for them; Gonville and Caius, known simply as Caius and pronounced as the anglicized "Keys," with its Gate of Honor through which the graduates go when leaving the college for the ceremonies at the Neo-Classical Senate Building next door; Christ's College with its succession of quads leading to the large garden with its famous mulberry tree, famous now at least to Stan. He walked around the ancient tree, its limbs held up by poles, and thought of Milton as well as the old American scholar who had hoped for some inspiration if not a visitation from the great man himself.

It was only in secluded places like the mulberry tree garden that Stan could escape the hoards of tourists, mostly non-English speaking, that crowd every street in Cambridge, even in September. The scholars had not yet arrived, but their worthy substitutes were still everywhere, and Stan was overwhelmed, coming as he did from a small Ohio town.

After all the walking Stan was beginning again to feel the jet lag setting in and decided to get a quick lunch and then go back to Mrs. Barton's for a rest and a bit of reading. By early evening he had fallen into a deep sleep.

The next day, overcast and threatening, Stan had his breakfast, read for a while and then in late morning, walked back over to the market in order to get his bearings, but on Benet Street he looked into what seemed to be an alley, and saw a pub, The Eagle. It looked old, its brick walls slanted and not quite square. It also looked intriguing, so Stan walked back the alley, into the small courtyard, and into the pub itself. Looking around, and up, he saw a ceiling full of signatures.

"That's the airmen's names," an older gentleman sitting alone at a nearby table said to him.

"What airmen?" Stan asked. The older gentleman – "Call me Graham. I was here then." – told Stan these were signatures signed by American airmen during World War II. According to Graham they were stationed up at the air-base north of Cambridge and came in often for a pint. "Fine men they were too," he said. "They bombed hell out of the Jerries. Some never came back."

Graham also mentioned something about some other young men, Watson and Crick. "Scientists," he said. "They came in all the time for lunch and mumbled to each other over there in the corner. They were always writing on the napkins. Strange pair, but I think they did all right." DNA. Stan knew about them. Graham recommended the Ploughman's for lunch, as well as a "fine bitter." Stan sat with Graham and despite the early hour enjoyed his meal immensely.

That evening, feeling somewhat refreshed after a walk along the Cam toward Trumpington and a rest back in his room, Stan wandered across the street to Jesus College and the large expanse of Jesus Green beyond it. Jesus College was another of the ancient colleges of the university, although nearly 150 years younger than Trinity. Stan found the medieval interior courtyard with its arched walkway intriguing and imagined Coleridge striding along here, verses cramming his brain. He then warned himself against over-sentimentalizing his stay in Cambridge. It's just another working town, he told himself, but he didn't believe it. He then crossed Jesus Green and stood beside the Cam, watching the white swans gliding majestically over its smooth surface. Finally, he found a pub and sat for a long time nursing another pint of good British bitter. He was pleased to discover he liked this quintessentially British brew.

CHAPTER FOUR

The next day Stan felt more like his normal self and decided to track down Byron's Pool, despite the threat of showers. First, he went back to Trinity and asked the porter there if he might know where it is. The porter just shook his head and said nothing like that around here, although Bryon's room is up there in the corner of that building, over there across the Great Court. Stan asked if he could visit it, but the Porter said no, it's off limits because the student using it still has his things there.

"Do you mean it's not a tourist site?" Stan asked.

"No," he said, "why would we do that? It's a perfectly good room for one of the boys, not the best but not the worst either."

Stan looked up at the room and across the court to the fountain where Byron's bear had once been attached. Oh, well, he thought and walked through to the next court where he admired Christopher Wren's perfectly proportioned Neo-Classical library masterpiece, and, beyond that to, once again, the River Cam. Standing with his back to the library he determined somehow to get to the other side of the Cam for a better perspective of the colleges.

After several false starts he finally got to the Backs, the area behind the half dozen or so colleges that line the Cam, by going through Clare College and crossing the bridge into a sunken garden. From this point he could look up at King's College Chapel with its perpendicular style buttresses and large end window. It has to be the most beautiful building I've ever seen, he thought. He determined at once to spend time inside. Rather than going directly to the building's entrance, however, he retraced his steps and arrived at the area behind the chapel where lush lawns cover the several hundred feet to the Cam. As he walked backwards to the river, he kept looking at King's Chapel, receding before him, providing him with changing perspectives, until he arrived at the bank. He turned and saw punters floating slowly on the river. It could be a hundred years ago, he thought.

After a few moments of quiet Stan noticed an old wooden bench up against the high stone wall that separated King's College from Clare. He walked over to it and sat down, not taking his eyes from the building. Tangled vines covered the ancient wall. He knew King's Chapel was hundreds of years old, and he realized that coming to England had given him a new perspective on age. I'm 55, he thought. I'm not old, but I'm not young. I suppose now I'm not even middle-aged any more. How many 110-year-old people do I know? No, I'm neither middle-aged nor old. What am I? It looks like I define myself by what I am not. "I am not old," he said aloud without realizing it.

"What?"

"What?" Stan turned to see a woman sitting at the other end of the bench. She looked at Stan as though she were viewing some strange creature.

"Excuse me," she said, "Were you talking to me?"

"Who? Me?" Stan was disoriented by the sudden appearance of this woman and by the fact that she was clearly an American. Where did she come from, he thought. How did she get here?

"No. Me," she said. "I thought you were talking to me. I thought you were addressing the statement to me."

"What statement?"

"You said something about not being old. I thought you were addressing it to me. Because of my age, you see. I thought you might be trying to insult me. Young people, younger people, do that, you see."

Stan looked at the woman closely, coming out of his confusion. She wore a long black skirt, a loose white blouse, and small, wire-rimmed glasses. She squinted despite the dullness of the day. Her hair, fine, thin, and grey, was pulled back. At first Stan thought she might be just a bit older than he, but when he looked more closely, he could see that she might be in her middle seventies. He could also see how she might take offense.

"Oh, I'm sorry," he said, " Guess I was just talking out loud without realizing it. I do that sometimes."

"Why did you say that?"

"Say what? About not being old?"

"Yes," The woman continued to sit at the end of the bench, her hands in her lap. She turned partway towards Stan. Stan looked away.

"I don't know."

"Then you weren't addressing me."

"No. No. I didn't mean you. You're not old. I meant me. I was talking about me."

"I can tell you something about old," she said, " but I won't. I'll just say you're not, so why worry about it?"

"I don't worry," Stan said. "Not really. It's this place. I guess age is relative." Profound, he thought to himself. The woman was looking ahead, over at the classical Gibbs building that comprised the other half of King's Backs. Stan looked at her, more closely he thought than he had ever looked at anyone her age, even his mother. She would look much younger, he thought, if she dyed her hair. Her skin was still smooth.

"My name's Mary," she said, looking back at Stan.

"My name's John," Stan said, too quickly, immediately embarrassed.

Mary sensed his embarrassment. "Really?"

"No, not really." Stan could feel himself blushing. "It's really Stan."

"Then why did you say your name was John?"

"I don't know. I just thought it would be amusing that we both had these common names. John and Mary. You know."

"Every Tom, Dick, and Mary, huh?"

"Sorry. You got me."

Mary sat up straight and looked away from Stan. "Anyway, I'm seventy-six."

Stan fumbled with his shirt sleeve, pulling it down. "Really? I didn't know. Would never have suspected. I mean I didn't think – "

"Really?"

Stan tried to regain his composure. "Why did you tell me how old you are?" he asked.

Mary turned and looked out at the Cam. "Because I wanted to tell you how old I am."

'Why?"

Mary turned to him. "Because I want to know how old you are"

"Why?"

"Because I want to know what you don't consider old."

"I'm fifty-five."

'Really? I didn't know. Would never have suspected."

Stan interrupted. "Look. I'm sorry. You don't have to get sarcastic." He stood up to leave and turned away.

"Okay. I'm sorry too." She paused and then added, "Why did you say that?"

"It sounded sarcastic, that's all."

"No, not that. Why did you say you weren't old?"

Stan turned back toward her. "Because I'm not."

"No," Mary insisted, "I mean there must be a reason you said it, even if you aren't. You know, old. Why did you say that particular thing at this particular time?" Mary was punctuating each point with a finger pointed at Stan.

Stan thought about it. "Maybe I'm afraid of getting old, even of being old." Stan sat back down.

Mary smiled, slid closer to him, and put her hand on his arm. "Why not let old up to me?"

Stan smiled shyly. "Okay."

"Actually," Mary said, "I'm not concerned about growing old for its own sake. It happens. I'm not even concerned about dying. That happens too. God knows no one will notice. I guess I'm concerned about growing old and being dependent on others. I've been living on social security and a small pension for ten years now. I could soon be a welfare case at a broken-down nursing home soon. Maybe I'll be a bag lady in New York City."

"You sound depressed," Stan said. More profundity.

"No, not really. It's just that I've been teaching in lots of places that don't have retirement benefits, and now I'm beginning to wonder what will happen to me."

"You're a teacher," Stan said and added, "So am I. Was."

"Of course you are. Why else would you be here in these hallowed halls? The only difference is that some of us teachers have generous retirement packages. Some of us don't. I don't."

Stan saw that Mary was sinking deeper into self-absorption. Hoping to change the subject he asked her where she had taught.

Mary said she had taught all over the world. "Name a place without retirement benefits and I've taught there. China. Indonesia. Bolivia." Stan asked her what she's doing in Cambridge. "Visiting the ghosts," she said. "You know. Milton. Byron. Wordsworth. Coleridge. Forster. Brooke. You know, I taught Milton's 'Lycidas' in China. I told them about the mulberry tree over at Christ's. You know about that?"

"Yeah. I know about it. I was there yesterday. So how did they like it?"

"What? The mulberry tree?"

"No. The poem. How did they like 'Lycidas'?"

"I don't know. We never got to the poetry. I was just telling them about Milton. We were studying American literature. I guess there was some influence or something. I don't remember. But they did like the story about the mulberry tree. 'Mulberry' is really hard for a Chinese to say. Did you know that?"

Stan confessed that he did not, and they lapsed into silence. Mary stared again at the Gibbs building. Stan brushed the dust from his shoes with his hand. He thought Mary might leave.

"So you're an English professor," he said. Mary said no, not exactly, more of an itinerant English professor. "I just took jobs wherever I could get them, preferably someplace interesting."

Stan said that he too teaches – taught – English. He said he had just retired and was in Cambridge doing a favor for a friend. His expense, he added. "That's some friend," Mary said, and then asked suddenly, "Are you married?"

Stan said no and then quickly tried to change the subject, saying he admires the poetry of Rupert Brooke and understands that he lived somewhere outside Cambridge.

"Grantchester," Mary said. "Are you gay?" Stan stiffened and said of course not. Mary asked why he said of course not. "It's okay to be gay. I was just curious. Forster was, you know. I don't know about Brooke. Probably not. God, he was handsome. I carried a picture of him all through high school. I visited his grave once on a Greek island. Years ago. I don't remember the name.

Stan said he's going there. "Wonderful place," Mary said, "You'll love it,"

She continued her story. "I was teaching in Athens at the time. An English language center."

"Without retirement benefits?"

"Without retirement benefits." Mary again looked out into the distance, across the Cam and added softly, "It was a great place."

"Athens?"

"No," she said. "The island." And Stan realized that Mary was remembering something special there. Suddenly, Mary turned back to Stan. "I'm not either," she said. "What, gay?" Stan asked. Mary said, "No, married. I've been married. A couple of times. Once to a man I met in Taiwan. He wanted me to take him to America for a green card. That didn't last long. I met the first one in graduate school. He took off as soon as he got his degree." Another pause, and then Mary apologized for boring Stan. He insisted she was not boring him. She asked him to tell her something about his life. Get back at me, she said. Stan said his life was not interesting enough to talk about.

"Go on," Mary insisted. "Tell me about your life. Tell me why you worry that way."

"Worry what way," Stan asked.

"About growing old." Stan didn't answer.

"It's lonely not being married, isn't it?" she said. Stan said he didn't know since he had never been married. Mary said she could answer that. It is lonely. "It's almost worse than being married," she said. Stan looked up and smiled. Mary returned the smile and went on. "So, do you regret it?"

"Not being married?"

"No, not that. Growing old. Not being young any longer. Do you regret that?"

"Not really," Stan said, "It hasn't been much of a life up til now, so there's not much to regret." Mary said nothing, and Stan didn't know what to say next, so he stood. "I'm going inside King's Chapel," he said. "Would you like to come along? We can talk about the architecture. I love that building."

"It is lovely," Mary said, "My favorite."

They walked back along the gravel path to the side entrance of the chapel, marveling at the flying buttresses, delicate despite their enormous responsibility. Stan explained that they hold up the whole thing. Mary said she knew that. Oh, yes, Stan said.

"But it is remarkable, isn't it?" Mary said.

"What's remarkable," Stan said, "is that it costs two pounds to enter. Think of that. Two pounds to go into a church. Mary replied that it's not a church, it's King's Chapel. Stan silently agreed.

Once inside and past the booth selling post cards, booklets and other souvenirs, Stan and Mary stood at the top of the nave and looked down the aisle for what seemed like miles, broken only by the sixteenth century wooden screen. A few people stood before the Rubens "Adoration of the Magi" at the other end of the nave; others sat in some of the pews, silent, some praying. As they walked down the aisle, saying nothing to each other, Stan looked up at the incredibly delicate fan vaulting, which covered the entire ceiling. Mary pointed out that the vaulting is so delicate that a foot would go through it if stepped on. Stan asked why it doesn't collapse. Mary said simply, architectural genius. That seemed enough for both of them.

After admiring the precise tracery and various figures on the wooden screen, they continued past the stalls where the boy's choir sat, as well as other dignitaries, to the Rubens. They looked up at the painting. Mother and Child.

"Do you have any children?" Stan asked. Mary said no. "That makes it even lonelier, doesn't it?" he continued. "Yes, I suppose it does," she said, and then, after a pause, asked Stan if had any children.

"Not that I know of," he said. "Isn't that the worldly thing to say?" Mary laughed but persisted. Stan said no, he had no children and continued to look at

the "Adoration of the Magi." After several minutes of silence, Stan asked Mary
if she would like to sit for a while. They sat in the front pew as the chapel filled
with shadows from the fading sun, a sun that eased through the stained glass
windows and cast delicate, sliding colors onto the opposing wall. Stan looked
at the colors on the wall and then at the windows. Mary told him that during
World War II the people of Cambridge took the windows out and put them
in a safe place, away from the German bombs. They talked of people they had
known, the places they had been, the past. Finally, the colors from the windows
faded completely, and the Rubens was difficult to see. A chill had slipped into
Stan's bones. He looked around; most people had left the chapel. They were
even more alone.

Mary broke the silence: "I think this is the time of day I most feel mortality," she said. "This is when Emily Dickinson most felt it. "There's a certain
slant of light, winter afternoons."

"You're not going to start quoting poetry at me, are you?" Stan asked. "Remember, I can do the same to you, and besides it's not winter."

"It could be," Mary said. "It could be."

When Stan did not reply, Mary said, "Poetry helps."

"What?" Stan said, "What does poetry help?" Both continued to look at
the fading painting.

"Facing your own mortality," Mary said. Stan laughed nervously and said
he's not going to die tomorrow. "I know I'm not young, but I'm not old either,"
he said.

"You will, of course," Mary said.

Stan was confused. He said, "Tomorrow? I hope not."

"Some tomorrow," Mary said. She continued to look at the painting and
then seemed to look through it, beyond it. Stan asked her if she was still talking about him.

Mary lowered her eyes to her lap and put her hands in her pockets. She then
said, "All I know is that I'm alone. No family. My few friends scattered all over
the world. And it's getting dark, very dark."

"I'm here," Stan said.

Mary spoke quietly. "But you're still young. You don't know." Stan looked
at Mary and put his hand on her shoulder. He insisted gently that he was no
longer young. "But you don't know," Mary said. "You're not looking down
the tunnel." Stan asked what tunnel. "The tunnel," Mary replied. "The one
you go down." Stan could only nod and say, "Oh." They sat a bit longer,
in silence.

Mary broke the silence, saying she had to go. "Thanks," she said to Stan, "you helped." She got up, looked one last time at the painting, and began to walk back up the aisle.

"Wait," Stan called out, "Let me come with you." Mary said without turning that he should not. Stan asked why, and Mary said, "No, you can't. No matter what you think, you can't." Mary walked back into the darkness.

Stan was shaken by the incident, even though he didn't know why. When he left the chapel several minutes later, he was surprised to see Mary waiting for him.

"Just wanted to say goodbye, now that we're outside," she said. Stan looked up at the buttresses flying out from the side of the chapel and then asked her of her plans for the next day. She said she had none.

"I have one chore to perform here, that favor for a friend" he said, "and I think you can help me." Mary looked at him, puzzled. "I'll tell you tomorrow," Stan said. "Let's meet out in front of the chapel, on King's Parade, nine o'clock. Okay?"

Mary didn't respond; she just looked at Stan as he turned and headed back to his room.

CHAPTER FIVE

At nine the next day Stan walked down King's Parade and saw Mary sitting on the small stone ledge that sets off King's College from the sidewalk. She had obviously anticipated something of an adventure since she was wearing black slacks, a long-sleeved jacket, and a pair of brown walking shoes. Stan smiled at her and asked what she thought he was up to. "You tell me," she said and reminded him of her age. He sat beside her, feeling the chill in the air.

While people, mostly students and mostly non-British students, swarmed around them, Stan told Mary of his plans and of his plan to scatter a bit of the remains of his teacher over an area near the River Cam known as Byron's Pool. She asked him why he needed her, reminding him that a few ashes don't really weigh that much.. No, not much, he said, and pulled out the packet, a small, clear plastic bag. Mary said she hoped the Zip-lock works. Stan smiled and said he planned to get one of the punts over behind the Graduate Student Center and take it up to the Pool, although he admitted he wasn't exactly sure where it was. He planned to stop by the Tourist Office near the market to ask if they have any suggestions.

They wandered about the market for a while before Stan led Mary across to Peas Hill Street and left on to Wheeler where the Tourist Office occupies a corner of a large building. After standing in line for a few minutes Stan was able to ask a young man about Byron.

The young man said he knew about Byron's Pool but wasn't sure where it is, although he thought it was not on the Cam itself. He then took Stan and Mary over to another young man, immersed in a computer, and asked him.

"Yeah," he said, "I know where it is, but you should have been here a couple months ago. End of term, you know. Lots of students went drinking up there – and swimming too. Some naked. It's always quite a sight. Ritual I guess. Anyway here's how you get there. You driving?"

Stan said no, they hoped to punt up the Cam to the site.

"Oh, yeah, you can do that, but you'll have to get off at The Orchard. You know about The Orchard? It's in Grantchester. No? Well, no problem. Just pull the punt up there. You'll know the place because it's the only spot along the Cam where there's a dock of sorts. Then just walk the path into The Orchard. Nice place for tea. Great scones.

"But what about Byron's Pool?" Stan asked.

"Right. Just go through The Orchard out onto the road, go left towards Trumpington a half mile or so, and you'll see a sign for Byron's Pool off to the right. Couple hundred yards. You can't miss it."

Stan thanked him, but he was already back at his computer.

"Well, I think we're ready," Stan said. "You still game?" Mary assured him that she wouldn't miss this for the world. "Who knows," she said, "maybe some of the students will still be there."

Then it was back to Kings Parade and up to Mill Lane, which emptied into the pool of the Cam where all the punts were kept. A small dam separates the punts going down to the Backs from those going up to Grantchester. They chose a punt from the Grantchester lot. Stan tested the pole used to push the punt, a flat-bottomed boat, along the shallow, narrow river, and soon they were on their way, pushing against the slight current and attempting to keep in the middle of the river or at least to keep from running into a shoreline. Mary sat in the bow of the boat looking past Stan at the ever receding town of Cambridge. The weather had warmed a bit, pushing tolerable.

She asked Stan why he wanted to spread his teacher's ashes over Byron's Pool. "Was Byron his favorite author?"

"Well," Stan said, "I don't think he was his favorite author, although he did like his more satiric work as I recall." Stan then told Mary why the pool is named after Byron. "He liked to go skinny-dipping here," he said. "I suppose that explains the student ritual. Apparently, it caused something of a stir when he was here at Cambridge. My teacher, Professor Schumer, liked that aspect of Byron's personality. You know, the rebel, the "Childe Harold" aspect I suppose. He may have thought he identified with Bryon somehow. I don't know exactly, I didn't know him all that well, personally I mean, but I do have my own theory."

"Which is —"

"Well, let's go back to Rupert Brooke," Stan said.

"My old flame?"

"Yes. Did you know that he too skinny-dipped in the Pool?"

"My God, don't tell me that. One more exciting moment I've missed in my life."

"He did." Stan pushed his pole against the shore to keep from bumping into it. "But it wasn't the thought of Byron naked in the water that excited him."

"I hope not," Mary said and the look in her eyes spoke volumes about lost opportunities.

"No," Stan said, "It was more the woman who was skinny-dipping with him."

"Anyone I know?" Mary asked.

"I think so, although you would never guess. I know I would never have guessed. I just happen to remember it from one of Professor Schumer's lectures. My long-term memory must be kicking in."

"I don't remember if mine is or not," Mary said and then added, "So who was this incredibly fortunate young lady?"

"Virginia Woolf," Stan said.

"You're kidding. Virginia Woolf? Were they about the same age? I thought Virginia would have been much older than Brooke."

"Older but not that much older," Stan said, "I looked up their ages, and she was only five years older. She was visiting him at the time, and I suppose she came under his spell. Apparently, there was a whole group of writers that gathered up at Grantchester before the war. They all seemed under Brooke's spell."

Mary said she could identify with that. "And they skinny-dipped together," she said, "alone or were there some others there too?

Stan said as far as he could determine it was just the two of them and it happened just once. At least, he said, that's the legend, and then added, "I guess that's why I want to drop a few of my teacher's ashes here. He liked Brooke's poetry, or at least Brooke himself, but he absolutely loved Virginia Woolf's fiction, especially <u>Mrs. Dalloway</u>. The thought of the two of them together, here, was too much for me to resist. I'm sure he came out here to the pool each time he visited Cambridge."

"Well, I'll tell you right now I have no intention of skinny-dipping, even in memory of your teacher." Mary thought for a moment and then said, "I might consider it in memory of Rupert Brooke if it were a little warmer."

Stan continued his slow, rhythmic poling as the flat-bottomed boat slid easily along the surface of the Cam. He liked Mary and respected her life. He was glad he had invited her along. She sat looking out at the pasture land and at the few young people walking along the path beside the river, her hand trailing in the water, apparently content with the moment.

As with many British rivers, the Cam is little more than a stream, forty or fifty feet across. And as with many British rivers, it's lovely: slow, meandering, banked by pasture land and small clumps of trees, some of them willows leaning out over the banks, their limbs and leaves dipping into the water. Occasionally, another punt drifted by in either direction, the occupants, mostly young people, smiling and nodding. Stan, standing tall, pole in hand, nodded back; Mary waved slightly and smiled. Soon expert, Stan pushed the boat effortlessly in the middle of the river and within an hour or so they saw the small wooden dock that marked the entrance to The Orchard. They pulled up and tied the punt securely.

"You think it will still be here when we get back?" Mary asked. Stan assured her it would be.

They walked across the meadow to a fence where a small sign hung, announcing "Morning Coffee, Light Luncheons, Afternoon Tea." "I like that," Stan said. "The Orchard has been here for a while. Maybe Rupert and Virginia had tea here before their adventure."

They walked through the gate and into an apple orchard with old wooden tables and chairs, all painted green, scattered among the trees. "It's from another time," Stan said. "I like it," Mary said.

By now, mid-day, the sun had warmed the air. It was absolutely hot, by British standards. Mary suggested they might have tea before going off to Bryon's Pool, so Stan went over to the dining area and came back with tea, scones, clotted cream, and strawberry jam. They enjoyed their tea and watched others, mostly couples, of all ages, sitting in the sun, reading a book or dozing. Mary said she couldn't remember anything quite this pleasant. Stan agreed and then told Mary to look behind her. Amazingly inventive, he said. A woman was sleeping with a napkin over her face, which she kept in place by putting her glasses on over the napkin, securing it by pinning her glasses behind her ears. "No wonder the English have been so successful," Mary said.

Soon, all too soon, the scones were gone, together with the clotted cream and jam, only the dregs of the tea remaining in the aluminum pot. Stan said he really would like to go on to Byron's Pool, and Mary agreed. "That's why we came here, isn't it?" she said. "In part, in part," Stan replied.

A brisk walk up the road and a short stroll up a tree-lined path beside the Granta River, a smaller stream which empties into the Cam, brought them to Byron's Pool, where several men were quietly fishing along the banks. Stan saw a concrete dam at the lower end of the pool. "My God," he said, "It's a pool because it's been dammed up, and it has to have been here since Brooke and Virginia were here, at least judging by the crumbling" Stan was confused. "The concrete couldn't have been here for Byron. Maybe this isn't the same spot. That's a bit disappointing."

Mary reassured him. "Despite dear Heraclitus," she said, "The spot is the same, even if the water is not." They looked on in silence.

Stan relaxed. He felt almost embarrassed to imagine Brooke and Virginia swimming here together. He was sure Mary was feeling something of the same thing, but neither said anything. For more than fifteen minutes they sat with their own thoughts. Byron, Brooke, Woolf. Who knew how many countless other Cambridge undergraduates and perhaps even a few tourists have swum here, naked, in admiration of their heroes?

Meanwhile, another fisherman took up a post across the pond, and several more walkers passed them, apparently heading for some unknown destination up the Granta. "I guess it would be difficult these days to duplicate their feat, unless, of course, you get here pretty early in the morning," Mary said. Stan mentioned that he's not an early riser. They both laughed.

Stan then reminded Mary of his mission and pulled the packet of ashes from his pocket. He told Mary to watch for any oncoming walkers, noting that the fishermen were much too engrossed in their activity to pay any attention. Mary asked if they should say something, maybe a short memorial speech. Stan said no, there was no need for that, but he did say he would take a moment and quietly remember his teacher. Mary bowed her head. "No need for that either," Stan said. "He wasn't very religious as I recall."

"So that's all there is. You just scatter the ashes," Mary said.

"No," Stan said, emptying the bag's contents into the water. "This is only the beginning." He told her he had a number of other locations to visit before he was finished. Greece, "Remember, the island?" China, Russia, Malaysia, Syria.

"My God," Mary said, "He really got around, didn't he? Are you up to that? He went to places even I didn't go to. Syria? How did he get there?

Stan said he thought he taught there for a while. A Fulbright.

The walk back to The Orchard and the trip along the Cam were pleasant, especially since they now had the current with them. Neither seemed in a hurry to have the day end. As they walked back Mill Lane to King's Parade, Mary apologized for her dark thoughts of the day before. "I get that way sometimes," she said. Stan assured her that she was right.

"If a bit gloomy?" she said.

"Maybe. But we're all looking down the tunnel, even if we don't think about it very much. I'm sure," he added, "that Brooke thought little about it until he found himself headed for battle, and Woolf must have thought about it often before her suicide. Even Byron, dead on a distant shore, young by any standard – ”

"Until then?" Mary said.

"Until then – now." Stan said, "It's all we have."

"It's enough," Mary added, and smiled.

At the corner, they noticed Fitzbilly's Pastries across the street. "One more indulgence," Stan said. Mary smiled. They each got a sticky, raisin-encrusted Chelsea bun and stood on the street eating them. "This might be as close to paradise as I get," Stan said.

Soon they said their goodbyes and headed off in opposite directions. Stan spent the next couple of weeks getting to know more of England, visiting the places associated with his teaching: The Lake District, Hardy Country, the Yorkshire fells, Canterbury, Stratford, and, of course, London, where he took in as many plays as he could. He didn't return to Cambridge. And then, too soon, he was off to his next destination, more ashes in hand, or at least in a pocket of his carry-on luggage.

PART THREE GREECE

CHAPTER SIX

"My God, there's a tank in front of the airport," Stan whispered to himself. He looked around. All seemed calm. Except him. So this is Greece, he thought. The cradle of democracy. The land of Plato, of Aristotle, of Sophocles. But also, he realized, the land of Creon, the reluctant dictator responsible for Antigone's death, the defiant Antigone, the Antigone that Stan had always admired. But never emulated. Better be careful, he thought. The tank is watching. Actually, the tank was empty, a silent warning perhaps to any would-be terrorist or perhaps drunken tourist.

Despite the tank Stan relaxed and basked in the warmth of Athens in late September. England had been pleasant but cool; Greece was Carlow in summer. He could have stood there on the curb of the terminal forever, he thought, but he also realized he had to get to the small hotel in central Athens he had contacted by e-mail. When he arrived at his hotel, after a harrowing ride through the crowded, lawless streets of Athens, he knew immediately he had made the right choice. He liked the location: several blocks from the Plaka, the old market area at the foot of the Acropolis. The hotel itself was a small four-story walk-up on a narrow, crowded, noisy street. Perfect, he thought as he walked out onto the tiny wrought-iron balcony of his fourth-story room, a room which overlooked the Plaka, and saw, off in the distance, one corner of the Acropolis. He could have afforded a much more expensive place, one with air-conditioning and a spacious lobby, but he was used to doing things on the cheap and just couldn't get out of the habit. He also knew he wouldn't feel comfortable in a place like that. While attending professional meetings in the States, he had stayed in those places — at the college's expense — but as he grew older he found himself at small hotels with few conveniences but lots of atmosphere. Plenty of atmosphere here, he thought, as he tried to find some place to put his suitcase. The only piece of furniture in the room was his bed, an iron contraption with a white, pebbly blanket stretched over it. He put his suitcase there. His one nod to convenience, the bathroom, cut out of one corner of the room, consisted of a toilet, a small sink, and a shower stall.

But Stan was hungry, so he left his bag unpacked, walked down the four floors to the street, and soon found himself sitting outside a small taverna at the end of his street, wrapped in a veil of contentment, watching the people, mostly tourists it seemed, walking by, arm in arm, hand in hand. He ate a Greek salad, with the best feta cheese he had ever tasted, and thought about ordering the mousaka. That can wait, he thought, as he watched one of the men in the kitchen slice off fine bits of meat from a large upright skewer and pack them into rolled-up pita bread. I'll have one of those, he told the waiter, pointing to the skewer and then also asked for a beer, although he thought perhaps he should have asked for ouzo. Tonight, he told himself.

After his late lunch Stan wandered through the winding streets in the direction of the Plaka. Although tired from his trip, having left his hotel in London at 4:00 a.m., he felt the needed to walk, and so he paid little attention to the map in his hip pocket (The only thing hip about me, he joked to himself) and just meandered, taking in the sights, the sounds, and the smells, particularly the smells, aromas of food cooking, spices, fruit trees, and, of course, in Athens the smell of exhaust and dirty air. Finally Stan saw ahead of him a narrow street lined with stalls. The main street in the Plaka, he thought.

As he started up the street, he was stopped by a man selling blankets. "English?" the man asked. Stan said no, he was American. "No," the man said, "You speak English?" Stan said yes, he did, of course, and then wondered why he had added "of course." The man tried to convince Stan that he needed to take a blanket back to the States with him. "Cold in America," he said. "My cousin, in Minnesota, say it cold there. You need blanket. Cheap." Stan thanked the man but assured him he did not need a wool blanket in Ohio. "Credit card okay," the man said and showed Stan his machinery for charging the blankets. At this rate, Stan thought as he looked ahead at vendor after vendor, I'll never even get up the street, and so he pulled himself away from the blanket vendor and proceeded toward the top of the street, smiling at the continuous stream of invitations along the way. Each time he passed an intersecting street he could see a part of the Acropolis looming off to his right. He pushed forward, through an endless crowd of tourists, resisting the temptation to buy wood carvings, maps, ice cream, small replicas of the Parthenon and every other notable ruin in Athens, even books. He also passed a number of small restaurants along the way and made mental notes of the ones that looked interesting.

Stan finished his walk at the base of the Acropolis, standing where Paul had preached to the Greeks. A bit more, he realized, and he could be at the top, viewing the Parthenon and the other ruined structures that make up one of the most hallowed spots for any teacher of literature. At the base of the Parthenon on the other side he knew the theatre of Dionysus waited, the theater where many of the great Greek plays of the Fifth Century B.C. were first performed. All that would have to wait for another day, however, as Stan was reaching the end of his energy for now.

After a short nap back in his room, Stan started to plan his stay in Greece. He kept reminding himself that he had to distribute a bit of Dr. Schumer's remains on one of the islands his teacher had visited, but there was no hurry. He was sure that part of Dr. Schumer's purpose in sending him to these places was to give him a chance to visit them in some depth. In fact, Stan had been thinking lately that Dr. Schumer had somehow kept up with his career and had noted his tendency to spend all his time in one place, namely Carlow, Ohio. So, Stan reasoned, Dr. Schumer really wanted me to spend some time in each of these places. His rationalization worked. The ashes could wait.

After returning to the Acropolis and visiting other portions of temples and after several days of obligatory guided tours around Greece, Stan was ready for ash disposal. He had stood before the Belly Button of the world at Delphi and looked out over the ruined splendor of the source of all wisdom, the place where the Oracle had once dwelt. He thought perhaps it still did, but he didn't see any wisdom coming his way, aware as he was that only one of the priests of Apollo could make sense of the garbled message. Still he luxuriated in the distant mountains and paused for a look, but not a drink, at the waters of the Castilian springs. I'm not willing to risk an upset stomach for purity, he told himself, adding with a smile, purity is overrated anyway. Stan had kept himself reasonably pure all through his life. Not that he wouldn't have preferred a bit of impurity from time to time, but it just never seemed to happen.

Stan also stood on the track at Olympia, spoke softly on the stage at Epidauros, and even sat on a toilet at Corinth, reputedly used by St. Paul. He took the one-day three-island tour that allowed him to taste briefly, with hundreds of other tourists, island life. He particularly liked the island of Hydra with its excruciatingly picturesque little village. In short he got his fill of all the touristy spots available, and he enjoyed them all, never imagining he would ever be in the land of the beginnings of western theater and philosophy. He had taught the playwrights so often they seemed like old friends, and now here he was in their home territory. This is what they were talking about, he thought, and he was as thrilled as a school boy.

But Stan had a job to do, and he knew it involved another island, Skyros, the island where Rupert Brooke is buried. So at the end of another long and exhausting day of visiting old friends, he returned to his hotel room and took a beer up to his room, intending to look out over Athens to the Acropolis one more time since he expected to leave the next day for Skyros; however, he promptly feel asleep and awoke that evening to see the shade descend on the Acropolis and the lights shine up at it. Magic, he thought and felt pangs of hunger. Each night in Athens he had ventured down to the Plaka to search out still one more small restaurant. This time he wandered through the dark streets that he by now knew reasonably well and worked his way partway up the hill toward the Acropolis, finding in the process a small rooftop taverna overlooking the city. In the distance he could see the tall thin hill of Likavitos, which dominates central Athens. The restaurant was full, but the waiter who had lured him in with offers of free ouzo said not to worry; he would find him a seat. While Stan stood at the steps leading up to the roof, he noticed the cats sitting along the steps and then saw them on a nearby railing. They seemed everywhere. Stan had never trusted cats, so he looked at them suspiciously, as they did him. Soon the waiter returned and told Stan he had found him a seat if he did not mind sitting with another gentleman. By now Stan was so hungry he would have eaten dinner with a cat.

"American?" the man asked in a clipped British accent. Stan acknowledged with a nod that he was indeed an American and sat at the table. "Geoffrey, with a G" the man said, and reached across to shake Stan's hand. "Geoffrey Griegson. Griegson's sort of a Danish name, you know." Geoffrey seemed older than Stan, perhaps because of his white hair in general disarray. It looks as though he's never combed it, Stan thought as he announced his name, adding that he thinks his name might be English. "I doubt it," Geoffrey said with a sniff. Geoffrey's face was clean shaven although ruddy and heavily creased as though he had spent much time out of doors, which Stan thought strange for a Brit, knowing the Brits as he did after his time there. Geoffrey was wearing grey, loose-fitting pants and a grey, not quite matching, crumply, collarless top. Stan felt overdressed in his khaki pants and blue, short-sleeved, buttoned-down dress shirt. One of the cats came over to Geoffrey and rubbed its back against his leg.

Stan asked Geoffrey if he was here on holiday, using the British holiday rather than the American vacation. No, no, Geoffrey replied, explaining that he now lives in Greece, having moved here more than six years ago. Stan said he must love Athens, but Geoffrey replied with disgust, "God, no. I hate the place. I just come here every few months to stock up on supplies I can't get back on the island. I can get most necessities there, but every once in a while I get on the ferry and get over here. I also like the meals here." Stan asked what he would recommend, and Geoffrey suggested lamb. "Any kind of lamb dish is wonderful," he said. "Even better than English lamb. I like it with some sort of unusual herbal flavoring, and of course with lots of ouzo." Geoffrey turned his head to look for a waiter and saw one coming with two small glasses of the colorless drink. The waiter sat one down before Stan and said, "As we promised." He then sat the other one before Geoffrey, "For your kind hospitality," he said. Geoffrey raised his glass and said, "Cheers," and then apologized. "I suppose there are some things we Brits just can't give up." "Drinking?" Stan asked. "No, no. I meant 'Cheers'."

During the meal Geoffrey talked almost non-stop. He explained how he had decided to leave England – "Berkshire, you know, north of London" – after his divorce, his second one – "I knew I didn't want to try it a third time" – and had come to Greece, a place he had been to several years earlier. He had made some money in real estate and had invested it safely, enough money in fact that he could live quite comfortably on a Greek island. Back in England, however, he would have been practically impoverished.

Stan asked him if by any chance his island was Skyros. "Oh, my, no," he said, "Too touristy for me. Of course, not as touristy as lots of other island, Santorini, for instance. And Mykonos, forget that. It's crammed with rich people and obnoxious young people. No, Skyros is not that touristy, although they probably do have a few hotels or guest houses there. Never been there myself, but that's what I hear." Geoffrey went on to explain that his island is Kea, which he pronounced as "Kay-yah." "It's a small island," he said, "and no tourists. Nothing much there except some grazing land and small mountains." Geoffrey said he lives in a small farmer's cottage at the end of the island opposite the small port of Korissia. The cottage has a well and an outdoor toilet, but no electricity. He said he walks down to the beach each day in place of a shower or bath and cooks over a propane heater which he keeps in a small shed near the house. It's absolutely wonderful, he said. When he wants a meal or just some sociability, he goes into a small village a mile or so from his home and eats at a taverna. "I read, and I walk all over the island," he said, "and I enjoy the solitude. It's heavenly. My nearest neighbor is across the valley, an old farmer who enjoys the solitude even more than I do."

Finally, Geoffrey stopped talking long enough to ask Stan why he had mentioned Skyros. "Oh, Stan said, "It's just that I'm going there tomorrow for a few days." He didn't want to volunteer too much information for fear that Geoffrey would launch into one of his soliloquies again. But Geoffrey was curious, offering the information that the trip, as he understands it, is easy. "Shouldn't take more than an hour of so, once you get over to Evia. That's the island, another Peloponnesus. The bus takes you right there. I think the port is Kimi." Stan explained that he intended to take the airplane since there's a small airport on Skyros. Geoffrey sat up straight in his seat, indignant. "An airplane. You're going to take an airplane to Skyros? Why, that would take about fifteen minutes, wouldn't it? What kind of adventure is that? Look, I can give you specific directions. Just go over to the main bus station; any taxi can take you there in no time. Then take the number 64 bus out to Kimi. I'm sure the boat goes every day, but let me check."

Geoffrey pulled out a battered schedule for the various ferries in the Aegean and announced that a boat does indeed go to Skyros tomorrow and told Stan to be at Kimi by four o'clock in the afternoon. As Stan stood to leave, Geoffrey asked him why he was going to Skyros. "A lady friend?" he asked, "sightseeing? Say, isn't that where the poet Brooke is buried? You said you used to teach literature. That's it, isn't it?"

"No," Stan said as he turned to go back down the stairs, "I'm going to scatter a friend's ashes there." For the first time that evening Geoffrey was speechless.

CHAPTER SEVEN

Skyros is two islands joined by a narrow isthmus, so it's really one island with the feel of two separate places. Both parts are mountainous, although the northern part seems more accessible, perhaps because of the trees and the one small green plain along the east coast. Perhaps too because the one town other than the port of Linaria is there. The town, also called Skyros, has about 2,000 inhabitants.

In the dust, Stan stood at the edge of Skyros town, his bus returning in the gloaming to Linaria about ten kilometers away. Skyros extends up the side of the mountain to near the jagged top, the acropolis. Clearly, the Venetian fort there, now in ruins, is the reason for the town's founding. Stan vowed to climb up there the next day.

But now he had to find a place to stay, especially since it was getting dark, and a wind, warm but beginning to chill, was howling in his face. He decided to walk up the main street and look for a "room for rent" sign, but before taking a step he realized the sign would probably be in Greek. He began to panic. Before going 100 yards, however, he was stopped, timidly, by a short, stooped old lady dressed in black. "Room?" she asked in English and smiled. "Oh, God, yes," Stan said and was led to a small building with several entrances. The old lady opened one of the doors and motioned for him to enter. The room was long; he liked that. The walls were white and bare, but the door and window frames were made of rich pine, and the floor was marble. He decided to take it, especially since he thought it might be his only offer. He held out some money for the woman, who carefully counted out a portion and slipped it into her dress pocket.

Later that evening Stan went out to buy some retsina and cheese, the cheese an excuse for the retsina, and the retsina an excuse for the cheese. He drank alone in his room and then went to sleep, waking sporadically to hear the wind tearing through the trees. It must be hell up on the acropolis, he thought, and turned back to sleep.

The next morning he left his room and started up the street, the wind still in his face, the narrow street winding through a maze of smaller streets on either side, white house piled on white house. Restaurants, tavernas, bistros were all there. He passed souvenir stands, woodworking shops, small clothing stores, ceramic shops, even a "Nice and Cheap" motorbike rental stand. He promised to rent one as soon as the wind died down. He wanted to see the countryside, the mountains, and the coves, and especially the grave of Rupert Brooke, buried on the southern half of the island. A good spot for a deposit, he thought.

But that was for later. Now he needed a cup of coffee and perhaps some breakfast. He found a simple restaurant, obviously not for tourists since he understood nothing on the menu posted in the window. He went in and sat down. "Cafe," he said to the elderly lady who ran the restaurant. "Nescafe," she said. "No Nescafe. Cafe, cafe," Stan insisted and settled down for his small cup of thick Greek coffee, which he had grown to admire if not actually like. She brought him a large cup of western instant coffee. "Breakfast?" he then asked. She nodded. "Omelet?" he asked. She nodded again. Five minutes later she returned with several slices from a roll and some butter. I guess it's never easy, Stan thought.

While he munched his bread, he thought about his walk to the top of the mountain. The guide book described the ruins of the Venetian fort there and a 10th century monastery near the summit, occasionally used by monks. But not today, he thought, as he listened to the wind. He had seen several clerics during his walk around the town last evening. They were impressive in their long black robes, flowing in the wind, and looked especially tall, he remembered, in their high black miter-like hats. All cardinals, he thought, smiling. Black-clad cardinals.

Stan wandered through the narrow streets, looking in shops, watching the people, satisfied that he would spend the next few days alone, a welcome treat after the madness of Athens. He spent the afternoon walking for miles outside the town, along roads where he saw no one, not even a car, past small farm houses, vacant looking. He sat for a while on a fence and watched the goats running wild over the hills. He nodded to the one shepherd he saw. The shepherd was following his sheep, a dog at his side, a staff in his hand. Maybe that's what I should be, he thought. Maybe that's what I was in a previous life. The thought of walking along those roads and over those hills with a dog and a herd of sheep somehow appealed to him.

Late that afternoon, on his way back to his room, he stopped in town at one of the few restaurants open and had a drink at an outside table. By then the wind had died down, and he leaned back comfortably, looking at the fort on the acropolis. Tomorrow, he thought and let his mind begin to wander, back to Maria. I wonder how she's doing, he thought, how she's getting along. Does she ever think of me? Probably not. So why am I thinking of her? He stared at his ouzo, with two ice cubes, the clear liquid slowly turning milky.

"Hello," he heard someone say. "I don't mean to be cheeky, but I thought you might speak English. You don't look Greek, if you know what I mean."

He turned to the voice and saw a woman standing there. She was about his age, with long, light brown hair, a pretty face. "Do you speak English?" she said. Stan nodded. "You're not British, are you?" she asked. Stan shook his head. "No, I didn't think so," she said. Stan knew she was British from the accent.

"You must be American," she said, "I can tell because you don't say anything. Americans are so reserved." Stan had heard the British were so reserved although there was Mrs. Barton of bed and breakfast fame. Nothing reserved about her.

"Do you mind if I sit with you for a bit?" she said, "Usually I'm not so forward, don't you know, but, well, here we are on a Greek island, so we're practically friends already." Stan tried to focus on her.

"Please, sit down," he said, "I'm sorry. I was thinking of someone, something else. I didn't mean to be rude."

"Never mind," she said and sat down.

Stan's first impression was not good. He thought she might be one of those British shop girls entering middle age and looking for a mate. He soon discovered, however, that she was simply there on holiday, spending a few weeks away from the accountancy firm where she works.

"No, I don't do the accounting myself," she said, "I supervise others. I see that they get the right work done and that they all get along together. Usually that's not a problem because they're all engrossed in their numbers, but sometimes I have to step in. Basically, I manage people. It's all a matter of making decisions and communicating. If I do something and don't tell them why, I usually get an 'Up yours, mate.' So I keep talking to them."

When the waiter came by, she said that she was hungry and asked if he would like to join her for dinner. He said yes, even though it was ludicrously early. They each ordered lamb.

"So you're a teacher," she said, "You know something about communicating, don't you? I'll bet you could tell me a story or two." Stan did not feel much like telling a story or two.

"But we do communicate anyway, don't we," she said, stopping him before he could begin. Stan was grateful for that. This time she waited until Stan had no choice but to respond. He discovered his mind was still on Maria, and he preferred that.

"Yes, but not much," he said. "There's much more we never know than what we do know, even in the longest and most intimate of relationships." Where did that come from, he thought.

"So how do you know that?" She was toying with the feta cheese in the salad.

Stan was also playing with his salad, picking out the tomato slices. "Know what?" he asked, backing off.

"What we don't know." She waved her hand theatrically. "It seems to me that we can't really know what we don't know. Maybe there's nothing else left to know and we just think there's more." She paused, fork in mid-air, and looked closely at Stan. "Did I miss something?"

"No, it's just that I think I know what we can't know."

"You do? That's amazing." She cupped her chin in her hands. "Are you sure?"

"Yes."

"How do you know that?"

Stan shrugged and said, "I just know."

She resumed working on the feta, which by now was crumbling under the probing of her fork. "Oh, it's like faith, is it?" she said.

"What?" Stan was lost.

"Faith. You just know. You haven't any proof now, have you?"

Stan stopped. Faith, he thought, What does faith have to do with it? She's telling me I have faith that something can't happen that doesn't happen. He then said to her, "Faith? I don't think so."

"Are you a religious person?"

"Religious? No, I don't think I'm religious," he said, "Why do you ask?"

"Faith," she said.

"Oh," he said, confused, then added, "Do you?"

"What?"

"Have faith. Do you have faith? Are you a religious person?"

"I am, sort of," she said, "Fact is, I suppose I'm a very religious person. I was a Buddhist for about seven years, and I liked it too, even the vegetarian part."

The waiter brought their dinner of lamb slices and small potatoes. She said something in Greek, which Stan assumed was thank you. "It pays to know the language," she said, smiling, "at least a few words."

"So why did you leave it?" Stan asked, relieved to be talking about her.

"Leave what?" she said.

"Buddhism."

"Oh, that. Obedience. I could never get the idea of obedience. The monk would tell me what I was supposed to do, and I would always ask why. It drove him batty. He told me once I had to learn obedience, and I asked him why. He just walked away. I think I also talked too much for them."

"So you're not a Buddhist anymore," Stan said, glancing at the lamb on her plate.

"No, I haven't been one for a while." She took a bite of the lamb and pronounced it excellent. After a pause to savor the moment, she continued, "Now I'm a Catholic, Roman Catholic. I like the ritual, you know. I think Catholic churches are beautiful and I like the smell of the incense. Ritual is very important."

"But religion is more than ritual," Stan said.

"No, it can be the same," she said.

Stan smiled and said, "Every day I get up I thank God I'm an atheist." He chewed on the potatoes, satisfied.

She laughed. "That's a good one. I laugh every time I hear it." She paused and thought for a moment before adding, "But are you really an atheist? Do you really not believe in anything?"

"I believe in the human spirit," he said, warming up to the challenge. "At least a bit of it. No, I guess I don't believe in anything, at least anything I can't know directly."

"Do you mean you don't believe in God?"

"Yes," Stan cut a piece of lamb. "I suppose that's what I mean." Stan realized it's not often he gets to be shocking.

"How do you know that God doesn't exist?

"I just know."

"Faith again," she said. Then she smiled at Stan and touched his hand lightly. "You might be a holy man," she said. He smiled, a bit embarrassed.

"That's okay," she said, "I believe lots of things I can't prove. I guess if I can't prove something, I just believe it. It seems as logical as not believing it, and a lot more useful." She then thought for a moment before adding, "I believe that a lot of communication goes on without words too."

"Like gestures?" Stan asked. At one time he had been interested in body language because one of his students had done an independent study project on it.

"No, mind to mind," she said. "I can know what other people are thinking sometimes." And then she added quickly, "Of course not now. Don't worry, not with you. But other times I do. I always have. One time I was into therapy with this woman who believed that most of our problems come from pre-birth trauma, most of my problems anyway. She put me back in my mother's womb under hypnosis and I relived what went on there. I knew what my mother was thinking of me then. I went back to see my mother and told her I knew what she had been thinking of me before I was born. She went bonkers, but she said it was true. I knew it, and I couldn't have very well heard it now, could I? I didn't even know what words were then."

They talked into the night, past the time when most of the local people came to eat dinner and past the time when some of them left. Despite the initial impression, Stan realized this woman was intelligent, rational, and even analytical, but he also realized that she had a strange side, a side that believed in all sorts of things that he had spent his life ridiculing. And yet he liked her. He just didn't believe her. Finally, they parted, but not before she gave Stan a hug. "I really liked talking with you," she said, and then added, "I also thought you needed a hug." She turned and started up the street toward her room; he watched her until she turned a corner. "I don't even know her name," he said to no one.

The next morning he woke early but stayed in bed for a while, enjoying that twilight state between sleep and waking. Finally, he said to himself, "I must do it today. Today I climb the mountain. It's easy. All I need do is keep going up. Eventually, I'll get there." Faith, he said to himself and smiled. The wind was back, however, and, once dressed, he looked out the window and saw the trees shaking violently. That damned wind, he thought.

Once again Stan put off climbing to the fort, convincing himself that he should wait for the wind to die, perhaps later in the day. He waited all day, read-ing, but by late afternoon the wind was still blowing. Stan wavered, but finally he decided to do it. He put on a light jacket and walked out into the town, sunlight slanting off the white buildings, the town a maze of small alleyways. Once off the main street, itself narrow and winding, Stan walked from alley to alley, around and past one chalk-white home after another, all with doors closed and windows shuttered. His only guide was his sense of up, and even here that guide sometimes wavered. Just when he thought he was on his way up, the al-ley would dip and he felt himself going down. He then had to catch the next alley going up. It was a slow process, and frustrating, but he felt himself making some progress. His heart pumped harder with each incline. This too was a sign of progress. The Canterbury pilgrims had it easier, he thought.

He kept climbing until he reached a narrow stone path just a hundred feet from the top. He looked across to the west and saw mountain after mountain vanishing in the distance. He looked down and saw the square white rooftops arranging themselves in a fine mosaic, a rounded church roof here and there. As Stan followed the path, which wound easily around the side to the summit, he passed a small hillside alive with wild flowers, tiny explosions of pinks and whites and purples and blues and yellows. He knew none of them.

And then, suddenly, Stan was at the top, his final steps battered by the wind, taking his breath away. He braced himself before looking around. Leaning into the wind, he saw the sea sweep around him. He stood there, dumb, trying to get his breath, trying to absorb and to comprehend.

The summit itself contained a small, cross-mounted white chapel and beyond that a slightly larger white building, some sort of refuge, he thought. But Stan was interested in the Venetian fort at the other end of the summit, and so he moved past the other two white buildings to the large mud-colored stone blocks, only the first level of the fort remaining. He entered and stepped down into the darkness of a room much smaller than he had imagined.

Stan sat in the room for a while, listening to the wind and trying to imagine what it must have been like for that handful of Venetian soldiers sent to guard the outer reaches of empire. Soon, however, he tired of the fort, of its blankness, and walked down past the first, larger building. It seemed locked. At least the door was shut tight. He went on to the smaller one, the chapel, and noticed the door slightly open. While in England, he had not gone into churches unless they were especially noteworthy or had some sort of literary association. This time, however, he nudged the door a bit and peered in. No one will see me, he thought, and stepped inside. It was tiny; certainly, more than four people would not fit comfortably. It was also dark, but as his eyes adjusted he could see three icons placed in a small alcove opposite the entrance. One had a picture of Jesus, one of the Madonna and Child, and one apparently of Jesus as King. In the middle of the room, on the floor, was a tiny bowl with the stub of an unlit candle sunk in melted wax. I guess someone uses it, he thought, but not on a day like this, not with this wind ripping up here. When he turned to leave, he heard something. He stopped. A cat, he thought. Then he heard it again. It sounded like a moan – or a prayer. Hoping not to find anything, he looked in the corner behind the door and saw a huddled mass of black, a man, a monk. The monk raised his bearded head and looked at Stan, mumbling something Stan didn't understand. "Are you okay?" Stan asked louder than necessary. Again, the monk mumbled something, and reached out his hand to Stan. "Are you sick?" Stan said, "Do you need help?" The monk stared at Stan and motioned for him to come. Now what'll I do, Stan thought. He moved cautiously to the monk, who grabbed Stan's wrist and gripped it tight. The monk pulled at him and said something in Greek. He looked emaciated, and Stan realized for the first time the monk might be dying. "I'll get some help," he said, but the monk wouldn't release his arm.

Stan pried the monk's fingers loose, but still he stayed with him. He sank beside the monk and said, slowly, "Look, I'll go and get someone, another monk, someone to help you. I'll be right back. You'll be okay till I get back." Stan was not afraid, but he was disturbed. He turned away and almost cursed the monk for putting him in this position. He wanted desperately to leave but he couldn't, and it wasn't just the monk's grip that kept him there. He knew he had to stay, and he had to understand the monk, to know what he wanted, needed.

Slowly he turned to the monk and looked him directly in the face. "What do you want me to do? Tell me." The monk kept looking at Stan, into him he felt. "I know you want to tell me something," he said to him, "but I'm sorry, I don't understand you."

Stan touched the monk's forehead. "You're cold," he said. He then put his arm around the monk, and felt the bones through the black cloth. They sat for a while quietly, Stan holding the monk, the monk looking at him, continuing to mutter. What is he saying, Stan thought. He's not asking for help, at least not for himself. Stan began to hear the same words, repeated with reverent regularity. "You're praying. "What are you praying for?" he asked. "To live? Are you afraid of dying?" Somehow he knew that was not it. "For what then, for what?" Stan repeated.

The monk again looked deeply into Stan. Stan looked back into the eyes of the monk and said softly, "For me. You're praying for me, aren't you? How did you know?" The monk closed his eyes. Stan held him tightly, afraid the bones might fall apart.

Outside, the day began to die, while inside Stan was confused, uncertain how to end this. Finally, two elderly monks entered the chapel and gently pulled their brother from Stan's arms. They said something, smiled, and half carried him from the chapel and down the path toward the town. What was he doing here, Stan wondered. Does he come here every day? Is this his way of worshipping? Is he really dying? Is this where he wishes to die? And what brought me here at this moment, this intersection of time and space? Stan had no answers and so he too left the chapel and returned to the town center and his room. He ate no dinner and did not sleep well that night.

CHAPTER EIGHT

By the next morning the wind had died, the sun was shining, and Stan felt surprisingly refreshed and even hungry as he wound through the town looking for breakfast. He hoped to avoid the accountancy woman. He was afraid she might ask what he had done the day before, and he was afraid he might tell her.

After a hard roll with honey and a cup of Nescafe, Stan looked for a moped rental. He had a delivery to make, and he knew it meant a trip to the southern part of the island, to a spot overlooking the Aegean. He had to visit Rupert Brooke.

Stan found the rental shop up near the town square, the one overlooking the Aegean. As he sat on it and followed the shopkeeper's instructions – in Greek – his eyes wandered to the end of the square and the large Greek statue there. It was clearly a later imitation but it looked like the many young male statues he had seen in Athens. He pointed to the statue and asked the shop keeper in English what it was. The man looked perplexed at first and then smiled and said "Rupert." Stan got off the moped in mid instruction and went over to the statue and saw "Rupert Brooke, 1887 – 1915." Doesn't look like him, Stan thought, so this doesn't count. He could not scatter ashes here. He had to make the fifteen miles or so down to the isthmus that connected the two parts of the island, and then down the western coast to where Rupert Brooke is buried.

Stan could find no map that indicated the site, except in the most general terms: somewhere on the southwest coast in an olive grove – not much narrowing down there – just up a ravine from the bay where the hospital ship had been docked, the one on which Brooke had died. He had read that the grave was surrounded by a low marble fence and could be seen from the road if you looked carefully. He had also been told that the bay was called the Tris Bouke Bay, at least that was the English approximation. He had written it down and now carried it in his wallet.

So, with a full tank of gas, he rolled carefully out of Skyros and back toward Linaria. Since there was no other traffic at this time of the morning, Stan had

no trouble navigating the macadam road, avoiding the stray sheep that meandered along and across the road. He balanced well enough and soon got used to
the hand gear shift. Although he had no helmet – he had seen none in Greece
and the shop owner had none to rent – he increased his speed, enjoying the wind
blowing through what was left of his hair, and thought of Marlon Brando. It
was a heady trip and soon he was across the isthmus and into the sparsely settled
southern part of the island, heading down the coast road. As he sped along at
20 miles an hour he thought of the day before and his encounter with the monk
on the acropolis. For some reason he felt less lonely today than he had before.

He also felt that it was time to try to find Brooke's final resting place, that
spot "that is for ever England," as Brooke had put it in one of his few poems
still anthologized. Somehow it sounded less sentimental now that Stan was
here, on the island, within a short distance, he hoped, of that spot. Although
he didn't expect to find a taverna down here, he did hope to find a person, any
person, who might be able to direct him to Brooke. He had noticed a few of
the typical white-washed homes sitting in ravines and thought he might stop at
one. He knew no one down here would speak English, but he thought some
sign language might help, and besides he did see a bay of sorts and a small ravine
coming up from it. He also knew there were dozens of places like it all along
the coast. Stan stopped and pulled his bike over to the side of the road.

Just then a man in black baggy pants and a loose white shirt came around
the corner and smiled at Stan, saying something in Greek. Perhaps a greeting,
Stan thought. They shook hands and Stan smiled back, nodding his head in
agreement with whatever the man was saying. The man then took Stan by the
arm and led him up the hill a short distance to his home. He motioned for Stan
to sit at a small wooden table on the porch while he went inside. Stan peered
into the darkened entrance to the home and noticed a wooden table and several
chairs, a colorful rug or blanket on the wall, and various religious icons sitting
around. He then looked out over the porch to the vivid blue of the Aegean.
Peaceful, he thought. I think I could live here. Soon, the man was back and sat
down with Stan. Before either could say anything, the man's wife came out with
a bottle and two small glasses. The man poured the pale yellow liquid into the
glasses and urged Stan to drink. They clinked glasses and Stan drank something
that burned all the way down. Good, he said, and smiled. The man refilled the
glass. Stan sipped this time.

Stan then got his map of Skyros from his pocket and spread it out on the
table. He pointed to where he thought he was, and the man smiled broadly,
pointed to that spot on the map and then to his house. "Yes, yes," Stan said.

Now for the real test. "Rupert Brooke," he said, and traced his finger along the coast. The man looked puzzled. Stan repeated, slowly. "Ru-pert Brooke." Again the man looked puzzled, but his wife, who had been listening in the doorway, came over to say something to her husband. "Ah," he said, "Rupert, Rupert," and he pointed down the road. The man then stood, took Stan's arm again, and led him back to the road. Stan went to his moped, but the man shook his head and pointed down the road. He and Stan walked along the road for several hundred yards, and then the man pointed up the hill, along a small ravine that came up from the bay. Stan started up the ravine with the man following him, and within 50 yards or so, he saw a small grove of olive trees and within it Brooke's grave marker. Its base and four corners were made of a white marble with black iron railings joining them Stan walked over to the grave and knelt to see what was inscribed on the monument. It was Brooke's poem, "The Soldier," the one about "some corner of a foreign field/ That is for ever England," the one Stan had quoted earlier. Stan was shocked that the poem which had always sounded so sentimental and phony, now sounded real. The man who had written it was buried here, reclining within feet of where Stan was standing. He looked at the monument again (Aug. 3, 1887 – April 23, 1915). So young, he thought. Twenty-seven. And I've lived so much longer. Why? The man, even older than Stan, stood by silently, making no effort to intrude on Stan's sacred moment. The monk was dying but old; that should be the natural order of things. Brooke was young. And I'm somewhere in between, Stan thought. What does that mean for me?

Finally, Stan stood and looked around, everything strangely familiar. The man continued to stand silently. Stan then took his plastic bag from his pocket and poured the ash into his hand. The man watched. Next Stan sprinkled the ash over Rupert Brooke's grave. The man relaxed. He understands, Stan thought.

The two of them stood for a while, looking at the grave. Here we are, Stan thought as he looked at the man, two people who cannot understand a word either says, and yet I feel I know him. Stan then walked over to the man, patted him on the shoulder, and took his arm. "Let's go," he said aloud and led the man back down the ravine.

Later, back in Athens, at the taverna around the corner from his hotel, Stan realized he had forgotten to thank the man. He knew he should have thanked him for showing him the grave of Rupert Brooke, but he also wanted to thank him for being there with him, another human being facing death.

Back in Athens Stan wandered down to the Plaka again for no particular reason, habit perhaps. After the solitude of Skyros, he wanted the ebb and flow of humanity that crowded the narrow streets in Athens. He bought nothing, but he enjoyed looking at the various crafts – the animals carved from wood, the rough woven blankets the color of earth, the delicate scarves and handkerchiefs, even the books in a language he couldn't begin to understand. The people were happy, and so was he.

As he fingered a white, loose shirt, the kind the man on the island had worn, he noticed a woman of forty-five or fifty who was looking at similar shirts. "Nice," she said and then asked Stan if he thought he would like something like that. Stan said, yes, he thought he would, but that he isn't buying things now because he still has a lot of traveling to do before he returns home to Ohio. The woman said she was from Michigan, but that she expects to be back home soon and wanted to buy something for her boyfriend, "if that's what you can call a fifty-year-old man," she said and laughed. She said she hadn't seen him for a year, since she had been living and working as a nurse in Saudi Arabia. "Fascinating," she said, "but really restrictive, especially if you're a woman." She then told him how she had to stay in the foreigners' compound and how she could never travel alone. "One time," she said, "I went for a ride with an American man and we were stopped and questioned. Basically, they wanted to know what I was doing with a man who wasn't my husband. It was scary."

They talked for a long time walking along the street, jostled by other shoppers and sightseers. Stan was intrigued by the woman's stories and finally confessed that his next destination was Syria. "Syria?" she said, "Why Syria? Not many Americans go to Syria." Stan said he was going on business but didn't expect to be there very long. He said he keeps hearing it's a dangerous place, hostages and terrorists, that sort of thing. The woman, who then introduced herself as Phyllis Deardorff, told Stan she had been in Syria just recently for about a week. "You'll love it," she said. Stan stared at her. "You will," she said and smiled. " You will. First of all it's beautiful, especially Damascus." She asked Stan if he will be in Damascus. He said yes, at least part of the time, but his business will probably take him just outside Damascus. He wasn't quite sure where. "I hope you get to Mount Qasioun," she said, "the mountain on the outskirts of Damascus. Stan assured her he would try. "I went up there," she said, "It's very dramatic, a great view of Damascus. You can see the entire city, even to the desert beyond it."

Phyllis told Stan of the couple she had met in Damascus, a Fulbright teacher and his wife, also from Michigan. "They were very helpful," she said, "and genuinely enjoyed showing me and my friend, another American nurse from Saudi, around the town, especially to the Souk, the bazaar." She then dug a small tablet from her purse and wrote down the name and address of the couple. "Just tell them Phyllis recommended them," she said and laughed again."

Stan had been trying not to think about his trip to Syria, but the conversation made him feel a bit better. They parted shortly after that. "I'm leaving tomorrow for home," Phyllis said, "but first I have to go back and get that shirt. I think my boyfriend will like it." She giggled softly as she turned and headed back down the street.

The next day Stan was high over the Mediterranean, headed for the not quite completely unknown.

PART FOUR SYRIA

CHAPTER NINE

The plane suddenly dipped and Stan's window filled with desert — empty, desolate desert. Damascus was just minutes away.

The trip from Athens was short, no more than two hours, and pleasant. Phyllis's reassurances had given Stan courage, but now as the plane slipped to within hundreds of feet of the ground, he could see the dirty dunes, the scrubby plants, and the darker patches that made up the landscape. And then he saw a road, dirt to be sure, but a road. There must be something around here, he thought. And suddenly there was. The plane landed with a jolt on a macadam runway, and as the afterburners kicked in and the plane slowed, Stan could see the charred remains of a burnt-out fighter plane along the runway. It does look like it's been here a while, he thought. He also saw the empty hulls of several other planes, commercial planes. They look like they died of natural causes, Stan thought. Such were his reassurances.

The woman who had been sitting beside him, a young woman dressed in a colorful blouse and pale blue skirt with a matching silk scarf neatly arranged around her head, had left her seat several minutes earlier, despite the warnings to passengers to take their seats. Now, she returned, this time wrapped in a long, black, loose-fitting garb with a black scarf on her head. Stan wondered what that was all about.

The plane parked some distance from the terminal, and as the passengers began to disembark down an airport stairs to the waiting bus, Stan saw several soldiers standing nearby with machine guns. He hoped they were there for protection. Inside, the terminal was chaos with the passengers from Stan's plane as well as from another, larger plane all crushed toward the immigration line. Fortunately, Stan's line for foreigners, the one sign so far he could read, was much shorter, and so soon he was ready to collect his luggage, although at the moment he was not sure just where it might be since he saw no evidence of a luggage carousel and no sign in English pointing the way. Stan wandered about the lounge for several minutes and then decided to look out the door where he saw a sign in English and Arabic pointing to a small corrugated building next to the terminal. When he entered it he saw all the luggage piled in the center of the building, and after some sorting, pushing, and shoving, found his suitcase and began to carry it out of the building. He was then stopped by an official who asked in English for his luggage sticker.

Finally, Stan was out to the taxi queue and soon carried through the outskirts of Damascus, past the dirty sand he had seen from the plane, past villages of small brown houses, poor in appearance and impression, past straggling crops striving to survive, past children playing among the debris, and, finally, into Damascus proper, a seemingly busy, even thriving city filled with cars, taxis, buses, and even some large, cumbersome trucks, moving slowly, all blowing their horns, the sidewalks filled with people, mostly men, walking leisurely, some dressed in the long galabeas he had read about, some in conservative western clothes, some in jeans. As he neared the center of the city, he saw hanging from several large buildings long banners with pictures he recognized as President Assad.

The taxi needed shocks and a muffler, perhaps an entirely new exhaust system, strange rumbling sounds coming from the engine, so Stan was delighted when he finally reached his hotel, the Meridian. He had chosen this hotel because it was the most modern in Damascus, one of only three which called itself modern. He had thought about going a bit rustic like he did in Athens, but Phyllis had warned him off. As Stan carried his luggage through the entrance into the large lobby and to the reception desk, he thought he could have been anywhere in America. Men were sitting on sofas and chairs reading newspapers. Again he saw no women. The lounge was decorated with large plants, paintings of local scenes on the walls, and several small statues, apparent imitations of antiquities, perhaps antiquities themselves. And as with the outside of buildings he saw several pictures of President Assad. He certainly seems popular here, Stan thought as he filled out the registration form and gave the clerk his passport. The receptionist, a young man, welcomed him to Damascus in almost perfect English.

Stan's room was equally impressive with all the usual amenities, including a shower. Stan stretched out on the bed, relieved that he had survived his entrance to fabled Damascus. If Saul can make it, he thought, so can I, although he wasn't sure just what to do next and he had no intention of converting. He did have the assurance, however, of the names of the American Fulbrighter and his wife, and he had the address of the American Embassy in case he had any serious trouble, so Stan's usual calm demeanor slowly returned and he decided to take a walk and then that evening phone the Fulbrighter. Beyond that he had no idea what he might do or what might be done to him.

After thinking for an hour of so about where he might go in Damascus, Stan put on his comfortable walking shoes and went out into the late afternoon heat. The sky was cloudless, a deep blue. Not too much pollution, Stan thought. He decided to walk one of the streets in one direction and to avoid side streets so he could find his way back to the hotel. He also took a sheet of instructions, what to do in case of fire, which had the hotel's name in both English and Arabic. He knew he could simply show this to a taxi driver and get back if it came to that. He told himself this would be easy, but he didn't sound all that convincing to himself.

The hotel is located on a major intersection, so Stan arbitrarily chose a street since they all looked the same to him. As he walked slowly and very conspicuously on the sidewalk, he felt surrounded by people, again mostly men and mostly smoking acrid smelling cigarettes. So much for clean air, he thought. He also realized that had he come first to Syria he would now be having far more difficulty grasping his situation; in fact, he thought he might have turned right around and gotten on the return flight. Now, however, surrounded by strange but clearly non-hostile people, mostly ignoring him and going about their business, he felt at ease. The few women he saw were a dissimilar lot. About half of them wore the traditional black outfits which covered them completely, some even covering their faces with a sort of black mesh through which they could see. The other half wore some variation of tight jeans, colorful blouses, and high heels. They would look at home anywhere in America, Stan thought, and then qualified that with, perhaps not in Carlow.

Stan passed curbside stands selling trinkets, fruit, even clothing. As the afternoon wore on, he saw more and more men on the streets, clogging the sidewalks, often forcing him to step into the curb to avoid them, especially the two or three soldiers walking side by side, some holding hands. No, it's not Carlow, he thought. The streets were equally clogged with traffic, a constant din of accelerating engines, screeching brakes, and horns. To Stan all the drivers seemed to be on their horns all the time. He also saw no one stop at intersections. They just blew their horns more insistently and kept moving. But in the midst of this sensory overload, Stan remained calm, thinking about his immediate future. He realized with some satisfaction, even pride, that he could cope with this.

That evening he called the American Fulbrighter, Anthony Burgess, who said he would come by the hotel after his afternoon class at the university, explaining that he usually walked the two miles out to his classes and the two miles back. The hotel was almost exactly in the middle of this walk. Stan spent the next day exploring further the area surrounding the hotel and had lunch at a small outdoor café on a boulevard lined with large plane trees. It looks like pictures of Paris, he thought. Phyllis had told him he could get by with three Arabic words – thank you, toilet, and beer. He asked for beer and was surprised when it came in a coffee cup. "Coffee," the waiter said and pointed to the people on the sidewalk. Stan knew Syria was not a formal Islamic state, but he also knew there was no point in offending his hosts, and so he quietly drank his coffee, which tasted for all the world like beer.

Stan returned to his hotel and waited in the lobby for Anthony Burgess. "I'll recognize you," Burgess had said. He did. They exchanged pleasantries; Burgess told Stan to call him Tony. He then asked Stan how Phyllis was doing. "I think she had a tough time in Saudi," Stan said. Burgess agreed. "I'll never forget her reaction to first being in Damascus. She kept talking about how free everything is here, how open the people are, and happy. We had been here for only a short while, and I was still trying to cope with the AKs on the streets and the Assad cult. You know," he said more softly, "We have a secret police headquarters across the street from our apartment." When Stan asked how he knows it's a secret police headquarters, Burgess explained that secret police all drive white Puegots with license plates beginning with 37 or 39. "Some secret," Burgess said, laughing, but he also told Stan that he was pretty sure they could hear everything that went on in their apartment. "We always try to say at least one nice thing about Assad each day," he said.

Burgess invited Stan back to his apartment for a meal that evening and offered to come get him. Later, on their way to the Burgess apartment, they passed the American Embassy. Burgess told Stan the people working at the Embassy have been very helpful to him and his wife and that they seem to enjoy working here in Damascus. "The big joke," Burgess said, "is that they receive extra pay for working in a difficult area, hazard pay I think they call it." Another few hundred yards and they were on a street with a narrow canal running down the middle of it. At the end of the street, Burgess stopped and pointed to the top of a four-story building. "That's our apartment up there," he said, "at the top. We have four balconies." And then he said in a mock whisper, "Over there is the Secret Police headquarters, but don't look, and especially don't try to take a picture." Stan didn't know how serious Burgess was, so he thought he would err on the side of caution.

The two men took the elevator to the fourth floor. It moved slowly and seemed to be on the verge of stopping every few seconds. Burgess said, "When I'm in a hurry, I walk up." They entered into a spacious room with a large glass chandelier in the middle and a long table surrounded by a dozen or so chairs with dark blue velvet seats. "The dining room," Burgess said, "as designed by Louis XIV." A woman came into the dining room from the kitchen and held out her hand. Burgess introduced his wife, Sue Ellen. "Call me Sue Ellen," she said, "Never Sue, Susan, or Susie, especially not Susie. I know Tony told you to call him Tony." She laughed easily, and Stan instantly liked her. She explained that she was making a chicken dish, and she hoped he could stay for dinner. Normally, Stan was uncomfortable with women, especially someone's wife, but he felt fine with Sue Ellen. She even reminded him a bit of Maria, back at Carlow, no pretension, just openness. Also married. He agreed to stay for dinner.

Tony was about Stan's age but much greyer. He said he taught American Literature at Michigan State and was teaching that here at Damascus University. He explained that he had large classes at both schools as well as one small graduate seminar. When Stan asked Sue Ellen what she's doing, she said she's working harder than Tony. She substitutes at the nearby American school for diplomat children and helps out around the Embassy. ""Usually," she said, "I put in more hours in a week than he does." She seemed genuinely proud of this.

After more conversation Tony asked Stan if he would like to visit his Western Literature class, suggesting it might be unlike anything he's ever seen in a small liberal arts college in Ohio. He told Stan he has approximately 2,000 students in three undergraduate classes and another dozen in a graduate American literature class for teachers. He said the graduate class is a delight, with bright, interesting students trying to soak up everything they can before going back to their village classrooms. The undergraduate classes are a different matter. The classes have 300-400 students on any one day, which is little more than half of those enrolled. He had been told not to expect more since a number of students sign up to stay out of the army and get their stipend but have no intention of actually going to class; in fact, most if not all can speak no English while even the majority of those who do come know so little English they can't understand anything they hear or read. Tony insisted, however, that each class contains a core of students who are intelligent, have good English, and want to learn. When Stan asked him what teaching methodology he uses with such large classes, he replied, "I lecture. I allowed time for questions at the end of the first few lectures, but no one spoke up. At the end of each lecture, however, a dozen or so students come forward and start asking questions, following me out to the campus and even down the street toward my apartment. And they always have interesting questions."

Stan was intrigued, so he made arrangements for Tony to stop by the hotel the next day on the way to the university. They would walk the second mile together. As much as Stan enjoyed talking with the Burgesses, he felt it was time to return to his hotel; he was still suffering from the new experiences he had encountered. By now it was dark, so Tony offered to walk back to the Embassy with him and help him get a cab from there, but Stan said he thought he remembered the way. They reviewed the route, and Stan walked down the steps to the street. He glanced at the building across the street and retraced his steps along the canal. As he walked, he thought how improbable it was that he was walking along a darkened street in Damascus and feeling perfectly safe. Maybe I'm just naïve, he thought, or maybe something else has happened.

CHAPTER TEN

At 9:30 the next morning Tony was at the hotel; Stan was waiting for him in the lobby. They walked to the university along a main highway leading out of town, chatting easily. Stan told Tony of his stay in Greece, and Tony said he and Sue Ellen hope to go there over the Christmas break. Stan asked if the Syrians really call it a Christmas break. Tony replied that it's really the semester break, but that he's told they do observe Christmas itself as a holiday, pointing out that Islam considers Jesus one of its prophets. And, besides, a number of Christians live in Syria.

Soon they entered the gate of the university and saw a campus not much different from a university campus in the States, except for the drab uniformity of its grey, concrete buildings and its poor grassy areas. Students milled around the entrance to Stan's building, boys in jeans, girls in modest dresses, some with scarves on their heads, all watching Stan and Tony as they entered the building. Tony smiled and nodded to them; they smiled back and followed the pair into the building. The interior was actually one large lecture hall, the only decorations pictures of President Assad hanging down from the side walls with one especially large picture across the back of the hall. Stan took a seat in the rear of the raked seating area.

Tony went to the desk sitting on a platform at the front of the room. Stan noted the pictures of the president on either side of Tony as he spread out his notes and fiddled with the microphone. It didn't work. Tony asked if anyone knew how to work the microphone, and several young men hurried forward to see if they could help. When they could not, one left to get a maintenance worker. Meanwhile, Tony began to shout out the outline for the lecture as he wrote some names on the blackboard. Before he got halfway through the names, the chalk disintegrated in his hand. By then a maintenance worker arrived and began to fiddle with the microphone. Finally he said something to Tony in Arabic, which a student translated as "It can't be fixed." Clearly resigned to his fate, Tony began to shout out the lecture on "The Iliad," which he continued for the next two hours, the students either taking furious notes or sitting completely still. The Trojan War itself, Stan thought, didn't take this much effort.

When the lecture was over and students were filing out of the room, six or seven rushed to the front and pinned Tony against the wall, asking question after question, not all related to the Trojan War. "Is it true President Reagan was a Jew?" Tony did not think so. "What about President Kennedy? Was he a Jew?" someone else asked. Tony said he was sure he was not. "Can you come to my village" another asked. Stan asked him where he lived, and he said, "Not too far. We can take a bus. No problem."

Meanwhile, Tony edged his way out of the room, onto the campus, and out the gate. As he and Stan walked down the road back to the hotel, the students gradually fell away, leaving only one student, obviously bright and inquiring. His name was Ahmed, tall with a full black beard, and he said how much he has enjoyed reading "The Iliad." "I have read it in Greek twice and once in Arabic, but I think I like the English version best," he said, adding, "It is so strong." He also asked about other western writers, finally growing silent before asking, "Is it true that all writers die young?" Tony seemed bemused and replied that not all writers die young, citing poets such as Wordsworth and Yeats, but he admitted that many poets have died young. He asked Ahmed why he asked such a question. "I just wondered," he said, "I visited my best friend in Lebanon; he is a poet . When we were walking down a street in Beirut, someone shot him in the head. I carried him to the hospital, but he died in my arms before I could get him there." And then he added, "I was just wondering. Maybe it was meant to be." Ahmed then excused himself and went back up the road toward the university.

Tony said he is often stunned at what he finds out about his students here. "Amazing," Stan said, "I had no idea. How does a student like that even function?" Tony assured him they do function, even at times with grace and humor.

Back at the hotel, Stan thanked Tony for allowing him to come to his class. "Glad you could make it," Tony said, and then asked Stan if he would be available on Saturday. He explained that some people from the Embassy were going up in the mountains to visit the village of Malula and said that he thought he would be able to get an invitation for him. "Malula is one of only five villages in the world, all five in Syria, where Aramaic is still spoken. That's the language Christ spoke," he said. "I think it would be interesting to hear that language, and it's supposed to be really beautiful up there. The Embassy people supply the vans and cars, so we just have to tag along. What do you think?"

"I don't know," Stan said, "I'm not very religious." Tony assured him he wasn't either, but then asked Stan, "When's the next time you'll hear Aramaic?

It's an adventure." Stan agreed to go, and so the arrangements were made to meet at the Embassy.

Over the next several days Stan walked on the ancient wall around Damascus, shopped on the Street Called Straight, visited the Omayyad Mosque, the third or fourth holiest site in Islam depending on whom he was talking to, and browsed through the Souk, the long, narrow bazaar with its tin roof filled with holes. "Bullet holes," one of the shopkeepers said. He was an older man with a graying full moustache, a Christian he called himself, saying he was open on Friday because of his faith. "I close on Sunday, he said, adding, "My neighbor over there is closed Saturday, and my other neighbor beside him is closed today because he is Jewish." Stan asked about the bullet holes. "They came at different times," he said, "Some came down through the roof after celebrations; others went up through the roof during troubles." He shrugged and suggested that Stan might like to buy some of the wooden inlaid mosaics in his shop.

Saturday morning at 9:30 Stan left his hotel and walked the mile or so to the Embassy. Since he was early he waited outside the wall until the Burgesses arrived, Sue Ellen carrying a basket. "Lunch," she said and added they had included some food for Stan as well. Stan realized he hadn't thought of food and wondered if the idea had been Tony's or Sue Ellen's. He already envied the easy relationship between Tony and his wife; they almost seemed to anticipate what the other's needs were.

Tony told Stan he should have gone into the Embassy, but Stan said he wasn't sure if he should. "The Marines at the entrance look pretty intimidating," he said. Sue Ellen laughed. "They're just kids," she said. "They're good at what they do, but they're just kids, nice kids at that." After going through identification, Stan was introduced to the other people going to Malula. There was Tim Stoppard, the Economic Attaché, and his wife, Marlene. Marlene said they have been at the Embassy the longest, more than three years. "They keep trying to send us somewhere else, but we really like it here. The US government doesn't want you to get too attached to one place, so they keep sending you to another post. I'm afraid it's too late for us," she said and looked up at Tim. He smiled awkwardly.

The other three people were introduced as Katherine Overmeyer, secretary to the Cultural Attaché, approximately 45 years old Stan judged, short, slight, with short brown hair and metal glasses a bit too large for her face. She told Stan she's in Damascus because she likes to try new things, although Stan didn't think she looked particularly adventuresome. Robert Townsend also worked in

the office of the Cultural Attaché as an assistant. "I book all the people coming through from the States," he said. Robert was short, slim, with short black
hair and a shy smile. The other person was Stu Diamond, a tall, robust man,
who talked easily and was the type of person who slapped you on the back and
laughed at some humorous remark he had just made. His hair was beginning to
grey and it was also short. I guess that's regulation Stan thought and decided he
needed to look up a barber. He also wondered what Stu did at the Embassy.

Stu took charge. "Okay, let's load up. The two couples can go in Tim's car.
The four singles will go in mine." Soon they were on their way out of Damascus,
expertly maneuvering the clogged streets amid the cars and trucks going in all
sorts of directions, following no particular pattern, all horns blowing all the
time. Stu seemed to be especially pleased to be honking his horn, laughing
and pointing out the most blatant violators, even waving to a few of them.
And then, almost suddenly, they were in the starkly impressive countryside, the
scruffy hills rolling by, tall crags of rocks sticking out from the sides. "Ever
been to the Black Hills?" Stu asked, "Same thing, only smaller. It gets more
impressive when we head into the mountains over there." He was right. Once
in the mountains Stan looked over the side of the road and down into sheer
valleys and across to the other side where, a short time later, he saw the pinks
and pale blues of as many as a hundred small square houses clinging to the side
of the hill. Malula.

They kept going up the winding road, and soon they reached the top of the
mountain and the Mar Sarkis Convent, a small concrete building with a large
blue dome over a central courtyard. The air was pure, and the sunshine brilliant.
From the convent they could look out in all directions at the miles and miles of
endless hills. "Lebanon is over there," Katherine said and pointed in a direction
which Stan assumed was west. He felt a bit uneasy. Tim took command and
herded the group into the courtyard where they sat on straight, wooden chairs
apparently arranged for the visit. A man with a long, black beard stood in front
of them. He wore a black robe hanging to his feet and a square black hat. Stan
thought he might be forty if his beard is not dyed; if dyed, he could be sixty.
He welcomed everyone in French. Tim asked if everyone understood French;
all said no. Clearly pleased with the answers, Tim offered to translate, which he
did easily. Impressive, Stan thought. Stan knew enough French to know they
had been welcomed, but after that he was lost.

The monk gave a history of the convent which went back to the fourth
century and then talked a bit about Aramaic, "the language of our Savior. Here
is where you can hear the actual words that Christ spoke." Stan realized he had

yet to hear any of the actual words Christ spoke or even any words he might have spoken since the Monk was speaking only French. He then realized that Tim probably didn't understand Aramaic. Who does, he thought. Once the monk finished his brief remarks, Tim said he had offered to recite the Lord's Prayer in Aramaic. Tim then sat down while the monk arranged himself in front of the group. He spoke the softly lilting language of Christ, repeating the very words which Jesus himself had spoken probably many times. Stan, not a particularly religious person as he had often described himself, was surprised to find himself affected by the words, his eyes misting and his jaw quivering, not noticeably he hoped. When he looked at the other people, he found them transfixed, not blinking, just staring at the monk. When the monk finished, Stan returned to his non-religious state of mind, but he realized even as he did what a rare opportunity it was to hear these words spoken here by this man. Two thousand years ago and it was as though he had been there.

"We're not done yet." Robert Townsend was tugging at Stan's sleeve. "We've got to see where St. Thecla split the rock and escaped. C'mon." They all piled back in their cars and headed back down toward Malula, which looked increasingly like a cubist painting, its flat, square, pale-colored roofs fitting together neatly. Just before entering the town they turned left and headed back up another road to another convent, this one larger than the first and comprised of several layers crawling up the side of the hill to another dome. They parked beside the convent and walked down past a terrace to a grotto, an opening of stones with water dripping from its roof. Tim explained to the group that the waters are supposed to have miraculous healing powers. There they go again, Stan thought. Why can't they stop when they're ahead? I guess I could stick my head under the drips and get my dandruff cured. A short walk down from the grotto brought them to a very narrow cleft in the hill. As they walked up through the cleft, Stan reached out with both hands and touched the sides, which were smooth and made of the grayish-brown stone he had seen all over the region.

When they reached the top of the cleft, Tim decided to give a short lecture. He had apparently done his homework; no one else had. He explained that Thecla was a young disciple of St. Paul, who at that time was preaching virginity for young girls. Her father, however, did not want her to follow Paul or his religion, and furthermore he apparently wanted her to marry. He and some soldiers chased Thecla up the mountain to this point where she found herself against a wall of solid stone, and certain death. When she prayed for help, the mountain wall split open forming this narrow cleft. Thecla escaped to safety.

Rumor has it that she's buried in the convent, but that's probably just rumor, since she's also supposed to be buried in Rome, despite never having actually been there. Nevertheless, she is the patron saint of Malula, and a martyr even though she died a peaceful death in old age. Tim looked around for questions, but none came. "Okay," he said, "Let's eat."

After lunch Tim offered to take anyone interested on a walk to inspect some nearby caves. Stan and Tony decided to stay there on top of the hill and relax a bit; Stan at least was a bit tired of Tim and suspected the same of Tony.

"Nice lunch," Stan said, "I really appreciate Sue Ellen including me. I guess I thought we would find a restaurant up here. I also appreciate the time you're giving me. I can't imagine how I would get around here by myself."

Tony assured Stan that he would have made out fine but added that he and Sue Ellen really do enjoy showing people around the area. "We like it here," he said, "The food is great, and everything is cheap." He then described a meal of chateaubriand, escargot, excellent French wine and breads, which they had recently at the Versailles Restaurant. "It's in the middle of Damascus," he said, "and it cost only about twelve dollars total."

Stan laughed and then turned serious. "You know," he said, "I can never get over how gullible people are. Of course, I'm not at all religious, so I guess I shouldn't be saying anything, but some people really do believe that stuff about St. Thecla, don't they?" Tony said he thought so, but he's no expert. "You'll have to ask Tim," he said, smiling. Stan pursued the topic: "I guess it's really no different than any other religious belief. I just don't get it. Perfectly rational people believing in superstitions. Life after death. God. Divine intervention. I guess I just don't get it."

"What's to get?" Tony said, "You either believe or you don't. Just look around. A thousand years ago, the Christians and the Moslems were killing each other around here. Saladin and all that. By the way, did you know that Saladin is buried at the Omayyad Mosque?" Stan nodded; Tony went on. "And now, just look over those hills and you'll see the same sort of killing going on. So, religion is capable of that. The Inquisition. The Intifada. What's the difference?"

"Right. What is the difference?" Stan said, "I mean who needs it, right?" Tony paused and thought. "It's needed," he said. "Whether it's true or not, it's needed. I can't imagine the world without it. True, in a billion years or so nothing will live on this planet. Maybe the planet won't even be here. But for now we have to make due, and religion, some belief in something larger, something in charge, something that will help make sense of this life, something that will insure this life will go on in some form or another, something – It's needed."

Stan said he didn't think he needed it. Tony agreed that some people don't need it. "I guess you're the lucky ones," he said and then added after a pause, "Or maybe not." Stan asked what he meant by that, and Tony tried to explain: "So what if this is all there is; we die and that's it. Life has lived and died for millions of years and will for another couple million at least. We're an obscure planet circling around an obscure sun in the obscure outer reaches of our universe. And we're here for a speck of that time. And that's time in a larger sense that has no beginning or end. We can't even comprehend endless space; even the term 'endless space' includes some concept of time. It's beyond us."

Stan squirmed a bit, picked up a small stone, rolled it down the hill, and said, "So?" "So," Tony said, "So why not make your life a bit easier by believing in something that puts limits around all of this and makes it comprehensible?" "Even if it's not true?" Stan asked. "Sure," Tony said, "Why not? You have nothing to lose. and besides – " "Besides what?" "Well," Tony said, "Maybe St. Thecla can heal with all that water dripping down the grotto."

Tony suggested they rejoin the others down at the caves. While walking there he asked Stan if he remembered the young man who held his dying friend in his arms. "Who can forget that?" Stan said. Tony then said the young man had asked him if he and his wife would like to visit his family up near Aleppo. "That's Syria's second largest city, up near Turkey," he said. Stan said he thought it was the other young man who had asked him to come to his village, and Tony explained that every week someone asks him to visit them. "I've decided to accept Ahmed's offer, however," he said, "because I trust him and respect his abilities. I think it would be a rare opportunity to see Syrian village life and talk with some people outside the city. Sue Ellen's going along, and we would like you to join us."

Stan said he couldn't intrude, and that he didn't even know Ahmed, but Tony assured him that Ahmed would be delighted to have another American come along. Tony said that he had already asked Ahmed if this would be acceptable, and Ahmed said he would be honored. "He even said his land has a number of houses on it, and that Sue Ellen and I could stay in one house, and you could stay in another. Your own house. What more could you ask? We can just take a bus to Aleppo, a straight shot of about four hours, and Ahmed will meet us there and take us to his village. He even offered to take us to Ebla, the ancient city they're just now beginning to excavate. You have to go."

CHAPTER ELEVEN

And so early the following Friday Sue Ellen, Tony, and Stan headed north on a comfortable bus, bound for adventures unanticipated, bound for, as far as they were concerned, the great unknown. However, as Tony told Stan, they were also going into the known since they would go through the city of Hama, several hours north of Damascus. Tony did not tell Stan why he was interested in Hama. After several hours of the gently rolling , brown, grubby sand of the Syrian countryside, they arrived in the center of the city where they stopped for lunch.

Sue Ellen, always prepared, had packed soft drinks and peanut butter and jelly sandwiches. Before they could even think of eating, however, they heard a low, groaning sound, which Stan said was one of two reasons he wanted to visit Hama. They walked in the direction of the sound until they saw a wooden water wheel, at least fifty feet high. As they sat on a low stone wall near the water wheel and ate their sandwiches, they watched the waters of the Orontes River turn the wheel, which lifted buckets of water high in the air. At the top of the arc, the buckets emptied into a wooden channel which then distributed the water to parts of the city. Tony explained that because it is turned by the river current, it runs ceaselessly and costs nothing. Hundreds of years old, its slow, ponderous turning spreads a heavy groan throughout the town, the weary moan of the ages, Tony called it. Somehow fitting, in this timeless place, Stan thought.

Soon, however, the bus loaded up and they were on their way out of the city. Block after block of squat square buildings floated by the window as Stan thought about the uncertainties of the trip. This might be more than I bargained for, he thought. I might be getting in over my head. As usual. But then he remembered what Tony had said earlier. "So," Stan asked Tony, "What's the second thing you want to see?" Sue Ellen looked over at him and smiled, which disconcerted Stan even more. "There," Tony said and pointed out the window at what looked like a wasteland of broken buildings, hundreds of them. "What happened?" Stan asked.

Tony explained that back in 1982, the Muslim Brotherhood led a rebellion against President Assad. In fact, Stan said, they were supposedly responsible for blowing up part of the Syrian Air Force building across the street from the American School. Stan remembered one of the teachers there telling him they had found body parts scattered across the school yard. "So what's that have to do with Hama?" Stan asked. Tony explained that the city was the center of the rebellion, and in retaliation, and as a lesson to future rebels, Assad leveled the part of the city where the Brotherhood was headquartered and killed as many as 5,000 people. Tony said he hasn't had any serious resistance since then; in fact, at the last election Assad got 99.8 percent of the vote. "What happened to the other .2 percent?" Stan asked. "Don't ask," Tony said. The next several hours to Aleppo passed mostly in silence as Stan watched the burnt landscape glide by.

In Aleppo, Ahmed met them at the bus station and took them to a café owned by one of his uncles, a crusty old local with a full graying mustache. At first Ahmed hesitated when asked about Sue Ellen joining them since there were no other women in the place, only men sipping tea and smoking the ubiquitous water pipes. Finally, however, Sue Ellen was allowed to sit with the men, one more of many uncomfortable experiences she encountered in this male dominated society. They picked among the small dishes of radish, baby turnips, vine leaves, lettuce hearts, and beans, and they dipped up humus with the flat pita bread found everywhere in Syria. When they were finished they were joined by several of Ahmed's friends, who whisked them off to another bus stop and a trip to Ahmed's home town of Binish. Unlike the large, comfortable bus to Aleppo, this was a microbus filled with local people carrying paper and cloth bags of all sorts and making frequent stops along the way. Stan had seen these buses in Damascus and had wondered what it would be like to ride in one since they were always bedecked, as was this one, with a colorful assortment of lights, feathers, and other geegaws. He decided it was fun.

Less than an hour later they arrived in Binish in a driving rain storm. Ahmed had said Binish has a population of 20,000, but it looked like a small town as the group walked a quarter mile in the rain through muddy streets, past dull, monotonous, dirt-colored buildings, past eyes staring from the windows. They must think we're mad, Stan thought. At that moment he agreed with them. Finally, they arrived at Ahmed's house dripping wet with large clumps of mud clinging to their shoes and stood before a single-story house consisting of four rooms arranged horizontally along the street, each room entered at the rear through its own door. Ahmed proudly said this is where his family lives. After an afternoon of tea all three visitors inquired about the toilet and were taken into the backyard to a Turkish toilet in a small, semi-enclosed concrete cubicle.

Afterwards Ahmed ushered the travelers back to his house and into one of the rooms. "This is your house," he said proudly. It had a small, sagging bed and several chairs and sofas lined up along the walls. There was a carpet on the floor and several more carpets shared the walls with various pictures of Islamic women praying. Also hanging from the wall was a diploma of Ahmed's older brother, the teacher. Stan figured that Tony and Sue Ellen were displacing the brother and wondered in which house he would spend the night, but before he could worry much about that, a dozen or so men entered the room and sat in the chairs and sofas lining the walls.

Tony had told Stan earlier that Arabic conversations go on for hours, often punctuated by long, uncomfortable for Westerners, lulls. Before Stan could confirm that description, however, Ahmed's mother came to the door; Ahmed ushered Sue Ellen to her. Sue Ellen's departure with Ahmed's mother was the last Stan and Tony saw of her for the rest of the evening. To Stan, Tony did not look particularly worried; however, Stan knew that before the evening was over, he will have worried enough for both of them.

But before the conversation there was dinner. Ahmed's mother and another young woman, clearly pregnant, came in with more small dishes, which they placed on a large metal tray. Stan saw the usual vegetables but he also noticed a dish of small meat balls and something that looked like a stew. He was hungry and looked forward to sopping up the stew with the round bread scattered among the dishes. The other men, clearly delighted, sat on the carpet around the food and invited the foreigners to join them, cross-legged, on the floor. At the insistence of the men, Stan and Tony joined in for what turned out to be a delicious meal. Fortunately everyone ate quickly and they finished just before Stan's knees gave out.

Ahmed's mother and the pregnant young woman reentered the room and took the remaining food away. Now, Stan thought, forgetting about the impending conversation, maybe we can have some time alone, perhaps even an early sleep. He was exhausted both from the trip and from the effort to keep up with a roomful of people speaking Arabic. His plan, however, was not to be, as the men returned to their chairs and sofas and looked at Ahmed.

"We will now have an intellectual conversation," Ahmed said, "and I will translate. This is my esteemed history teacher who taught me so well when I was in school here in Binish, and – he pointed to Tony – here is my esteemed English teacher and – pointing now to Stan – here is his esteemed friend from America. We shall now discuss." Ahmed nodded in the direction of his history teacher, an older gentleman, slight, with gray hair and obviously used to deference.

He nodded back to Ahmed and slowly began to speak in Arabic. When he finished, Ahmed translated. "My teacher would like to ask you several questions," he said, "the first one being what is your opinion of the Bermuda Triangle." All the other men leaned in Tony's direction; their obvious function at this discussion was to listen carefully.

Stan's first inclination was to say the Bermuda Triangle was nonsense, but when he realized that was not what the men there wanted to hear, he stayed silent while Tony began to speak about the need for urban legends in the west. "Not that the locale is urban," he said, "but you know what I mean." By the look on their faces, they did not. Undaunted, the teacher asked if Tony thought that cryogenics is merely a modern extension of the embalming practices of ancient Egypt. Tony thought for a moment, looked desperately at Stan, and then said, "Yes and no." Nodding to each other, the men seemed satisfied with the answer so Tony didn't try to elaborate.

As the men began to wiggle impatiently in their seats and look around the room, the history teacher smiled, said something to Ahmed and then spoke directly to Tony and Stan. Ahmed translated: "What do you think of Toynbee's cyclical theory of history?" At last Stan thought he could make a useful comment, so he gave a short summary only to be interrupted by the history teacher. Ahmed then picked up the history teacher's line of reasoning: "My teacher knows about the cyclical theory of history as it applies to the West," he said, "but he wants to know if it can be applied usefully to our land." Tony asked if by our land he meant Syria. "Yes," replied Ahmed, "but remember we mean Greater Syria." "Which is?" Tony asked. Ahmed looked over at his history teacher, said something, and then turned back to Tony and Stan. "You know," he said, "Greater Syria. From the Taurus to the Sinai, natural borders." Tony pointed out carefully that these are not now the borders of Syria, but Ahmed said just as carefully, "They have been, and they will be again."

With that stipulation the four men spent the next several hours discussing the history and current dilemma of the Middle East. Stan could not believe he was talking about issues he had only read about, and he was talking with the people most affected. He heard their side of the story, about ancient Assyria, about the Palestinians and the loss of their land, about the Israelis, never mentioned by name, about the French occupation between the wars, and about occupied Palestine, which Stan quickly discovered was Israel. All the men seemed to hang on every word Tony and Stan said. It was heady stuff, Stan decided, not at all like the reception he got in his classes back home.

Finally, Tony told Ahmed they had to get some sleep since the next day, their trip to Ebla, would be very tiring, and besides, he said, I would like to see my wife again. Ahmed said something to the men, and they dutifully left the room, bowing and smiling at Tony and Stan, saying what Stan thought must be a thank you. Within minutes Sue Ellen was brought back by Ahmed's mother, and Stan was ushered out to his own house, the small room next door. Despite the exhilaration and strangeness of the experience, Stan fell instantly asleep.

CHAPTER TWELVE

Stan awoke the next morning to voices outside his door and a rattle of his doorknob. Time to get up, he said to himself. Moments later he joined Tony and Sue Ellen in their room for a breakfast of hot, sweet milk and dry, hard rolls, and soon they were walking back across town, this time in dry weather, to the bus stop and the beginning of their journey to the recently discovered ruins of the ancient city of Ebla. They were followed by an entourage of Ahmed's friends, relatives and children, with other women and young girls peering from doors and windows along the way.

Soon they were on another microbus, similar to the one they had arrived on the day before, except this one was decorated even more outlandishly and had a much stranger assortment of passengers, a dozen or more people standing in the aisle. At one point as they were entering a town, the driver turned around and motioned to all the standing passengers to get down. They quickly knelt in the aisle, and Stan thought it must be prayer time. Sue Ellen said she thought the driver simply wanted to use the rear-view mirror. Soon, however, the bus stopped, and the reason became clear when a police officer entered and saw the people kneeling in the aisle. Tony whispered to Stan that it must be illegal to have passengers standing in the aisle. Stan remembered the total chaos of people at the airport and could not believe that anyone would care about people standing in a bus; however, Tony's assumption proved true when the driver handed the police officer a small amount of cash. The driver did not receive a receipt.

Ahmed then told them they were entering Mara, a town where they could get another bus which would take them to Ebla. There they would find, as promised, the remains of a 5,000-year-old civilization, just recently discovered and in only the beginning stages of excavation. When they arrived in Mara Tony asked Ahmed how far to Ebla. Ahmed said not far but first he wanted them to see the home of Syria's most famous poet, and so off they went once more hiking through dirty streets and past the dirt-colored houses toward what to Ahmed was clearly a shrine. Soon they stood before a two-story house, which looked almost identical to all the other houses in the town, but the look on Ahmed's face showed that this was indeed the house of Syria's most famous poet. "This is where Mari wrote his most famous poems," Ahmed said and spread his arms out in front of him. Tony looked at Stan with a question mark on his face. Stan looked back and shook his head. Clearly, neither one had ever heard of Syria's most famous poet.

After walking around the house and peeking in the windows, Ahmed wandered back to the front of the house and stood solemnly. "Now you are in the presence of Mari," he said, "What is your poem?" Stan was confused and then he realized that Ahmed thought that just being at the home of Syria's most famous poet would produce poetry. Tony looked around with a confused expression and muttered something about his specialty being fiction. He then turned to Stan and said, "Why don't you make up a suitable poem here on the spot? This will give you something to tell your colleagues back home." At that moment Stan wanted to be anywhere but here at the home of Syria's most famous poet, but he thought for a while, considered something like "There once was a poet from Mara," but quickly rejected that possibility. He then came up with a quatrain about the beautiful Syrian countryside and how it is reflected in the poetry of Syria's most famous poet. Unfortunately, he could not think of a rhyme for Syria. "Blank verse," he said to Ahmed, who smiled and nodded. "Well done," Tony said to Stan in a soft voice. Sue Ellen just rolled her eyes as if to say, "How do I get myself into things like this?" A rhetorical question, to be sure. After all, she had married Tony.

By now Stan had the distinct feeling that they would never get to Ebla since it was already the middle of the afternoon. Quickly, however, Ahmed flagged down a bus, and soon they were bouncing in yet another festooned microbus, this time with just two other passengers, who remained silent, even, Stan thought, sullen. In the middle of nowhere the bus stopped, and Ahmed said this is where they should get off. Here, Stan thought, but there's nothing here; it's just an intersection with a dirt road apparently going into the desert. Nevertheless, they got off the bus and soon were walking up the dirt road into the desert. After a mile or so of walking they entered a small village filled with brown homes and the beehive livestock buildings typical of the area. Within seconds they were followed by another entourage of children, and then a woman came out of a house carrying a pitcher of water for them. By now the three travelers were so thirsty they cared nothing for the assorted ailments they were told they would contract if they drank the local water. Stan thought it was the best water he had ever tasted. Refreshed, they walked the remaining mile to the ancient site of Ebla.

The Tel of Ebla is huge and crater-like with the edge of the crater formed by the city wall. Inside the crater the ground slopes gently down to the floor, giving a graceful, bowl effect. Sheep graze on part of the land; other parts are farmed, the farmers apparently little impressed by the importance of the site. Ahmed stood proudly on the edge of the crater, swept one hand across the horizon, and said simply, "Ebla." Tony and Sue Ellen were silent. Stan too stared, realizing that beneath this cratered land lay the remains of a civilization old beyond his ability to comprehend. At one time, 5,000 years ago, the circumference of this crater enclosed and protected a complete civilization lost to history until sometime in the 1970's he seemed to remember, and now he stood on its cusp. Across the way he saw a shepherd sitting back on the heels of his feet, exactly as his ancestors five thousand years ago had sat, caring for the sheep in exactly the same way. Stan was struck by the utter tranquility of the place, by the peacefulness of the shepherd. "He doesn't have a care in the world," he said, softly he thought, to himself. "He doesn't have a thought in his head," Tony said. Stan looked over at Ahmed and Sue Ellen and then back at Tony. Tony continued, "Don't get any romantic ideas about the lives these people live. It's a hard life, and it's a life without the things we take for granted: literature, philosophy, the arts, all those things that elevate the mind and make life really worth living." Stan asked if Tony might be too harsh on the people. "No," Tony said, "They can tell you something about harsh, about surviving, about sheep, but that's about all."

Stan nodded and smiled as Ahmed and Sue Ellen joined them. "So, Ahmed," Stan asked, "Do you think that shepherd over there is happy?" Ahmed said he is happy. Stan asked how he can be happy since he has not had Ahmed's opportunities to learn at the university, or Ahmed's future of interesting work, or even the travel that Ahmed will surely enjoy some day, the chance to go to other lands and to learn of other people. He will never know the rich history and heritage of this place. Ahmed said nothing. Tony broke the silence by saying that even he now knows more about this place than the shepherd who lives here. Ahmed looked at the ground, nudged a small rock, and pushed it over the edge of the crater. It rolled a short way down and stopped. "He knows this place," Ahmed said, "He is this rich history and this heritage. He knows it in his bones. It is not separate from him. With me it is separate because I have opened a divide between myself and the land. It is the price I pay for my education." Stan asked if it is worth the price. Ahmed said he did not know. "Maybe some day I will know," he said.

Ahmed told them to look across the crater, over there, he said, where they have been digging. We'll go there, he said. The four of them went down onto the floor of the crater and walked the quarter mile or so to the other side. There were no excavators, no one working the site, digging carefully, picking, sifting. Ahmed said it is Saturday. They did see, however, what appeared to be the walls of rooms, comprising houses much like the ones they had seen while walking to this site. Ahmed took them to one of the rooms. The library, he said. Tony asked if this is where they found the more than 15,000 cuneiforms he had read about. Yes, Ahmed said, and they speak to us from 5,000 years ago. Stan could only stand in awe, thinking that was 3,000 years before Jesus spoke those words he had heard at Malula. His whole concept of time imploded.

They roamed the site for a while longer, Stan thinking more about the existence beneath his feet of a complete civilization completely gone. Could it happen again, he wondered, but then he realized that the sun was low on the horizon and suggested that perhaps they should think about returning to Binish. Soon Ahmed had them back through the small town and waiting for a bus to come by and pick them up. There they waited as loaded bus after loaded bus passed them by. Even Ahmed seemed concerned. Tony, Sue Ellen, and Stan were increasingly nervous, their faith in Ahmed beginning to waver. Stan wondered if they would have to spend the night sleeping by the side of the road. Just before dark, however, a bus, crammed as full as the previous dozen or so, stopped and picked them up. They jammed themselves through the door and held on to straps as the locals all smiled at them. "They are very pleased to meet you," Ahmed said, apparently enjoying being the center of attention again, at least the attention of those people close enough to see him. "Tell them we are honored to be here," Tony said. Ahmed translated and they all smiled even more. Stan felt comfortable there, almost at home in a way.

When they arrived back in Mara Tony suggested they get a taxi to Binish since by now it was completely dark. On the ride back Sue Ellen fell asleep with her head on Tony's shoulder, and Ahmed apparently took it as a sign that the trio should be spared another late night of conversation. Stan for one slept soundly that night but was awakened again in the morning by the sound of the doorknob rattling. It was obviously time to rise, and Stan looked forward to the return to Damascus.

But first another breakfast of hot milk and hard rolls, after which Stan, Sue Ellen, and Tony emerged with Ahmed into the morning sunlight, where they were met by thirty or so relatives and friends of Ahmed. The foreign trio was asked to sit in three chairs directly facing the sun while every possible combination of people stood beside and behind them, all squinting into the sun, all having their pictures taken with these creatures from another world. As the photography wound down, Stan noticed that the people seemed increasingly crestfallen; he worried that something terrible might have happened. Tony also apparently noticed this change and asked Ahmed what was wrong. "They are sad," Ahmed said, "because you are leaving." More heady stuff.

While Tony was talking with Ahmed, Stan wandered away from the crowd, down toward the end of the property where he saw a young woman sitting on a rock, staring into the distance. That's Ahmed's brother's pregnant wife, he thought. During Friday evening's discussion, Ahmed's brother, the teacher, had pointed her out as she helped bring food into the room. To Stan she looked shy, but he also noticed that she carefully took in everything that was happening. Ahmed's brother said they have a daughter and then, pointing to his obviously pregnant wife, said that if this is another daughter, he will take another wife and try for a son. At that time Stan ignored the biological ignorance of such a statement and said nothing, deciding not to question the practices of a culture which was hosting him. Now, however, as he looked at this young woman and remembered the brightness of her eyes and her curiosity even during the brief time he saw her, he worried about her future.

Ever since his first days in Syria Stan had been troubled by the men's attitude toward the women. He could accept the different foods; in fact, he grew to love some of them. He also grew used to the almost claustrophobic sense of space as Syrians crowded around him and thrust their faces near to his. Even the pace of life grew familiar as he began to understand what one of Ahmed's friends explained to him: Time is like a rubber band; sometimes it's like this, as he pulled his hands apart, and sometimes it's like this, as he pushed his hands more closely together. He could even accept though not understand the Turkish toilets widely used here. But the one thing he could neither understand nor accept was the relegation of women to second class citizenship, and this young woman brought all of this together for him.

Stan had noticed that generally women were ignored, except when the men wanted something, and then they jumped up, prepared the tea, and left it outside the door. But Stan realized it was much more than this, more than the separation of men and women, more even than the male attitude which seemed to Stan to reduce women to the role of servants or even domestic animals. Stan looked again at the young, pregnant woman sitting on a rock, staring into space, and thought of this obviously bright, sensitive, inquisitive person, and realized that she has little or no chance of developing into the interesting and fulfilled human being she could be. Instead she will continue doing what she is now doing – having babies and languishing all day, so bored she does not even know what boredom is. Sitting on that rock, staring into space, she was looking at her future. But then Stan remembered all those young women in Tony's class, the women comprising half of the students at Damascus University. Perhaps it's only in the countryside, he thought. Perhaps there's hope. Stan kept that thought as he turned and walked back up to the house, back to Tony and Sue Ellen, who were obviously trying to get Ahmed moving toward the bus stop, toward Aleppo, toward Damascus. "We're going home," Sue Ellen said later on the bus as they left Aleppo, and then she took a deep breath and added, "I never thought I would say that about Damascus."

On the way back to Damascus, Stan told Tony of the one additional task he had to perform, a task he had nearly forgotten in this magical place. He had some ashes to deliver. Shortly after arriving in Damascus Stan knew where he would fulfill his obligation to his teacher. He knew that Mark Twain had stood on Mt. Qasioun, the 1,100 foot mountain west of Damascus, and he also knew he would release the ashes to the wind and let them glide down into the city many consider the site of the Garden of Eden. "You should look at Twain's Innocents Abroad," Stan told Tony. "He has a passage there about standing on the mountain and looking down on the beauty of Damascus. It's one of the few times in his book that he's not mocking someone or some place." Tony then told Stan the story of Mohammed standing on that spot, looking down on Damascus and saying that he would not enter the city since he wanted to enter Paradise only once. Two good reasons to spread some ashes there, Stan said. But you should do it at night, Tony said.

And so the next night Stan took his small packet and rode a bus to the top of the mountain. Upon arrival he walked over to the terrace where he stood with a dozen or so people and looked down on Damascus. The street and house lights sparkled in the clean air, and the city was clearly outlined by the darkness of the desert beyond. It reminded Stan of the Christmas yard his father used to put up each year. Stan loved it when his father turned off all the lights in the house and he could look down upon the tiny houses glittering there. On top of Mount Qasioun Stan felt the slightly cooler air as a small breeze came up behind him. He walked over to the edge of the terrace, noted that no one was watching, and scattered the ashes, the breeze lifting them and carrying them into the magic.

Two days later, after a final walk around the city and a final look at the Souk and the Ommayed Mosque, after a farewell meal with Tony and Sue Ellen, Stan was back at the airport and soon looking down at the receding landscape of Syria, at the scrubby sand he had only begun to understand.

CHAPTER THIRTEEN

A railroad station out of the Arabian Nights. Stan stood in wonder in the middle of old Kuala Lumpur and looked at the station bursting with minarets, spires, towers, arches, all salmon and white stripes, and all flamboyant. He didn't know whether to stare or simply stand there and applaud. He knew it was built by the British early in the 20th century, but he didn't know if they were serious. Were they trying to incorporate Islamic architectural motifs into their colonial style or was this simply Moorish kitsch? He did know, however, that at some point he would have to return here to take the train north to Penang. His dissertation advisor, Professor Schumer, wants his ashes delivered there.

In stark contrast, Stan had just arrived earlier at the ultra-modern KL airport, a bright, light-filled structure of glass and aluminum. It struck Stan as straight out of a science fiction movie he had seen as a child. The people moved silently on the gleaming monorail that transported him from one axis of the airport wheel back to the hub and a waiting taxi.

Now, he was in Chinatown, old KL, checking into one of the small hotels in the area. Once checked in he walked over to the Central Market area, just a short distance away. His taxi driver had told him he could get just about anything there, from produce to clothing to jewelry to souvenirs, but Stan was mostly interested in indulging himself. Perhaps Stan had been in Syria too long. When the taxi driver had mentioned the Baskin-Robbins store located just outside the market, Stan knew he would allow himself two dips of chocolate chip ice cream on a waffle cone. Not bad, he thought, licking the melting sides, I think I'm going to like this place.

Stan sat with his ice cream cone in front of the Central Market at Merdeka Square, a small park where two small rivers meet, streams really. From his tour book he knew this as the site of the founding of KL. Even after his ice cream was gone, Stan continued to sit there watching the people moving up and down the adjoining streets, going in and out of the market. Finally, he realized that, except for the ice cream, he had eaten nothing since the bit of airplane food many hours earlier, and so he decided to visit one of the small restaurants attached to the market. He entered the restaurant through the market and suddenly found himself outside the building on a worn wooden patio overlooking one of the small rivers. Stan asked the waiter what he might suggest. "Laksa," he said, adding, "Very good. Malays like it. Soup and coconut." Stan ordered that and some Satay, the chicken on a stick dipped in a peanut butter sauce. Before starting his trip Stan would not have ordered anything like this, especially on first arriving in the country, but in recent weeks he had eaten all sorts of things he never thought he would eat. He had even tried steamed sheep brain in Syria. After that, he thought, peanut butter chicken on a stick is little more exotic than a Big Mac. At that point he looked across the street and saw a McDonalds.

After his leisurely dinner Stan decided to walk back to his hotel on the other side of Chinatown, perhaps a mile away. He had read that Malaysia had large numbers of Chinese and it seemed like they were all around him now. He also knew that the country had many Indians, as well as the majority of native Malays. At the moment, however, they all seemed to be living together peacefully, but Stan had also read about earlier conflicts. He hoped the peace would last at least for the next several weeks.

Stan's modest, three-story hotel was located on a busy street across from a large student hostel. He thought it was comfortable, although it seemed a bit musty and even mildewed if you look closely enough. Stan decided not to look closely. The single bed sagged, and the television got only a few snowy channels, all in languages other than English. Stan knew he could have afforded something better, even the tall luxury hotels he had passed on his way to Chinatown, gleaming tributes to KL's growing tourism, but, as in Athens, he wanted a local experience before heading off to Penang.

Over the next few days Stan walked all over central KL. He especially liked the area around the Petronas twin towers and even the towers themselves, then the tallest structures in the world. He took the elevator up to the walkway connecting the two towers; the view was spectacular if a bit dizzying. He also liked to spend time sitting in the park beside the towers, watching young couples walking by, holding hands, and watching families at the pond, the children wading in the water, splashing each other and then running giggling back to their parents. He enjoyed the serenity of the place, protected against the frantic traffic surrounding it. But he knew at some point he would have to go to Penang, and he also knew that at some point before that he would have to attend to some other business here in KL.

While at Carlow Stan had befriended a young woman from KL by the name of Chelsea Jalan. A student in Stan's Freshman English class, she showed up one late afternoon in his office and began to talk to him about her home. Stan listened as Chelsea, obviously homesick, told Stan about her mother and father, descendents of Chinese who had emigrated from Fujian Province in Southeast China some time in the last century. Stan remembered asking Chelsea after class one day early in the semester where her name came from. "The British," she said and explained that the British colonialists had left two important institutions when they departed in the fifties, an excellent educational system and first names. After that Chelsea stopped by at least once a week to talk about things with Stan, things like a possible major. She likes political science, she said, but her parents want her to major in business. She explained that she is the only child and that her parents sold their house so she could come study in the States. "They expect a lot of me," she said, adding after a moment, "perhaps too much."

Stan enjoyed their conversations, and Chelsea seemed at ease with him. And then one day Chelsea asked Stan if she could tell him a secret. Stan was surprised, but said of course, even though he was reluctant to get involved with female students' secrets.

"I don't ever want to go back home," she said. Stan asked if she meant her home with her parents or her home in Malaysia. "Both," she said. She began to explain, holding back tears. "I don't want to go back to Malaysia because of a terrible thing that happened to me there, and I don't want to go back to my parents because I'm too embarrassed of what happened to me. If they ever found out, I think it would kill them."

Stan knew this was something he would rather not explore, but by now Chelsea clearly was compelled to explain her situation.

"You see," she said, "just before I left my home to come here, my uncle raped me." Stan was stunned. No student, male or female, had even confided anything to him this intimate. He wondered why she was doing it now.

"I'm sorry, Professor Pickering. I know I shouldn't be telling you this, but I don't know who else to tell."

"That's okay," Stan said, "Perhaps with time you'll feel better."

"No, there's more. I was pregnant when I arrived here, so I had an abortion."

"Oh," Stan said, "I can see — " But Stan could think of nothing to say.

"So you can understand that I can never go home, and my parents are too elderly to start over again. I guess I'll never see them."

Stan fumbled for his handkerchief and handed it to her.

"I write letters to them to tell them that everything here is fine, but I don't know what to do."

For the rest of that semester, Stan was able to distance himself slowly from Chelsea and her situation. Perhaps she will go back home after all, he thought. So when Stan had told her he was coming to Malaysia, Chelsea insisted that he look up her parents. Stan was surprised. "I have told them about you," she said, "They would like to show you Kuala Lumpur and take you out to dinner. I told them you have been very helpful to me. Perhaps you can reassure them that I am fine."

Now that he was here in KL Stan had to contact the parents and spend some time with them, parents who obviously don't know their daughter will never be returning to them. It could be awkward, he thought, but he also realized he had to do it.

A telephone call from his hotel lobby had set up the meeting at Merdeka Square for 2:00 p.m. the following Tuesday, which gave Stan two days to figure out what he would say to them, especially if they have any suspicion of their daughter's decision. The truth, he thought, but then he realized he would tell them anything but the truth. Chelsea had told him many times that her experience would cause unmeasured grief to her parents, perhaps even tainting them in their society. They would be devastated, she had said.

The two days went by quickly as Stan took buses around KL and even spent one afternoon at Kuala Besut, a small fishing village, mostly sitting on a bench, watching the boats going in and out of the small port, and walking on the scrubby shore line, looking for sand crabs. It was a pleasant interlude as well as a distraction from what would come next.

At precisely 2:00 p.m. on Tuesday an older Chinese couple came up to Stan at Merdeka Square and introduced themselves, explaining that Chelsea had sent them a picture of him that had appeared in the school newspaper. They smiled and chatted happily, obviously pleased to see one of their daughter's teachers. "Education is the most important thing in the world," Mr. Jalan said, "and you are one of the teachers at Chelsea's school. We are most grateful." Mr. Jalan bowed slightly when he said that, and Mrs. Jalan smiled. Despite what Chelsea had said about them, both parents were older than Stan had expected, the father tall with a full head of white hair, erect, even stately, the mother much shorter, heavier, and stooped. Her hair too was white.

The Jalans invited Stan back to their home. When they arrived by bus, Mr. Jalan explained that this home was not really theirs, that they were renting it only temporarily. Stan had a hard time swallowing, remembering the sacrifice they had made for their daughter.

Throughout the small meal Mrs. Jalan had prepared, they chatted easily about their life in Malaysia and about the college. Stan asked if they had been back to their home town in China. Mr. Jalan said no and smiled. "It has been at least three generations," he said, "since any of my family have been to China. We often wonder what it is like there." Stan asked if they have any contact at all with his village. "Oh, yes," he said. "All of us here in Malaysia send money back there to help with their schools." Stan was surprised. "And you do this after all these years." Mr. Jalan assured Stan that they did. "Education is very important," he said, and Stan swallowed hard again.

The Jalans wanted to talk about their daughter's experience at Carlow College. Stan assured them their daughter was a very good student and that she worked very hard at her studies. They beamed. They asked if she has many friends, and Stan assured them that Chelsea was very popular on campus. All of this was true, so Stan had no trouble filling the Jalans in on Chelsea's time at Carlow. Mr. Jalan said that the most important thing in their lives is for Chelsea to have a good education. Stan nodded. Mr. Jalan then said that the next most important thing is for them to have grandchildren around them. "We wait the day," Mr. Jalan said, "when Chelsea can come back home, marry, and begin her family. We will be very old then, but we will be very happy in our last days." Mrs. Jalan nodded in agreement and smiled broadly. Stan forced a smile and felt his stomach tighten. Later he remembered saying something about that being a nice thing.

That evening Stan lay on his sagging bed. When a movie in Chinese played on the TV, Stan thought about the Jalans. Will they ever find out, he wondered. And if they do, what will it do to them? He thought he might be able to talk Chelsea into returning home and forgetting her past and what happened to her, but he immediately knew that would not happen. Who's right here? He could not believe that her parents would react the way Chelsea described, but then he did not know their culture. He only knew that a family has been destroyed.

The questions kept coming. And I thought life was simple, Stan said aloud to an empty room as he dozed off, only to wake up hours later with a blank TV before him and his questions remaining. He turned off the TV and rolled over for several hours of sleeplessness.

Next morning the Moorish extravaganza of a railroad station beckoned and Stan packed his luggage for the ride to Penang. He looked forward to the train ride. He knew it would go along the western coast, much of it through jungle, and although he had gotten a sleeper berth he would be leaving early enough to see some of the scenery and would arrive in Penang several hours after daybreak.

As the train pulled out of the station and made its way through the city into the countryside, Stan went to the rear car and stood on a small balcony looking back down the tracks. Soon the deep tree covering of the jungle enclosed the tracks, and Stan watched the rails and the jungle itself disappear into the far point of the perspective. It all seemed perfectly ordered, and perfectly natural. This is the way life should be, he thought, and knew instantly it was not.

CHAPTER FOURTEEN

Early the next morning the train pulled into Butterworth, just across the water from the island of Penang. It was raining lightly. Stan left the train and walked across the station, up a long walkway, and into the ferry station, the ferry that would take him across the water to Penang. After a few quiet days of sightseeing and resting, Stan knew he would be ready to leave, but at some point during that time he would have to make a delivery.

Stan knew the ferry crossing normally takes only twenty minutes, but part-way across, it already seemed longer, perhaps because of the rain. Although he thought at first he would sit inside, he decided he needed the fresh air so he sat on one of the deck benches and let the wind blow a light mist over him. He liked the mist because he thought it might clear his mind,; he was still thinking about Chelsea and her parents. A woman, another westerner, walked onto the deck, looked at the only other bench, one occupied by a young couple, and then turned to look at Stan. Please don't sit here, he thought. He wanted the time to think. She walked over to him.

"Do you mind?" she asked.

"No. Please," Stan said without looking at her. The Herald Tribune he had brought from KL was beginning to droop from the mist.

She sat next to him, but not too close, and he was grateful for that. He kept looking at his newspaper, not turning a page, while she looked straight ahead, shifting in her seat. Both were getting wet from the mist.

Finally, she said without looking at him, "Why are we sitting here?"

"What?"

"Here. Why are we sitting here?" She held up both hands to the sky as though she were questioning the gods. She then looked at Stan, who finally looked at her.

"You mean here, on this ship?" he said.

"Yes." She looked around the ship. "Here."

He explained he was going to Penang, and wondered why she wanted to know that since she was obviously going there too.

She leaned back on the bench and laughed lightly. "It was raining when we got on this boat," she said.

"Yes. It was." Stan was lost by the conversation but didn't want to admit it. Instead he carefully turned the page of his newspaper, smoothed out the edge, folded it in half and began reading again.

"So why didn't you take a taxi?"

Stan put the paper on his lap, realizing that this conversation was going on with or without him.

"Oh. Good question." He looked across the water. "I suppose I like simplicity."

She turned toward him. "You're sitting on a boat in the rain because you like simplicity?"

He nodded, hoping that would end the conversation, but knowing it would not.

"I guess I like stupidity" she continued. "Look at me. I'll never dry out."

Stan looked. By now she was soaked by the rain. Trying to console her he said the rain will probably stop by the time they reach Penang. "Monsoon rains are like that," he added, not knowing the first thing about monsoon rains.

"I've heard." She didn't look convinced, but she did look at Stan and thanked him.

"You'll dry out quickly," he assured her. "You'll be fine."

The woman shrugged and then walked over to the side of the boat. She stood there, slowly swiping beads of mist from the wooden railing. Stan guessed she was in her middle to late forties, five to seven, perhaps ten, years younger than he. She was wearing a yellow, flowered, loose fitting dress, the kind that tries to hide an extra ten pounds. When she turned toward the front of the boat, Stan noticed her short dark brown hair, hanging straight and cut across in front. He thought she probably had long hair when she was young. She was probably thin then, in a short skirt, laughing easily. The image of this woman recalled an earlier image, one he wished to forget. Maria.

She made a quarter turn in his direction but didn't look at him directly. It was then he saw her eyes, large, slightly feline, and green. Easily her best feature.

She turned her head even more and looked at him. "You know why I took the ferry?"

Stan suddenly realized he had been staring at her and hoped she hadn't noticed. He dropped his eyes.

"No," he said.

"Twenty ringgots," she said, and laughed. "That's 15 cents. How could I pass that up?"

"Me, too," he said, and then realized he was smiling and stopped.

"Really? I wouldn't have thought so. You look like you could come up with ten dollars for a taxi."

"It's simpler this way," he said.

"How?" She again sat beside him. "What could be simpler than getting in a taxi?"

Stan explained that the cab goes south for a couple of miles, then across the Butterworth-Penang Bridge with a toll attached, and then back north, through Georgetown, to the hotel. "The ferry is a straight shot," he said.

"Which hotel?"

"It doesn't matter." He said, "They're all north of the bridge." He then began to talk quickly about the resort hotels strung along the coast above Georgetown, how ghastly they are, how overpriced, and how you cannot even swim on the beaches because the water is so contaminated. He said he had read about them in a magazine in KL. The woman interrupted.

"No. Which hotel are you staying at?"

Stan was confused, not knowing why she wanted to know that, but he told her anyway. "Oh, that. The E & O." he said. "The Eastern and Oriental. It's on the —"

"I know," she said. "So am I. That's where I'm staying. We can share a cab. You're not walking, are you? In this rain?"

"I guess I'll take a cab," Stan said. He had no idea how else to get to the hotel.

"You've been here before?"

Stan shook his head and looked at the Penang shore.

The woman then explained how this was also her first time in Penang. She looked straight ahead. "Some friends in Japan told me to stay at the E & O. I teach in Japan. English. Been there about a year. You can make some money, but you have to run around a lot. It's expensive too. I've saved some. So I decided to take my first vacation, and everyone said go to Penang, and stay at the E & O. They said it's like Singapore used to be but isn't anymore. My name's Anne. Annie. Truax."

"Hi. Stan. Pickering."

Stan thought again of Maria, a younger version of Annie. He thought of the only time he had acted without calculating the results beforehand, one of the few times he had allowed his emotions to overrule his head. Just a few months ago. It seemed like years.

"We could go inside," she said.

"No, I like it out here," he said. He thought perhaps she might seek dryer quarters.

"Me, too," she said, and relaxed into the mist.

Stan tried to put Maria out of his mind.

"You were right," she said suddenly.

"What?"

"The rain is stopping."

Annie stood and walked to the railing. Stan followed her and stood beside her. They watched the ferry slip into its berth, and with the mist almost gone, they followed the other people through the winding passageways, into and through the waiting room, and out to the taxi stand, where Annie piled her two suitcases into the trunk of the next available taxi.

"Sorry," she said, "I seem to have filled the trunk."

"That's okay," he said. "I just have this one bag. I'll hold it."

"It's awfully big."

"I can do it," Stan said and hoped it would be a short ride to the hotel.

The ride took just five minutes, through the shop-lined streets of Georgetown, Penang's only city, past the hawkers and trishaws, past the colonial buildings, England's leftovers, past the men and women going about their business, past a world Stan never knew existed.

And then he and Annie were there: the E & O Hotel.

Annie stared at the entrance. "I love Somerset Maugham," she said softly.

The hotel's exterior was white, with colonial arches announcing it had been here with the British. For more than one hundred years this hotel had looked out onto Georgetown with its back to the Straits of Penang, a fortress of sorts. It had been built by the same family that had built the Raffles Hotel in Singapore. That hotel had recently been renovated and modernized as only Singapore can do, and it was no more. In its place is a sanitized version with suites going for $500 a night. The old E & O was still here in Penang, a fresh coat of paint but the same. You could still get a large room overlooking the water for $70. It was perfect.

A porter grabbed their bags and took them to the desk.

"Together?" he asked.

"No. Separate," Stan said quickly, and then to the clerk, "Reservation for Pickering. Stan Pickering."

"Yes, sir," the clerk said. "Please fill this out."

Annie also filled out her form. The formalities over, they walked over to the elevator. While waiting for the elevator, Annie continued to stare at the lobby, which opened into a rotunda of white, reaching up several stories. Beyond the rotunda was an open staircase and around that were large glass doors with views of the esplanade and the Straits of Penang beyond.

"It's gorgeous," Annie said. "This must be the way life used to be."

"It is nice," Stan said. "It's relaxing. Don't look too closely though or you'll see the paint flecking beneath the fresh coat."

"I won't," she said.

The elevator arrived, a wrought-iron, open, clattering contraption from the early twentieth century with an equally old operator and room for just one other person with luggage.

"You go first," Stan said. "You're on the fourth floor. I'm only on the second."

Annie got in, piling her luggage in with her. The elevator started slowly, hesitating its way up. Suddenly, halfway out of sight, she shouted down through the iron openings, "Dinner tonight? At seven. Okay?"

"Okay," he said as she disappeared up the shaft.

He stood there, not knowing what to think. He had come to the Penang to make his delivery and then to enjoy a couple days of reading and some rest. Now, dinner.

CHAPTER FIFTEEN

They had dinner that evening on the esplanade, shaded by palm trees, a breeze blowing off the water, waves shooshing gently against the stone sea wall. Four eighteenth-century cannons aimed across the straits at the mainland. The lawn was perfectly manicured.

"It is lovely here," Annie said. "I can see why my friends wanted me to come."

They shared a steamboat meal, the Malaysian equivalent of the Chinese hot pot, a mixture of meat, eggs, vegetables, and shrimp, which they put in the steaming water themselves and then picked out what they wanted when they thought it was done. Stan loved the thin slices of meat, Annie seemed to favor the long Chinese cabbage.

Stan told her that just outside the walls of this hotel, Malays, Chinese, and Indians live, but here, he said, "Everything is peaceful and just so. No complications." Stan hoped that was the truth. He was no expert, however.

"It's another world," she said. "I feel different here. It's this hotel, isn't it?"

They ate quietly, saying little fillers. It's hard to get crisp salad in Asia. Where's the best place for souvenirs? Stan grew increasingly uncomfortable despite Annie's attempts to keep the conversation going. He smiled once. She smiled back. He looked down. He sensed he would have to be careful.

Finally, she said, "I don't feel as though I have to fill in the gaps with you."

"What do you mean?"

"I don't know. It's like with most people I just talk whenever there's silence. I'm compulsive, in case you haven't noticed."

"No, I hadn't noticed. I mean I did. Some. But that's okay."

She looked at him until he looked up at her.

"I don't have to do that with you, you know, fill in the gaps. Somehow I feel that here silence is okay."

"It's okay with me," he said, looking at his fork. "I often prefer it."

She looked at him and smiled. "Thanks. I'll be quiet."

"No, I didn't mean that. I enjoy talking with you. I mean when I'm alone I don't mind the silence." Stan was talking more easily now. Maybe he was beginning to forget Maria.

"At any rate," she said, "I usually never go that long without saying something."

Annie picked up the beverage menu and looked through it.

"So what are you doing here?" she asked without taking her eyes off the menu.

"You asked me to dinner. Remember? Through the wrought iron?"

"No, what are you doing in this place? Now?"

Stan still wasn't sure how to respond. Is she really interested in knowing why I am here, he thought, or is this just more talk to fill the space? He decided to be open and told her he had a delivery to make. She didn't ask what kind. He then added, "Maybe the real reason is what you said. Maybe I didn't know that until now."

"What I said?"

"Yeah, you said it's another world. It's an old world feel, I suppose. The slower pace. I can breathe here, without disruptions, interferences. The E & O has a certain elegance, a falling down elegance but an elegance, and it soothes and revives, and allows you to forget." Stan was surprised he could talk that way.

"You sound sort of spiritual."

"I'm not," he said quickly.

"I saw a cockroach in my room in KL."

"I can tell you how to take care of that," he said, grateful for the change of subject.

"I thought you might like to change the subject," she said.

She smiled at him. He looked in her eyes for the first time all evening and they seemed even larger and greener than before.

"So," she said, "You came halfway around the world to make a delivery?"

"No, not really. I mean I did, at least I will."

"Is it a package?"

"Yeah."

"What sort of package?"

"What? Oh, just a package. Nothing exciting."

"Sorry. I shouldn't have asked. I do that all the time. Sorry."

Stan sensed that she really wanted to know, that she wasn't just filling time. "I'm a teacher," he said.

"A teacher? Why didn't you tell me before, when I told you I was teaching in Japan? What kind of teacher?

"English. In a college, a small college, in Ohio. Actually I'm sort of retired. I quit." Stan wasn't sure what to say, how much to say. Just saying it brought him back to a kind of reality he had almost lost in his travels.

"Wow. English, huh. You could at least have agreed with me about this place and Somerset Maugham. That's a little embarrassing. So you're an English professor. Ph.D. and all I suppose."

Stan mumbled something. He knew Annie was angry about his not confiding more in her, but he didn't know why she would care.

"You don't talk much for an English professor," she said.

Stan looked at his plate and wished he were somewhere else. "No, I suppose not," he said, hoping Annie would change the subject again.

Annie looked at Stan until she forced him to look at her. "I'm divorced," she said.

"Oh, I'm sorry." Stan never knew what to say when people tell him that.

"It's okay. I'm over it now." Annie paused, fingering her napkin, and then added, "He got nervous when our child was born — I have a twelve-year-old son, in boarding school — and he just left, like that." She snapped her fingers. "Now that Julian is old enough to be a pal, he wants him part of the summer. Legally, I wouldn't have to do it, but I feel that Julian should know his father, even if he is a bastard."

Stan desperately wanted her to talk about something else. He squirmed in his seat and looked over the Straits.

"Oh, I'm sorry," she said. "I shouldn't go on like that. It's embarrassing you." She touched his hand.

"No, it's okay," he said. "I don't mind. I mean. It's just that —" Stan carefully removed his hand from under hers.

"What?"

"Well, I've never been married, so you can see I can't understand."

"Oh, sorry. Are you gay?"

"No, of course not."

"It's okay, really. I have lots of gay friends."

"No. It's just that since I haven't had the experience of marriage, it stands to reason I can't react to problems of marriage."

Stan was beginning to feel discomfort again; discomfort for Stan bordered on pain. He began to hope all this would simply go away. Why must just talking with someone become so complicated?

"Are you a virgin?"

"What?"

"Sorry. That was a stupid question."

"No, it's not stupid."

"You want to change the subject?"

"No. We can talk about marriage and divorce. It's just that I can't help."

Stan was unsure what Annie wanted. He supposed he could be a sympathetic listener, although he rarely had been, but he didn't want to start wallowing in the misery of another human being, especially when he knew he couldn't help.

"It's okay," she said, "You don't need to help, but it's sweet of you to be concerned. I'm just talking. It helps sometimes to talk. Doesn't it help sometimes for you to talk?"

"Well, no. Not usually anyway, but I don't mind listening."

And then they were finished. They stood, and both waited for the other to move or say something.

Finally, Annie said, "Thanks for the company." And then after a pause she added with a smile, "Sorry about getting upset about you not telling me you're a teacher. It's just that it seemed more natural for you to tell me earlier, my being a teacher and all. I'm just that way. Hope it wasn't too uncomfortable."

"No, of course not. Why would you say that? I enjoyed the meal, and the company."

Stan had enjoyed the evening, despite the embarrassments. When she wasn't talking about her problems, or, unbeknownst to her, his problems, Annie was refreshing, like the E & O, something unique, and she made him forget what she reminded him of.

"Well, anyway, thanks," she said. "Good night."

She turned to go and then turned back. "Look, she said, "You can ignore this. Just tell me you have to meet someone or something, maybe deliver your package, but do you have any plans for tomorrow?"

Stan hadn't even thought about tomorrow.

"No," he said, "I just thought I might take some buses around the island. I have a bus schedule; it's just a matter of getting the right bus at the right time. I think I've figured out which buses to take to do it."

He didn't know why he had said he thought he had figured it out since he had carefully memorized the schedule on the train. Before he could even think, he said, "Would you like to come with me?"

"I would, Dr. Pickering." She smiled. "It sounds like you have everything under control. When do you want to start?"

Stan regretted the invitation as soon as he had said it, but he knew now he was locked in. "Nine?"

CHAPTER SIXTEEN

The next day turned out to be the same as the day before, hot and humid. They got the first bus at the terminal and succeeding ones fell into place, just as Stan knew they would. They spent most of the day exploring villages close to the roads where the buses changed, guessing whether they were Malay, Chinese, or Indian. She liked to walk even further into the jungle. He was more cautious.

When they got back to the hotel, Stan realized he had enjoyed the outing and suggested they get a quick meal and go up to the top of Penang Hill.

"The view must be spectacular from up there," Annie said.

"They say it is," Stan said. "You go up this long funicular railroad. It's over seventy years old, but it still runs perfectly."

"Okay," Annie said, "I like the sound of funicular."

"But first you have to get over to the hill. We'll have to take the bus again."

After the meal, which they ate at a small noodle shop, they walked through Georgetown back to the bus terminal, took the No. 1 bus, changed to the No. 8, and soon were standing in line for tickets up Penang Hill.

"You'll love it," he said. "The whole concept is really simple. They just ratchet you up, and ratchet you down. They have one in Hong Kong that takes you up Victoria Peak. And the one in Pittsburgh."

"Pittsburgh?"

"Pittsburgh. It's shorter, of course, but it works the same way. Automobiles made them unnecessary. Sort of like what happened to trains."

Soon they were ratcheting their way up the side of the mountain, a click at a time. As they did, the view opened up beneath them, becoming more magical with each moment. They stopped.

"Now what?" Annie said.

"We switch cars. Come on." They moved across the landing to another car and settled in.

"It's more efficient this way," Stan said. "That's a long way for one source of energy."

Stan was thinking the same thing about himself. He was not sure he had the emotional energy to carry this out, but he knew for some reason he wanted to, even though it was beginning to disrupt his plans for Penang and perhaps, he feared, everything he had been keeping under control since he had left the States.

At the top, all of Georgetown, the Straits of Penang, Butterworth across the water lay beneath them, lit and sparkling, spreading out it seemed forever. Before them, the tiny ferries were taking people back and forth; to their right, the bridge glittered with lights from cars. Stars glowed in the black sky.

"It's stunning," she said. "I feel I can reach down and touch it, like a toy." Stan thought again of his father's train set.

They watched the lights dancing in the distance and felt the darkness. After a while Annie said, "Silences again."

"Yes," Stan said. He sensed it was okay, and he relaxed for the first time since he had arrived.

They walked around Penang Hill and explored the old hotel there.

"My guide book says this hotel is haunted," Annie said.

"I don't think so."

"Don't you believe ghosts are possible?"

He did not.

"Are you sure they don't exist or do you just not believe they exist?"

His conversation with the woman on Skyros — what was her name? — came back to him. "I'm sure," he said.

They searched out the good vantage spots, standing close together, arms touching, alone under the black sky.

"I feel good here," she said and put her arm in his and squeezed it gently.

"So do I," he said.

Finally, late in the evening, they returned from Penang Hill, tired. The E & O Hotel welcomed them.

"I think I'll shower," she said.

"Yes,"

"Well, good night. I enjoyed the day."

"Me, too," he said.

As they walked to the elevator, she asked if he would like a drink after showering.

"I'll treat," she said. "You did all the work today."

They entered the dark mahogany paneling of the hotel's Anchor Bar and Library. Books lined one wall, and brown leather chairs stood in front of the books, musty without the smell.

"I love this place," she said. "It is just like Somerset Maugham, clear but understated, ironic even, in a way. Maugham never goes on and on about a place. He just says it in as few words as possible — sort of like you, Stan."

"He's a writer," Stan said. "It's his job to use words well."

"But he was also a scientist, a doctor first."

"Probably not a very good one."

"Why do you say that? Do you think he became a writer because he couldn't be a scientist?"

"No, I didn't mean that."

"Lots of writers are scientists, especially doctors."

"You're right, of course." he said.

They each had a scotch, and then another. They talked of small things. Where they went to school. What the Japanese are really like. The future of Asia. All the usual things people talk about when they've had several scotches in a glory-gone hotel in Malaysia. Stan relaxed again into the evening.

"So, Stan, have you ever had a girl friend?"

"Sure."

"Lots?"

"No, not lots."

"Serious?"

Stan thought for a moment before answering, not knowing how to answer, and then he did.

"One," he said.

"Care to tell me about her?"

"No. I'd rather not. I mean it's not that I'm not over her or anything. It's just that — . Do you mind?"

Stan wanted to tell Annie about Maria, but that would have meant a commitment of sorts, a commitment to a truth that he didn't want to reveal. He was sure it would open up all the old feelings, the regrets, the second thoughts, the despair at what he couldn't have, but more than that he was afraid it would tie him emotionally to Annie.

"No, of course not. Sorry," she said.

Annie swirled the ice around in her glass slowly.

"You know Stan," she said, looking at him over her glass, "I'm usually pretty good at sizing up people, but I can't with you. I'm not sure who you are. I can't figure you out, Stan."

"Why should you?"

"You interest me. I like the challenge. I like you."

Stan thought this is how it all started. Perhaps Maria was just interested in figuring him out.

"Don't you ever just let loose?" she said.

"What do you mean?"

"You know. Do something just for the hell of it."

Stan thought about letting loose. He knew he had.

"No," he said.

"You are relaxing here at the hotel, though. That's something."

"Yes. It's the hotel. Like I said, it's another time."

"And another you?"

"Maybe," he said. "Yes, I suppose so. A little bit anyway."

Their conversation again lapsed into the usual traveler's tales — other places, good deals, cheap flights. She told him about teaching in Japan. He told her about trying to coax freshmen to say something, anything. More silences.

Finally, she said, "I really must turn in. You look exhausted too."

"I am," he said.

"Tomorrow?"

No, he thought. This is a good time to end it. And then he nodded.

They walked toward the elevator.

"I was going to invite you to my room for one last drink," she said, "but they didn't fill my refrigerator. Sorry."

Stan felt relief. He was out. And yet he knew this was somehow different. He didn't know how it was different, but he did know that. Annie was not Maria, he said to himself, several times.

Finally, as Annie turned to the elevator, he said, "I have something I picked up at the airport in Kuala Lumpur. I don't suppose. I mean — We are on vacation after all."

"Are you sure?"

He was never less sure of anything in his life.

His room, like all the rooms at the E& O, was large but simple with a window across one wall looking out onto the water.

"Look at the size of this room," she said. "It's thirty feet long. I walked mine off."

"Thirty feet, nine inches," he said.

"You measured it?"

Stan nodded, not knowing why he felt embarrassed about that. Annie closed the door and looked up at Stan.

"It's okay," she said. "We can just sit and have our drink. We can talk."

Stan knew he could not just talk. There was too much to talk about. He would have to be careful.

So they talked, sitting side by side on the sofa, in front of the window. Annie tried to get Stan to talk about himself. He kept ignoring the invitation, asking about Japan, about the Temples, about the Ginza.

"Did you climb Mt. Fuji?" he said.

"No. Maybe one day though."

Finally, she said, "I don't know you, Stan, and I know I never will, but I wonder if you even know yourself. Do you know who you are, really?"

New Age mumbo-jumbo, Stan thought. Of course I don't know who I am. Who does? That's the nature of the beast. So much for that.

Annie turned to him and leaned her face toward his. "This is really stupid, Stan." And she kissed him. He was stunned, and then he returned the kiss and tried to put one arm around her. She turned, letting his arm encircle more of her waist.

Suddenly, she pulled herself free and stood up.

"Wait," she said. "This is going somewhere, and I'm not sure you want to go there."

"Do you want to go there?" he said

"Only if you do. I don't want to force you, and I sure as hell don't want to seduce you."

Stan thought of Maria. Maybe this would be different. Annie's not married, and Maria is.

"Yes," he said.

Annie told him she would go to the bathroom to undress. He was grateful for that. He undressed, turned off the light, and curled under the covers of his bed. When he turned on his side, he saw Annie standing in the door of the bathroom, silhouetted, and then it was dark.

They made love, at first a slow, easy love but then increasingly awkward, hurried.

"Relax, Stan," she said. "Really. There's no need. We can just hold each other."

Stan could not just hold her because this would give him time to remember. He pressed against her, groping, knowing that this was going somewhere new. He was afraid.

When it was over, they lay side by side. Annie held his hand until he fell asleep.

CHAPTER SEVENTEEN

When Stan woke well into the next day, Annie was gone. He opened the curtains, looked down, and saw her in a blue sun dress sitting by the pool, reading through large sun glasses. He didn't know what to do or what to say. He could not explain anything. Finally, he showered, got dressed and went down.

"Hello," he said.

She turned and looked up at him, lowering her sun glasses. "So you finally got awake. You were tired."

"I was," he said.

"Big day."

"Yeah."

"Would you like some breakfast? I've been waiting for you. I had just about given up. I'm famished.

I don't think so," he said.

"Really?"

"Maybe just some toast and coffee."

"Okay. Do you mind if I have the American breakfast?"

"No, no. Of course not."

Annie looked down at her menu and then up at Stan.

"Are you okay?" she said.

"What do you mean?"

"About last night."

"Sure. I mean, fine."

Stan sat down across from her and Annie looked back at her menu. She straightened her napkin, lined up her silverware, and then looked back at Stan.

"When are you leaving" she said.

"Friday."

"I'm leaving Wednesday." The napkin again. "I would like to spend some of that time with you. No commitment. We can just enjoy the island together."

"Sure," he said. "There's still lots more to see here. There's a butterfly farm on the other side of the island. Maybe we can rent a car."

"Let's do that."

They were together several more times and pretended that everything was normal. She bought souvenirs and showed him. He bargained with the trishaw drivers. They had dinner at a Chinese restaurant they found, sitting on a balcony, overlooking one of the busy streets. The days went by.

Then it was time for her to leave, and they were walking back through the ferry terminal. He carried her suitcases.

"Back to being a Gaijin," she said, and laughed.

"Good luck."

"Thanks."

"Don't forget to climb Mt. Fuji," he said

"You too."

Stan wondered what she meant by that. "I doubt that I'll ever get to Japan," he said.

"I know," she said.

The whistle blew.

"Should I write to you?" he asked.

"Do you want to write to me?"

Stan seemed distracted somehow, like he was in another place, but she was here, with him, and he didn't know what to say.

"Then perhaps not," she said.

She reached up and kissed him lightly on the lips. "My card," she said and handed him a business card. He looked at it dumbly and put it in his shirt pocket. He looked up at her and saw a smile.

"Goodbye," she said.

"Goodbye," he said.

Annie walked up the ramp and stood at the railing looking down at him. The whistle blew again. The ferry pulled away, and she began to recede.

"Stan," she called. "Let me know if you ever climb Mt. Fuji." She waved.

He pretended she was too far away for him to hear and merely cupped his hand around his ear and shrugged.

She was gone, and he was alone on the pier.

Stan walked back to the hotel, stopping often for no good reason, taking detours. It's a nice day, he told himself, I might as well enjoy it while I can. But he knew the real reason was he dreaded going back to the hotel, back to the life he led before Annie.

Finally, he was there, looking up at the rotunda, at the open cage elevator, at the floor. What now? He walked out through the rear door, a double door comprised of small, square windows, and onto the small, grass-covered esplanade. He walked over to a bench that looked out over the water to the mainland and sat beneath a gently swaying palm tree . Annie was by now on the train heading for KL and then Japan. Kyoto. She had said it's beautiful there. Would he like to visit it someday? He would, but he thought he wouldn't. He told himself he had a job to do here in Penang. Ashes. After that he had other places to go, other obligations, and then a return to his home. Home. At the moment it seemed as remote as the moon, as remote as Kyoto. So this is what loneliness feels like? He had been alone all his life, and yet this is the first time he had ever felt loneliness, not just lonely, he had felt that often, but loneliness, a feeling of nothing there where something was at one time. Maybe it's just homesickness, he thought, but he knew it was much more than that. He knew he could write to Annie, maybe even e-mail or phone, he had her card, but the thought overwhelmed him. Where would that take him? How would that upset his little world? What if it didn't work out? Like Maria. He wasn't sure he was ready for another risk. Safer this way, he thought. No risk, no harm, no hurt. So what was this he was feeling now?

Stan sat there until the sun went down behind him, the sky to the west reflected in the east as a dark red cover thrown over the horizon of the mainland. He went into the library bar, ordered an Anchor beer, and stared at it for an hour or so. He then went up to his room, tried to read from a collection of Maugham's short stories, Malaysian Stories, he had found on one of the shelves in the bar, and fell asleep.

The next morning he felt better, even with a monsoon pelting his window. He could barely hear with all the noise the rain was making, but he realized there was nothing to listen to anyway, no one to listen to. He wanted to finish his task, deliver the ashes, and get away from Penang, from Malaysia. Start over at the next place. But first he had to decide just where to deliver the ashes. After thinking about it for a few moments he decided to deposit them at the most obvious place, here at the E & O Hotel because he thought Dr. Schumer would approve – Somerset Maugham and all – but he also knew it was more for himself. Where in the hotel could he deposit them? He thought he might simply throw them into the water from the esplanade, but that didn't seem quite right. Could he find a little used place in the hotel? Perhaps he could simply scatter them widely enough that they would not be noticed. But then they would be swept up with all the other dust and deposited in a trash container, ending up in a dump somewhere. Surely, Dr. Schumer deserved better than that. It was at that point that the absurdity of it all hit Stan and he began to laugh out loud. It's just ashes, he said to himself. Nothing sacred there. I could just dump my

packet and the rest of the little bags of Dr. Schumer anywhere and get back to
Ohio in a day. It was tempting, but Stan had agreed to the arrangement, and he
knew he would have to go through with it. He also knew he had had enough of
traveling to know he wanted to go on, to find out what was next, what was over
the next hill. It was a new feeling for him. He had always been satisfied with
what was on this side of the hill.

Later that afternoon, Stan walked into the library bar thinking he might as
well stare at another Anchor while deciding where to scatter the ashes. As he sat
there, fingering his glass and looking around the bar, he suddenly realized what
he would do. What better place to scatter an English professor's ashes than in
a library, and better yet a library that's also a bar. Perfect. But he also knew he
had to be discreet; somehow he had to distract the bartender, the only other
person in the bar. He began to ask questions. How long have you worked at
the E&O? How do you like it? What drink do you most like to make? How
much longer do you hope to work here? The bartender answered the last question quickly, leaning on the bar, a towel flung over his shoulder. Not too much
longer, he said. Stan asked why since he seemed relatively young, perhaps late
40's. The bartender explained that within a year the owners of the hotel, a con-
glomerate in Singapore, will gut the building and erect a sparkling new E & O
within its walls. All of this will soon be gone, including me, he said. Now
what, Stan thought. I can't leave ashes here that will be just swept up with the
remains of a discarded building and hauled off to a landfill somewhere. He
was stumped.

That evening Stan took a walk through the town and returned by dusk. He
was told the neighborhood was safe, but he still thought he should be cautious.
He took the cage elevator to his floor, chatting with the old man who ran it.

"Too bad about the building being torn down," Stan said as they started
slowly shuddering up the cage. "I guess that means you'll be retiring soon,"
he said as an afterthought. The old man didn't look at Stan. He only said,
"No."

Stan was suddenly interested. "Will they give you another job with the
hotel," he asked, wondering how the old man could do any other job.

The old man said, "No, I'll just keep running this elevator like I always
have. Sixty-two years. I guess I'm good for another couple years."

Denial, Stan thought. The old man is losing it. He knew he should just let
it go, but he still wasn't to his floor, so he asked the old man how he could run
his elevator if they are going to gut the hotel.

"Oh, they're going to gut it all right," he said, "all except for this elevator. They won't touch it because it's important. It'll be the only thing left over from the old hotel. They'll keep it running. Of course, there'll be a couple new elevators for most people, but this one will be for the people who come back here. Old time's sake, I guess you could say."

"The whole elevator?" Stan asked. The old man assured him it would remain. "The cage too?" The man nodded his head. "Everything."

Suddenly, the elevator jerked to a stop, and Stan knew where he would deposit the ashes. Tonight. After the elevator operator leaves.

At midnight Stan walked down the steps to the lobby. No one was there except the night clerk, his head down on the desk, apparently asleep. Stan walked over to a chair, sat down, picked up a newspaper on the stand next to the chair, paged through it briefly, stood up, stretched, and walked slowly over to the elevator. To an observer he looked like a man having trouble sleeping and deciding to walk around a bit. At least that's what Stan hoped would be interpreted by anyone watching him from cover. I've never done anything where I actually had to sneak around, he thought. He enjoyed the bit of drama attached to his actions. When he stood beside the elevator, he slowly reached into his pocket and pulled out the small plastic bag. What if someone does see me doing this, he thought. They might think I'm placing some sort of poison or even explosive materials in the elevator shaft. They might even think I'm some sort of terrorist. Stan's heart was racing now, but he had made up his mind. This is the only place where Professor Schumer's ashes could remain intact, or at least as intact as ashes can be, right into the completion of the building's renovation. It's the only place. Stan then knelt on one knee and slowly emptied the plastic bag into the small opening between the bottom of the resting elevator and the hole at the bottom of the shaft. In the dim light he could see the ashes float to the bottom. Rest in peace, he said to himself, and then wondered how Professor Schumer, or at least this small part of him, could rest in peace with a cage elevator clattering up and down on top of him endless times throughout the history of this new building, which hasn't even been started yet. Stan stood up, looked around, saw no one but the sleeping night clerk, and then walked back up to his room and sleep.

When Stan woke up the next morning he was amazed at how well he had slept. I guess that comes from doing a good job, he thought. He also thought he was ready to leave Malaysia and made arrangements to fly back to KL and take a flight to China, his next destination. He also thought of Annie and doubts returned. There was nothing he could do now, he said to himself. I might as well get on with it. He still had several small plastic bags to deliver.

PART SIX CHINA

CHAPTER EIGHTEEN

The crush was unbelievable. Stan had read about the crowds in China, but he was not prepared for the thousands pressed up against the exit gate at Shanghai airport. While all other airports he had visited had ropes defining an exit lane, with relatives, friends, and waiting limo drivers behind the ropes, Shanghai airport had people, lots of them, all straining to get a glimpse of a debarking passenger, all pushed mercilessly up against each other and, consequently, all pushed mercilessly up against Stan as he turned the corner and suddenly confronted this immovable mass.

At first Stan panicked, wondering how he was ever going to get through all these people, but then he realized he need not worry; in fact, he had no choice but to get through them since the mass of people behind him formed its own push through the waiting people, sweeping Stan and his suitcase along on its own momentum. Before he realized it, Stan was out into a huge hall, what passed he thought for the concourse. Still being pushed along, he was whisked out a door, one of many he assumed, and into the dirty air of China. He realized he had no idea what the interior of the airport looked like.

As Stan stood among the people coming from and going into the airport, he knew he needed a taxi to get into Shanghai but had no idea where to find one. There must be a taxi queue somewhere, he thought. Suddenly, a young woman pulled at his shirt sleeve. "Taxi?" she said. Yes, yes, Stan thought and shook his head vigorously. The woman quickly pulled out the handle of Stan's luggage and motioned for him to follow her. As they walked quickly through the crowd of people in front of the airport, Stan said he wanted to go to the Peace Hotel. The woman nodded vigorously and kept moving, dragging Stan's luggage, refusing his offers of help. They continued for several hundred feet and then stopped before a twenty-year-old pick-up truck of indeterminate origin with a cap over the bed. "Taxi," the woman said, smiling, and pointed to the truck. "How much?" Stan asked slowly and carefully. "Twenty," the woman said and added, "FEC." Stan recognized the FEC as China's monetary system, the one for foreigners, but he had not had the opportunity to change money in the terminal and now stood before this woman with no way to pay her. He got a $20 bill out of his wallet and showed her. She smiled again, took the bill, and said, "Okay," motioning for him to get in the back of the pick-up truck where she threw the luggage. The rear entrance was covered with a piece of canvas, which Stan pushed aside. Inside he saw a small wooden bench lining each side of the truck and his luggage up against the cab. Oh, well, he thought and sat on one of the benches just as the taxi lurched forward. Throughout the half hour trip into Shanghai, Stan bounced on his seat, shock absorbers obviously unknown in China. The truck did not have the small windows Stan was used to seeing elsewhere in the world, so he had to push the canvas aside to look out into the road. There he saw a continuous line of trucks, decades-old cars, and buses, lots of buses, all spewing out a lethal dose of carbon monoxide and who knows what other poisons, much of it aimed directly at Stan's lungs. At that point Stan had no idea if he were actually being taken to his destination or even that he would live long enough to get there. As he passed through the outskirts and then the interior of Shanghai, his fears began to mount, until, suddenly, the truck stopped and the woman pushed the canvas aside and stuck her head inside. "Peace Hotel," she said. Stan carefully unbent his cramped knees, stepped out of the truck, and looked around. A sign did indeed say Peace Hotel, in English. When he turned around, his luggage was on the sidewalk, a sidewalk packed with people, and the taxi was gone. The good news is, Stan thought, I didn't have to tip her. The bad news is that I was probably woefully overcharged. Nevertheless, he concluded that $20 was well worth his safe arrival at the hotel where he had made reservations for a few days.

Stan carried his luggage up the steps of the hotel and inside the lobby, ornate in a 1920's sort of way with its dark, elaborately carved woodwork , with its columns where columns were not really needed, and with its art deco stained glass and worn maroon carpeting. Stan went over to the reception desk and announced himself. To his relief, the receptionist located his name in a large ledger, the sort Stan remembered from his childhood. As a child he had found one in his attic, apparently serving, at one time, his grandparents as a record keeper for their expenses. He loved to lift the heavy pages and look at the carefully crafted numbers. Now here they were again, this time in exotic China. He peeked at the perfect Chinese characters in the ledger and wondered which one was his. He was excited.

The receptionist shook a small bell, and a bell hop, dressed in typical 1930's American bell hop uniform, including the small round bell hop cap, walked over, picked up Stan's luggage, and walked slowly toward the elevators. Stan followed closely, wondering if he should perhaps take the stairs instead, although he had no idea what floor he might be on.

Stan remembered reading in the tour book he had picked up at the KL airport (a world away) that the Peace Hotel had been a favorite hang-out of the privileged foreigners between the wars, a western oasis on the edge of the various western concession areas, the enclaves resented so much by the Chinese. Similar to the Baron Hotel in Aleppo and the E & O in Penang, it had provided shelter for many famous people traveling through Shanghai, and had in the eyes of foreign visitors become something of a legend. That was why Stan wanted to stay there. He knew Shanghai had built a number of huge, Western joint-venture hotels that could be considered world class, but he wanted to taste something of the real Shanghai without giving up all creature comforts. So here he was staying in a legend, a somewhat run-down, even seedy legend, but a legend. Nothing new here, he thought.

His room too was somewhat run-down, also seedy, but Stan knew he had been in seedier and felt comfortable here, so much so in fact that he lay on the single bed and fell asleep. But not for long. When he awoke, he realized he was also very hungry, and so that evening he went to the Peace Hotel dining room, a comfortable, if fading, almost elegant area with straight back chairs and lace napkins. After a completely western meal of steak and french fries, Stan settled back and waited for the promised orchestral entertainment while sipping instant coffee. When the orchestra members arrived and set up, they began to play big band tunes from the forties and fifties. At that point Stan decided he had to get out of there and into the real China, something resembling what he saw through the flapping canvas of his taxi/truck. He also decided he would do it the next day since the combination of a heavy meal, travel fatigue, and the trip from the airport had exhausted him.

Stan had been told in KL that the first thing he should get in China was a train ticket to Nanjing, since tickets were often difficult to obtain in China. He also wanted to get to Nanjing because that's where he needed to deposit some of his dwindling supply of ashes. And so with map in hand and a good night's sleep Stan plunged into the mass of humanity that is Nanjing Road, Shanghai's main shopping street, and off to the train station as best he could determine.

His journey took him through the most densely populated intersection in the most densely populated city in the world, a fact he did not contend as torrents of Chinese pedestrians swirled around him, all content with being there, apparently seeing nothing out of the ordinary. At times Stan found himself swept up in a rush of people that took him out into the street where he dodged cars, trucks, but mostly bicycles, bells tinkling, expressionless women sitting side-saddle on the rear luggage racks, small children riding in bamboo seats strapped to the front of the bicycle. It was all exhilarating, and Stan didn't worry since he knew he had only to turn around and walk back Nanjing Road to the Peace Hotel and something approximating privacy.

Soon, Stan saw the street he needed, the one that would lead to the train station. When he arrived, he found himself in another mass of people in a large open area in front of the station. Many people were coming and going but most seemed to be parked there, sitting on blankets, bundles of colored plastic surrounding them, children playing, men smoking and chatting, women busying themselves with small domestic chores, all settled in for the long haul. These are the peasants from the countryside that Stan had read about, whole families coming to the city looking for jobs, finding nothing, and camping more or less permanently before the train station and in other public places.

Pushing through the people and into the station, he found the soft seat ticket booth with no trouble and bought a ticket to Nanjing with no trouble. It can't be this easy, he thought, and then he realized that most Chinese had been packed into the hard seat line for tickets. He was a privileged foreigner. That privilege disappeared when he left the station and found himself back among the masses.

At that point Stan made his first bad decision. He had been watching with fascination the large, articulated buses moving slowly along the streets, jammed with people who hung halfway out of windows. He wanted that experience, and so he consulted his map of Shanghai, determined which numbered bus would take him back to his hotel, and waited at what he was sure was the appropriate stop. Soon the bus came along and stopped in front of Stan. The doors opened, and Stan was swamped by the disgorge as men, women, and children swept everything before them. Instantaneously, however, a counter wave began and Stan was caught in the swell of people moving to the bus. Seconds later he was in the bus, not merely inside but in the middle of the bus, people pushing him from all sides, inches from his face. Stan felt panic because he couldn't see any window and realized that he would not be able to tell when to get off the bus. As he tried unsuccessfully to get the map out of his pocket, a young man standing in front of him and staring at him said in almost perfect English, "Why are you here?" Stan acknowledged the appropriateness of the question and wondered that himself before realizing that this young man was speaking English. Stan said he was a tourist. "No," the young man said, "Why are you on a bus? Tourists take taxis." Stan smiled and said he was going back to the Peace Hotel. The young man smiled in return. "Oh," he said, "It is only a short distance up here. I can tell you when to get off. I am studying English at my technical institute, so this is good for me."

The young man chatted on about his school, about Shanghai, about his interest in America, and then he stopped suddenly in the middle of a sentence as the bus stopped and frantically began pushing Stan toward the door through the unyielding people. As with his entrance to the bus, so his exit was accompanied by the miracle of far too many people going through a door far too small for the number. He was in effect shot through the door and, once outside, stumbled to a stop. When he turned around, he saw that another group was already packing itself into the bus; in fact, his last view of the bus was of several people actually trying to push potential riders through the entrance to the bus as it began to pull away.

The Peace Hotel stood before him. It was still early in the day, however, so Stan decided to walk up to the Bund, that strand of river front along the Pudong River. A combination of narrow parks and a concrete walking path that fronted many of the early commercial buildings of Shanghai, it too was packed with people. Stan thought he might gain some anonymity there. Stan was wrong. As soon as he crossed the busy street leading to the Bund, he was surrounded by people of all ages, all, like the young man on the bus, wanting to try out their English. "Where are you from?" one asked. "What do you think of China?" another asked. "How old are you?" "What do you think of Michael Jackson?" The questions came furiously from all directions, and Stan tried to answer as many as he could. He was the center of attention again, as he had been in the Syrian village, but now with a vengeance.

After an hour or so of this Stan excused himself, no easy task, and returned to the Peace Hotel. That evening he wandered through some of the side streets of Shanghai, trying to ignore the crowds and gaining more confidence the further he went. After several hours he returned to the hotel for another Western meal and another well-earned good night's sleep. The next day he was off to the train station, by taxi, and a leisurely five-hour trip to Nanjing. The soft seat car, which really did have soft seats, carried only Stan and a few obviously important overseas Chinese and military officers. They ignored Stan. Stan was grateful.

CHAPTER NINETEEN

Nanjing. Stan didn't know what to expect, except for crowds of people, and he was not disappointed at the train station, although it was nothing like Shanghai, milling rather than packed. It was almost a relief as Stan walked out to the street fronting the station and hailed a taxi. He had changed some money at the Peace Hotel, so he negotiated with the driver using his fingers. Both satisfied, they rode madly into the evening and down Zhongshan Lu, Nanjing's main shopping street, to the Jinling Hotel, the tall Western hotel in the center of the city. As the taxi entered the gates of the hotel, Stan noticed the crowds of Chinese standing outside the fence, staring in at the hotel, obviously peasants from the countryside getting as close to the exotic foreigners as possible. The Jinling Hotel was newer than the Peace Hotel but without its character. It could, in fact, have been found anywhere in the world. When Stan opened the door to his room, he thought he might be back in Cleveland or Detroit.

The only literary association Stan knew about Nanjing was that Pearl Buck had lived there for a time before she wrote <u>The Good Earth</u>, a book Professor Schumer had praised and, therefore, a book which Stan had read. He thought he might deliver the ashes somewhere in the town where she was born and raised. Before leaving the States Stan had contacted Meng Dijin, the chair of the English section of the Foreign Languages Department at Nanjing University, since he had published a book on Pearl Buck in China. Stan thought Meng Dijin might be able to get him to her home, although he wasn't sure just how he would raise the subject of the ashes. He thought about it as he fell asleep that night, deciding not to tell Meng Dijin the reason for going to Pearl Buck's town. He would just say he was interested in her. The next morning, Stan walked the mile or so up Zhongshan Lu and back one block to the university.

As he approached the entrance to the university, Stan passed a number of sidewalk stalls and even small outdoor restaurants. He was particularly intrigued by an old woman serving noodles to a young couple. She cooked the noodles over a charcoal fire enclosed in a large discarded food can and served the two bowls steaming hot to the couple seated at a small table and bench. They slurped happily away. He was also intrigued by an older man wearing a

Mao-type blue coat grinding out new keys and by a stall with various books and magazines spread out on a long table. He walked down the street paralleling the wall and saw, over the wall, various buildings he assumed to be dormitories of some sort because they all had colorful clothing hanging from the windows, producing a Mondrian-type appearance. Finally, Stan turned a corner into a small alley and came upon another, even smaller alley. As he turned into this passageway, he saw a gate ahead of him. The entrance, he thought.

When he arrived at the entrance, Stan saw, among hundreds of students, a western-looking couple, both much taller and heavier than the students, and both in their sixties, perhaps early seventies. Stan stopped them and asked if they speak English. "We invented English," the man said, explaining that they were from England, Devon to be exact. "Do you know where that is?" he asked Stan. Stan did not but said he had been in England recently and loved it. "Yes, of course," the man sniffed. Stan then asked if he could direct him to the English Department. The man said there is no English Department. Rather it's the English Section of the Foreign Languages Department. Stan then asked if he could tell him where that is, where Meng Dejin can be found. "Meng Dejin," the man said, "You know Meng Dejin. Great chap. Splendid." After a short pause, he added, "Oh yes, the location. Just go through the gate here, up to the intersection, turn right, north that is, and go to the end. You'll find him in the English Section building, the one on the left. He's always there. Good fellow. Good fellow. Cracking good." He gave Stan a big smile and said his name was Field, Ian Field. My wife, Fiona." As Ian and the silent Fiona departed, heading off into the wilds of Nanjing, Stan thought, of course, what other names would this British couple have?

Stan walked into the campus, past a large pile of soft coal and an extensive bulletin board with neat Chinese calligraphy, messages he assumed to the students, although few were paying any attention. The campus was cooler than the city, perhaps because of the many trees that lined the walkways and covered the grassy areas. Stan enjoyed the five minute walk. He especially enjoyed the students, many sitting on the grass, despite the chill in the air, reading or resting. They reminded him of his own students back in Ohio and he felt a pang of homesickness. It doesn't matter, he thought. They're not my students anymore.

Finally, he reached the northern edge of the campus and stood in the midst of three buildings forming three sides of a small grassy area. Each building was just two stories high, and the grassy area was unkempt, grass and weeds of various lengths sprouting among the dirt patches. Despite the unattractive, to Stan, look of the area, even more students milled about, many sitting on the grass patches in twos or threes, chatting happily away. This was the area described to him by Ian as the Foreign Languages buildings, and over to his left the offices of the English Section. Stan walked into that building, looking for Meng Dejin or anyone who could help him get to his destination.

Stan looked around several rooms on the ground floor but saw no one, so he decided to go up the narrow stairs. At the top of the stairs, he saw what he took to be a young, female Chinese student and asked for Meng Dejin. She replied in excellent English that he was in the room at the far end of the corridor. Stan complimented her on her English, and she replied that she had just returned from three years in the States, Harvard, where she had earned her Ph.D. She said she's on the English faculty. Oh, was Stan's response.

At the end of the hall before an open door, Stan looked in at a small room containing five desks. No one noticed him so he cleared his throat and asked for Meng Dejin. A man Stan guessed to be about fifty, although Stan had lost all confidence in his ability to guess the ages of Chinese, stood up and came over. "I am Meng Dejin, please come in." Stan took two steps into the room and said that he is Stan Pickering from Ohio, from the States. Meng Dejin interrupted him. "Of course," he said. "I remember you are interested in Pearl Buck, a wonderful writer. You wrote to me. Would you like some tea? Please sit down." Meng Dejin offered Stan the only other chair, a straight-backed wooden chair like all the other chairs in the room, and poured hot water from a thermos over some loose tea leaves in a china cup and then topped up his own. While they talked, Meng Dejin occasionally blew over the surface of his tea, blowing the leaves floating there out of the way so he could take another sip. Stan tried to do the same thing, although he more often than not ended up with a leaf on his tongue. Nevertheless, he felt entirely comfortable with this man and looked forward to spending some time with him, perhaps even discussing Pearl Buck.

During the next several days Stan stopped in to chat with Meng Dejin. Stan told him about his small school in Ohio, and he told Stan about his year at Harvard as a visiting scholar. At one point he mentioned that he had graduated from Nanjing University in 1969, and "went directly to the river to help build the Yangtze River bridge." Stan was curious. "Oh," Meng Dejin said, "We all did manual labor at that time. You see it was the Cultural Revolution. I was lucky. Many of my friends were sent to the countryside. It was very painful." Stan wanted to know more, but realized Meng Dejin didn't want to talk about it, so he let it drop. Another time, he thought, but he also decided he needed to know more about the Cultural Revolution since so many of the participants on both sides are still alive. Stan had remembered reading about the Cultural Revolution during the late Sixties, when American college campuses were going through their own revolution. He had been fascinated by the grainy images of rampaging students on the nightly newsreels and had always wanted to know more about it. Living history, Stan thought, and now was his chance to get first-hand accounts.

Over the next two days one of the graduate students escorted Stan around the city, Stan objecting to taking up her time, but Meng Dejin insisting this was a good opportunity for her to practice her English. And Nanjing has its share of tourist things to see. He visited Stone City, the red sandstone remnants of a third century citadel located in the western part of Nanjing, easily missed unless pointed out by a guide. He visited other parts of Nanjing even more spectacular. He was told the city wall dates back to the 14th century and is still the largest city wall ever built anywhere, approximately 37 kilometers, much of it remaining. He also visited the Zhonghua Gate on the southern section of the wall, actually a series of four successive gates, each huge and each containing vaults housing at one time as many as 3000 soldiers. And just a few blocks from the university Stan was shown a well-preserved 14th century drum tower and a museum containing a spectacular third century jade burial suit. But he enjoyed most wandering through the Taiping Museum in the center of the city.

The story of the Taiping Rebellion captivated Stan. He learned that Nanjing was the center of this particular rebellion, which lasted from 1851 to 1864, a revolution which at one point controlled most of southern China. The movement was heavily Christianized; in fact, the leader, Hong Xiuquan, claimed to be the younger brother of Jesus. Modesty, Stan thought, prohibited him from claiming to be the older brother. The rebellion was finally ended after a devastating bombardment of the city by Chinese and British troops. Despite the western religious attachment, the Chinese see this rebellion as a precursor to the Nationalist movement early in the twentieth century, and the museum itself contains many artifacts of the rebellion. Stan was pleased to discover that the gardens, which now form part of the grounds and were originally part of the palace of the first Ming Emperor, are being restored. That might make up for some of the many sites and artifacts destroyed during the Cultural Revolution as the students followed Mao's dictum to destroy all that is old.

But the real tourist stops, Stan discovered, are found just outside the city, in a hilly area called the Eastern Suburbs, where he saw the location of the tomb of Hong Wu, the first Ming emperor, who ruled during the 14th century.

But Stan was most impressed by the Sun Yatsen Memorial, a massive structure sliding 323 meters up the side of a mountain. Stan stared at the white marble and blue glazed tiles gleaming in the sunlight and then walked to the top of the monument where a large crypt supports a reclining statue of the dead Sun Yatsen and beneath that, some say, lay the body of China's George Washington. Stan's guide, however, told him some people think the Nationalists under Chiang Kai-Chek took the body with them when they retreated to Taiwan, but the Chinese surrounding Stan didn't seem to care as they crushed into the single lane entrance to the crypt and then crushed out again.

Stan enjoyed all of it; however, he was growing impatient to make his deposit and returned once more to Meng Dejin's office. "Yes, I've been thinking about your interest in Pearl Buck," Meng Dejin said, "and I think you should visit her home in Zhenjiang. It's only ninety miles away, but it will take hours to get there because of the bad roads. I think someone will be going there soon. I'll let you know when." Perfect, Stan thought and immediately began to rethink the plan. He had seen the terrible roads of the countryside through the train window.

In the meantime Stan got to know some of the foreign teachers, mostly Americans, teaching at the university, usually meeting them for dinner at their favorite local eatery. Zhou's, or Joe's as it was known in the Western community, was a narrow restaurant with a half dozen tables and painfully narrow benches. Mrs. Zhou, Stan assumed, did all the cooking over a charcoal fire located in an opening between the interior of the restaurant and the exterior. She fired up the charcoal with a hand bellows and then expertly manipulated three or four dishes simultaneously over the single fire, holding one over the fire until it was steaming and then quickly switching to another. In this way she could feed everyone in the restaurant as quickly as if she had a full array of kitchen stoves and utensils. This must be what they mean by expert Chinese juggling, Stan thought. Each night for the first week of his stay Stan enjoyed a different meal. He also enjoyed the local beer, Jinling, which was sold only in quart bottles and opened with bottle openers hanging on strings from nails in the wall.

In the short time Stan had been in Nanjing he had met and even become friends with a number of Westerners and even some of the Chinese teachers and students. So far his stay in China had been the most social of his stops, eating out almost every night with a group of friendly, chatty, interesting people, discussing China's present course of modernization and even Westernization as well as the international implications of such almost revolutionary change.

On one hand, he could buy for almost nothing originals of Chairman Mao's little red book, the collection of quotations that everyone had to memorize and repeat on demand during the Cultural Revolution, while on the other hand he saw posters of Madonna, the material girl, for sale here in one of the last bastions of communism.

Stan tried to grasp what was happening in China while sitting on a bench near the library. He realized this was all very exciting, and he loved every moment of his stay in Nanjing, but at the same time he felt something was missing, a longing he had never felt before. It would be good to have someone here to share all of this, he thought, and he thought of Annie and realized that he missed her. I wonder how she's doing, he said to himself and wondered if she ever thinks of him.

Stan's thoughts were interrupted by one of the American teachers he had gotten to know. He liked Jesse Chambers immediately, despite some of her attitudes and behavior. She had told him she had come to China six years earlier with her husband, an English professor at the University of Wisconsin, to teach English in Shanghai. He went back, and she stayed. She goes home each summer for a month or so, but can not wait to return to China.

Stan figured that Jesse was probably in her middle 50's, short and, unlike the Chinese, somewhat squat. Stan had even made notes of her mannerisms and appearance. She walked straight-ahead, a barrage of quick steps. When she entered any group, she immediately launched into the subject she wished to discuss, until someone reminded her the group was talking about something else. At that point, she sheepishly backed down, apologized, and said she did not realize what she was doing. She wore jeans, always, and they swung low on her hips. She also preferred flannel shirts and leather boots and wore a blue knitted hat with a knitted bill projecting over her eyes. Her wardrobe was always accented with a heavy metal chain dangling keys from her belt, the sort of thing construction workers wear in the West. And she always had a cigarette drooping from her lips, even when she was talking.

Stan also discovered through some of the students that all the Chinese love her, in part, he thought, because her outlandish behavior, outlandish wardrobe, and outlandish language reinforced their stereotype of the frontier American. But he also knew they loved her because of her kindness and her generosity of time and money. Students said it was nothing for her to spend hours with a student needing help or to give that student a few hundred dollars to tide him or her over when arriving for graduate school in the States. She was obviously a good teacher and she worked hard. She told Stan that she had built up a personal library over the time she was in China, grouping works that might be useful to students doing M.A. theses. She called herself an old-time itinerant teacher who carries her books with her.

But as kind and generous as Jesse was, Stan discovered that she also had her dislikes, which she broadcast loudly and to all, primary among these being American diplomats and journalists. She had a tendency to group people and then to denounce the entire group, without exception. There was, therefore, no such thing to Jesse as a competent diplomat and no such thing as an honest journalist. She particularly disliked journalists who wrote books about China because, she insisted, they didn't know what they were talking about. Stan made a note not to write a book about China, especially if there would be any chance Jesse might get hold of it.

Only once did Stan see Jesse drop her tough pose. He had asked her why she didn't go back to America and get a job at a university there. He thought he already knew the answer: she loves China and wants to contribute to China's modernization. But she gave him another answer. She said she had had a successful early career in teaching, having received a Ph.D. from a good school and having landed a good teaching assignment. But then her son came down with a disease, which necessitated her giving him full-time care for a number of years. By the time he had recovered, she had lost ten years of her career and, because of the tight job market, could not pick it up again. "Oh," she said, "I might have gotten a job at Podunk U. teaching Freshman English forever, but here I can teach literature to graduate students." Ten years lost, Stan thought, Jesse's own Cultural Revolution, one more thing she has in common with many of her Chinese colleagues. Despite everything, Stan grew to like this curmudgeon, about his age, but with several more lifetimes of experience.

CHAPTER TWENTY

One afternoon Stan got a message from Meng Dejin, asking him to stop by. At last, Stan thought, a trip to Pearl Buck's home. When he arrived, however, and was blowing and sipping his tea, Meng Dejin said he thought Stan might enjoy a trip to a literary conference up in Jinan province. "Is that close to where Pearl Buck lived?" Stan asked. Meng Dejin said no, it's an eight-hour train ride on the way to Beijing, but he thought Stan might enjoy getting to see another part of China and meeting some other academics. He explained that one of his graduate students, one with excellent English, was going there and that Stan might provide some companionship for her as well as security. He said the conference was on the topic of Post-Modernism. Great, Stan thought, but he decided to go anyway, almost as a favor to Meng Dejin.

Fu Lan was in her thirties, Stan guessed, and quite outgoing. She said in impeccable English she was happy he was going with her, explaining that they would be in a soft sleeping compartment with two other people, probably men. When Fu Lan got on the train they walked through the hard-seat compartments, four narrow bunk beds for eight people crammed into a small area. The travelers, mostly men, stretched out into whatever space they could find with luggage piled high everywhere. They were sipping tea, playing cards, smoking foul-smelling cigarettes, and generally having a jovial social time. By contrast their soft-sleeping arrangement was luxurious, with only two other occupants in the upper and lower bunks along one side. The compartment also had a small table at the lace-draped window.

Fu Lan said something to their compartment mates, whom Stan took to be Chinese, but she then told him they are Japanese, who do not speak English. She turned from them and made a scowl. "I do not like them," she said, and then added almost as an afterthought, "They were terrible to us during the War of Resistance," which Stan took to be World War II. He remembered reading about the Rape of Nanjing in 1937, an atrocity in which many thousands of Chinese were ruthlessly massacred by the occupying Japanese.

Fu Lan told Stan to take the bottom bunk. "I don't mind being up there," she said. "I'm most happy to be in a soft-sleeper. This is my first time. Even when I traveled from my home in Inner Mongolia I traveled hard seat and had to sleep sitting up." Fu Lan was obviously delighted with the arrangement, as was Stan. Stan was also pleased with the rolls which Fu Lan had brought with her and held out his porcelain cup for tea leaves. Once his cup was filled with hot water from the thermos, which had been placed in the compartment for them, he and Fu Lan sat back and relaxed.

Fu Lan asked Stan how he has been enjoying China, the usual question he had received from just about every Chinese he had met. "Fine," he said, "Everyone has been very kind." His usual response. "Is there anything you would like to know about?" she asked, "Anything I can help you understand." Stan wondered just how sincere Fu Lan was in her offer since he had one topic he had wished to discuss with someone. He asked her if she remembers the Cultural Revolution. "Oh, yes," she said, "I was a child in elementary school when it began. I missed years of schooling." Stan asked her what she remembers about it.

"I loved my grandmother very much," Fu Lan said suddenly. "When I was small, just after the Cultural Revolution started, she was attacked in big character posters because my grandfather had been a landlord. The woman in charge of our work unit did not like my grandmother and always found things to criticize.

"I remember one day I asked my grandmother to buy me another Chairman Mao pin. Everyone wore them then and we had many in our house. She said she would not buy me another pin because I already had so many. 'You cannot eat a Chairman Mao pin,' she told me. The woman heard her say that and reported what she said in a big character poster."

Fu Lan said not only was her grandmother criticized but also her father because he too was associated with his father's bourgeois background and because he was a teacher. "For one whole year," she said, "my father was kept in a cow shed at the school where he taught because he needed reeducation. He was denounced and told to reexamine his mistakes and to confess his crimes. They called him names."

She said her father never really capitulated to his tormenters but rather excessively agreed with them. "Instead of bowing before them and mumbling his crimes," she said, "he stood up straight before them and shouted them out, calling himself the names the guards were calling him. The Red Guards did not like this."

During the time her father was at school, Fu Lan stayed at home with her mother and grandmother. Stan asked her what she thought of what the Red

Guards were doing to her father. She said at the time she thought they were doing the right thing because her father was from the wrong background. "You see," she said, "that was all we heard. I just thought how unlucky I was to have a father like that. I used to dream my father had died and my mother had married someone from a good family because then the other children would like me and I would have friends. I pleaded with my mother to divorce my father. But she would not do that. I was depressed throughout my childhood," she said, "and I cried a lot."

During the first years of the Cultural Revolution, she said her school as most schools was closed. Although she didn't have a formal education from grades two to five, each day she went to school anyway, only to be told there was no school that day. At first, she said, the children were happy about not having school, but soon they wanted school. Occasionally, one of the teachers would do some tutoring, and the children often studied together and taught each other. Since her parents were both teachers, they also helped her. "But they did not help much," she said, "because they did not see what good education would do me. The future looked hopeless to them," she said.

The double indictment of landowner and teacher continued to place the family in danger. "We were always in fear that the Red Guards would come and take something from us or do something to us," Fu Lan said. "One time they came in and began to tear through all our belongings. They found my parents' collection of records, and we had many western classical records – Mozart, Haydn – because my parents loved music. The Guards said this was western influence and took all our records." She lived in fear of the next door knock, all the time thinking how unlucky she was to have this family.

By the beginning of the Seventies, the schools reopened and education resumed. Fu Lan said she was a bright young girl and quickly earned the respect of her classmates, despite her undesirable background. "We had an election," she said, "to choose two students from our class to be Little Red Guards. All Schools were supposed to have these. I was chosen by my classmates, but my teacher came to me and told me I could not be a Little Red Guard because of my father. They had another election and another girl was chosen. When the school had the ceremony making her the Little Red Guard, I sat in the back and silently cried through the whole thing."

The next year Fu Lan was again elected by her classmates, and this time the teacher allowed her to assume the title. When she entered Middle School, where elections to Red Guards were also held, she won that election as well and for the next several years was a Red Guard.

Stan told her he was astonished to hear she had become a Red Guard, especially after what they had done to her father. "Didn't you feel like you were betraying your father?" he asked. "No," she said. "First of all, the Red Guards were no longer destroying things and persecuting people. They were more like propaganda or cultural leaders. I remember we put on plays and concerts. I loved that because I loved to sing and dance. I was happier then."

"But," Stan persisted, "These were the people who had humiliated your family. Didn't that bother you?" "No," she again insisted, "I still thought the fault was with my father and his family, and we were just unlucky. By being a Red Guard, I thought this was a lucky thing for me. I was grateful to be chosen despite not really feeling worthy of it."

When Fu Lan reached the eleventh grade in school, her parents told her she should leave school. Stan was surprised to hear this since both parents had been teachers and since the Chinese value education. "If I had graduated," she explained, "I would have been sent to the countryside, away from my parents, and they did not want this to happen." Stan asked her what she did then, thinking that she had probably been assigned to some sort of manual labor. "I became a teacher," she said, "a teacher of English at the Middle School where I had just been a student. I even taught my old classmates and even some twelfth grade students." She added with a laugh, "I was a very good teacher and knew more than most of the other teachers anyway."

Fu Lan explained to Stan that finally, in 1976, the Cultural Revolution ended with the death of Mao and the arrest of the "Gang of Four." Once again the universities were opened to students on the basis of competitive examinations rather than just to peasants and students from correct family backgrounds or with political connections. Despite having missed the last year of high school, Fu Lan passed the university entrance examination, allowing her to enter the university in her home town in Inner Mongolia. When she graduated, she was made a teacher at that university.

And then, she continued, three years ago, now married with a small daughter, she decided to study for a Master's degree at Nanjing University. This meant leaving her husband behind and her daughter with her parents while living in a student dormitory at the university and working for three years on her degree. As she now approached her degree, she looked forward to returning to her husband and daughter in Inner Mongolia and getting a teaching position at a university there, for a very small salary.

"Do you ever regret working on your degree for the past three years, especially since you will receive very little pay in return?" Stan asked her. "No," she said, "I like to teach and I think that teaching is important to my country. I could translate popular novels or something and make much more money, but I do not think it is worth it, even for a lot of money. Many people think I am wrong, even my husband, but that is what I believe."

As the light outside the train window faded and they prepared for sleep, Stan asked Fu Lan what she really wanted. "I want power," she said. "I do not want to stay just a teacher because a teacher just does what others tell her. I want to be able to tell other people what to do because I think my ideas are good." As Stan was about to close his eyes, she added, "That is why I want to become a member of the Communist Party."

Stan's eyes popped open wide. "Wait a minute," he said, "I thought all young people believe Communism is wrong and all party members are corrupt." Fu Lan agreed but then added, "Unless I can become a Party member, I will not be able to become a Dean of the university, and I will not have any power unless I'm a Dean." Stan countered: "Then, you're saying you want to join the party for pragmatic reasons, that it has nothing to do with ideology or with what you believe." "Of course," she replied, "That is why everyone joins the Party. I just hope they accept me."

As Stan drifted into sleep, he thought about that and about the life she had so far survived. Finally, he rolled over and said to the darkness, "Good night, Dean Fu."

CHAPTER TWENTY-ONE

Late the next morning Stan and Fu Lan arrived at the Jinan train station and took a taxi to the university where the conference on Post-Modernism was being held. While Fu Lan began to work on her thesis, Stan went off in search of the Fulbrighters Meng Dejin said would be at the conference. He soon found two of them sitting at a round concrete table outside a large concrete building that could have been a classroom building or a heating plant. They introduced themselves as Rufus James, a Fulbrighter from Florida and Larry Pendelton, a California Fulbrighter, who was teaching in Beijing. During their conversation Stan found Rufus irrepressible, always moving, always working on ideas, always enthusiastic about the latest literary theory. Despite this reminder of Stan's own unpleasant encounters with the latest literary theory back home, he liked Rufus. But he was fascinated with Larry, a clearly brilliant and eclectic teacher from San Diego State where he taught courses in Rock Music, Post-Modernist Fiction, and Post-Structural Criticism. But what fascinated him most was the way he could drop back into the 1960's, complete with jeans and jean jacket and a constant patter of 60's type language, punctuated by "likes" and "you knows." Even his face looked young, much as it must have looked when he was a college student, except for a slight fraying at the edges and a slight graying of the hair, longish and unkempt. Stan looked forward to several days of conversation with Larry during the conference. Little did he suspect they would share a mutual fascination with another man, this one from the Pittsburgh area.

Later that afternoon Stan began to make a cup of coffee in his room when he discovered the service people had not given him the usual thermos of hot water. He went to the adjoining apartment and knocked on the door. A Chinese woman, of indeterminate age, opened the door and smiled broadly. Stan showed her his empty cup and said, "hot water." She motioned him into her kitchen, still smiling. While she was getting Stan a thermos, he peeked around the corner of another room and saw a man, wearing a pair of those thick, black, plastic-framed glasses all Chinese used to wear. He looked back at Stan. "Ni hao," Stan said, using the only Chinese he had managed to pick up so far. "Hey. You American?" the man shouted with a perfect western Pennsylvania accent, the kind Stan imagined steel workers must have had forty years ago. Stan was instantly disoriented.

"Yeah," Stan said, "Sorry, I thought you were Chinese." "I am," he said, "but I'm also American. I'm Jim Aftosmos, from Pennsylvania," and he grabbed Stan's hand and shook it hard. Stan didn't even think to ask what he was doing here, but instead he took the thermos from the woman, who had by now returned, mumbled something about nice to see you, and stumbled out the door. The man followed Stan and called from the door for him to stop back and "chew the fat for a while."

The next morning Stan saw Larry. "You won't believe what I saw," he said, "This guy in the apartment next to me is from Pennsylvania —"

"I know, I know," Larry interrupted, "I saw him too, in the garden. He's one of those Korean War POW's who stayed in China. It was like psychedelic, man. I mean he talks the way people used to talk, and right here in China. It blew me away. Talk about a time warp. I have to talk with him some more. I couldn't believe it." Stan suggested they set up a meeting, but Larry was already around the curve. "He told me to come by this evening," he said, "I'll get some beer and cigarettes. Maybe we can take him out to dinner or something. It's really wild." Larry was now running at 100 miles an hour, but Stan was satisfied that the "we" included him, so he went along with his plans.

Stan and the conference participants ate in the foreign compound, convenient but nothing special, except that everyone there knew Jim. "Hey, Jim, good to see you back. How've you been doing?" Gary Cunningham, an American economics lecturer at the university, shook his hand. Gary's five-year-old daughter also greeted him happily and asked why he had been in the hospital. "What did you have, Jim?" Jim smiled, "Just a little heart trouble, but it's okay now." Everyone, including Stan, chatted through the meal. When Gary's wife and children left, he said to them, "Don't take any wooden nickels," and laughed.

Jim, Larry, Gary, and Stan all drifted back to Jim's apartment. "I teach oral English here," Jim said. "We talk a lot. My students all want to learn English. It's fun." His apartment was the same as those for all the other foreigners in the compound. "Excuse the mess," he said, as they walked through the kitchen and into the room that serves as a living room and study, the room where Stan had seen him sitting earlier in the day. "They just gave me another room," he explained, "and I'm moving things around."

The living room/study, mostly study, was cluttered, but not from moving. It was filled with the comfortable clutter of books and papers found in any teacher's study,the top of the desk a disaster, books in ragged piles on a dresser or in a corner.

Stan also met there two young men, one Chinese in his mid-20's, short, powerfully built, and animated; the other Westerner, about 20, hair dark and long but neat. He had the cool attractiveness of a successful Harvard senior. He was Russian. The Chinese young man spoke no English but didn't have to because the Russian moved easily between Chinese and English.

"This is my nominal son," Jim said of the Chinese young man. "His father and I were good friends. When his father died, I sort of adopted him. He likes to come here. The young man spoke enthusiastically in Chinese as the Russian translated for us. "I used to fight a lot," he said, "and always argued with everyone. Now I never fight and think only good thoughts. My father taught me that," and he pointed to Jim. Jim smiled and changed the subject. "Dimitri is studying Chinese, but he comes by to practice English," Jim said of the other young man. Dimitri smiled softly.

I asked Dimitri if he was studying anything other than Chinese here. "Recent Chinese history," he said, "especially the Cultural Revolution. That interests me very much." Me too, Stan thought. As his eyes wandered about the room, he noticed the front of a bookcase, covered with Christmas cards, here in November, and on top of the bookcase a shrine: two small flags, one American and one Chinese, about ten inches apart. Between them was a black and white photograph of a young man in uniform, with black hair, full and combed back, handsome in the typical mid-twentieth century sort of way, sharp features, strong nose. Stan looked back at Jim's full head of grey hair, swept back in the same way.

"I was a Greek god in those days," he laughed. "Now I'm just ordinary. My parents came from one of the Greek islands. I would love to go there. You ever been there? Dimitri here has the same name as my father." Jim rambled on excitedly. Stan was eager to ask Jim about the Korean War, but once again Larry anticipated him. "So, Jim," Larry said, offering him another American cigarette. "Coffin nails, right?" Jim said to me and laughed. "What was it like in the Korean War? You were captured, right? I mean, how did they treat you and everything?"

Jim started to tell his story. It had the tone of a tale told many times but one he had to keep telling. Stan thought of the Ancient Mariner. Gary excused himself; he had obviously heard this story before. "It was when we were pushing the North Koreans up to the Yalu," he said. "I was given my orders to join my regiment at the front and was pointed north. I kept going north and then I started to see American troops and things going south, past me. But you know the army; I followed orders and kept going north. Then I climbed a hill with a little Korean kid, who was sort of my guide, and when I looked down, all I saw was lots of Chinese soldiers, all over the fields, so I figured I might as well go down and surrender, so I did."

"What was the prison camp like?" Stan asked. He remembered as a kid all those stories about Chinese atrocities in the prison camps and especially the subtle, mind-altering brain-washing techniques they used there. "Those Chinese are clever devils," he remembered hearing as a kind of refrain throughout his childhood. He also remembered reading about the scandal when 26 American POW's decided to go to China instead of returning to America. How could they choose China over America, he remembered thinking. The only explanation that made sense was brainwashing, augmented probably by subtle forms of torture, such as water dripping for days on a forehead.

"There really was no prison," Jim said. "We just lived in a Korean village up near the Yalu. There were guards around, but not many. There wasn't any reason to escape. We didn't know where we were or which way to go anyway. Of course, some of the guys tried to escape but they always came back. The only trouble was when some of the young guys started to smoke the hashish the Koreans grew. I think the Koreans made shirts or something out of it. If you behaved yourself, you got along okay."

Jim told the story of one young GI who began to cry when he was given paper and an envelope to write a letter home. "The Chinese guards took him away," Jim said, "and we didn't see him for six months. When he came back, he could write a little bit. They taught him to write."

Jim said he had joined the army a few years before World War II started. He grew up in a steel town near Pittsburgh, during the Depression, and didn't see much future there. So he joined the army. He fought throughout the Pacific Theater in World War II, left the army for a few years, and then reenlisted in time for Korea.

"I liked the Chinese I met in Korea," he said, "When the war was over, the US government told us we had a choice. We could either go home to America or go to China to live. It said so right in the agreement. Then when we decided to stay, they gave us a dishonorable discharge. The agreement didn't say anything about that. But I'm still an American citizen," he said, adding, "I love both my countries."

Jim explained that when he was taken to Beijing in 1953, he was amazed and embarrassed to discover that he had been eating better than the Chinese people themselves. "It was a hard time for them," he said, "but it was a good time because everyone believed in China and worked hard for it. It wasn't like now with everyone wanting money for themselves. Then people worked overtime and refused the extra pay. They told the government to keep it. China will be okay. It won't be easy, but they'll make it. I have faith."

In Beijing Jim said he was given the choice among four possibilities. He could have gone to a university with a stipend, worked in a factory with a stipend, worked on a farm with a stipend, or done nothing with a stipend. He chose to work in a factory and in 1954 was sent to Jinan, his current location, where he worked in a paper factory until 1963. It was in Jinan that he met and married his first wife. "One of the other workers introduced us," he said, "and I still know him." They were given a small apartment and they worked hard, even through the difficult years of the early Sixties. Then in 1963 Jim was offered a chance to attend the People's University in Beijing and get a degree. "I wrote my thesis in Chinese characters," he said proudly. "It was about the good things in Americans."

Stan asked him what the good things were. "Oh, you know," he said, "about the settlers working hard to make the nation and about how Americans always help out when things get tough, about compassion. I just wanted the Chinese to know the Americans better than they did. I thought that was a way of bridging the gap. I saw that as my job. I still do."

Just as Jim finished his degree in 1966, the Cultural Revolution exploded all over China. "I stayed in Beijing for a while," he said, "but I tried to keep low because I was a foreigner and also now an intellectual." Finally, since the universities were closed, he decided to return to Jinan, back to manual labor, including among other jobs pulling carts through the streets, because he thought that would keep him out of the spotlight. "I didn't have trouble with the Red Guards," he said. "They called me names, things like 'Rotten Element,' but they called everyone names."

The Cultural Revolution did, however, take its toll. After the death of his first wife from tuberculosis in 1966, Jim married again, a marriage that failed partly because of the stress of the Cultural Revolution. "We didn't agree on the Cultural Revolution," he said, "but I was as much to blame as she was. It was just a bad time."

So now he was teaching English and hosting visiting Americans for a little chewing the fat. At 67, with a bad heart, Jim could have been content to just sit back and take things easy, but instead he kept working. In addition to his teaching, he said he had one more task to accomplish. Recently someone from the States had sent him a bottle filled with dirt from all 50 states. "Before I kick the bucket," he said, "I'm going to scatter that dirt somewhere in China.

And when I die I want my ashes scattered too: forty-nine percent in the Yellow River and fifty-one percent in the Mississippi." There must be something about ashes, Stan thought.

By the end of the evening Jim was beginning to tell his stories a second time, and Stan decided to leave. Larry however stayed. Enveloped by smoke in a darkened room in China this child of the Fifties and this other child of the Sixties continued talking far into the night.

The conference for Stan was anti-climactic, the usual jargon-ridden language of self-congratulating literary theorists. What little interest Stan had vanished from the meetings when Rufus told him he doesn't really like literature, he just likes to write about it. It sounded familiar. Stan wandered the streets of Jinan and bought a New York Yankees baseball hat, obviously a knock-off since "Yankees" lacked one e. Meanwhile Fu Lan attended the meetings and continued working on her thesis.

The train ride back was quiet because Fu Lan was exhausted, sleeping much of the time. When not sleeping, she tried to answer Stan's questions about the Cultural Revolution, describing how one of her friends was forced to watch as her father was publicly humiliated on a sports field before everyone in town, how hordes of Red Guards swept over the countryside ransacking towns and even killing villagers for having a foreign book or a letter in English from a relative. "It was terrible," she said sleepily, "but we survived. The Chinese always survive."

Stan was still exhilarated from his encounters in Jinan. He thought of how enjoyable it had been to share experiences with others, especially with Fu Lan, now sleeping in the bunk above him. He realized, however, that in his travels, no matter how interesting or how enlightening, no matter how much he had learned of the world and of himself, something was missing, perhaps someone. He thought of the forbidden Maria back home in Carlow, and he thought of the inaccessible Annie, in one sense a million miles away but in another sense just across the China sea in Japan, practically next door. Despite her invitation, he had not written to her since their separation in Malaysia. He wondered if she even remembered him. If so, he was convinced she remembered him much less than he remembered her and the ease with which they confided in each other, at least after his initial reticence. She could do that for him. China, as much as he liked being here, would be better with her. He held that thought in his mind as he fell asleep to the calming monotony of the train carrying him a thousand miles through a culture many thousands of years old.

CHAPTER TWENTY-TWO

Meanwhile, back in Nanjing, Stan still had to worry about depositing his ashes. When he raised the subject once more, Meng Dejin told him that he himself would accompany Stan to the town where Pearl Buck was born; in fact they would go to the very house she had lived in. Meng Dejin explained that the local authorities had recently decided to buy the house and make it into a tourist stop, hoping to cash in on its proximity to Shanghai. "The house is in Zhenjiang, a small town where the Yangtze River and the Grand Canal meet," Meng Dejin said, "Not too far, but it will take several hours at least since the roads are so bad. We can leave in three days."

Three days, Stan thought. That's not very long to arrange a flight to his next destination, Moscow, and then St. Petersburg. He decided to contact people at the university's office that helps foreigners make travel arrangements. He had heard they are not particularly helpful, but he also knew he could not navigate the confusion himself. He had also decided to make a phone call. Annie.

First the phone call, which as with everything in China, Stan discovered, is easier said than done. He went to an office on campus that specialized in making overseas phone calls. First he had to get in line since others were also planning to phone someone. Then he had to give them the phone number he wanted to call. Next he was motioned to sit over there on a chair and wait until his turn and then until the person working the phone actually got through. He knew it might be a while but he was prepared to wait. I don't even know if she's still in Japan, he thought, or if she will be in when the call gets through. Maybe I should just cancel the whole thing.

He waited for what seemed like forever, his courage fading with each passing minute. Just as he was about to cancel the call, however, the person with the phone, a middle-aged woman with short black hair, and uncharacteristically heavy, motioned for him to take the phone. He did, while she sat across the desk from him. He assumed she did not understand English but he wasn't sure.

"Hello. Hello," the voice on the other end said. "Anyone there? Who is this? Stan forced himself to speak.

"It's Stan."

"Stan?"

"Stan Pickering."

"I know, Stan. Of course I know. How are you? Where are you? What are you doing?" Annie was obviously pleased to hear from him, and she was clearly in control. Stan was also pleased to hear her voice, but he was clearly not in control. He had no idea what to say next. Which question to answer?

"I'm in China."

"You're calling from China? That's exciting. Are you enjoying yourself there?

"Yes, yes. I am. I'm — I'm in Nanjing, delivering my ashes. You know."

"Yes, the ashes. How long will you be there?"

"About a week, I think."

"Then where"

"Russia. Moscow. Then St. Petersburg."

"More ashes."

"Yes, the last ones."

"And then home?"

"Yes. Home."

"Stan."

"Yes."

"I'll be in Russia then. I'm leaving next week. Vacation, I suppose. Education. I don't know. It's just something I've always wanted to do. I'll be in Moscow, at first. Then I don't know where. I just take it as it comes."

Stan surprised himself with his next response. "Can you come to St. Petersburg?"

For a moment there was no response.

"Annie?"

"Yes, Stan. I'm still here. I suppose — I suppose I could. I mean it's certainly one of the places I should visit. The Hermitage is a place I've always wanted to see. It's supposed to be fantastic. I mean — It would be good to see you again, Stan. It would be fun seeing St. Petersburg with you."

Stan felt the same way.

"I can meet you in Moscow," Stan said, "Then we can go to St. Petersburg." Annie did not respond.

"Annie?"

"Yes, I'm here."

"Is that all right? I mean I can —"

"No, Stan. It's fine. It's good. It's just sort of sudden."

"I would really like to see you there, Annie."

"Look," Annie said, "Make your plans for when you'll be there, and let me know. I'm sure it's a lot easier for me to adapt my plans to yours than for you to do that. Let me know in a few days. Can you call me at this time?"

"I think so," Stan said, and then added, "The system here isn't all that reliable but I'll keep trying until I get through. Okay?"

"Sure," Annie said. "I'll be waiting. It will be good to see you again, or did I already say that?"

"I don't know," Stan said, "but it's good to hear it."

Annie laughed

"Annie?"

Stan surprised himself again. "Maybe," he said, "Maybe we can climb Mt. Fuji, together."

Annie was silent for a moment. "I hope so," she said but then added, "We'll see, Stan. We'll see. I'll be waiting for your call."

"Okay," Stan said, " Goodbye." He handed the phone back to the lady behind the desk, who was mercifully oblivious to what had just happened.

Stan was surprised to notice that he was slightly trembling. Never in his life had he done anything so daring. Calling someone in Japan from China. Who would have thought? And it felt right to him. Oh yes, let's meet in Moscow in a week or so. The most natural thing in the world. Well, hardly. But still – he did it, didn't he?

And yet, there were still those ashes.

As he left the phone office, he met Martha Kennicut, an American married to a Canadian. They had both retired recently, she from a secretarial position in a municipal office in Winnipeg and he, Horace, from the faculty of the University of Winnipeg, where he taught in the English Department. They had told him earlier over some hot chicken and peanuts and some soothing Jingling beer that they had decided to spend their first year after retirement giving something back to society, so they signed up to teach English in China. Martha was the stable one, insisting they teach according to the wishes of the department, while Horace went periodically ballistic with his unresponsive students.

"They just sit there," he had said, "saying absolutely nothing. I finally got fed up and told them we should discuss why this class is not going anywhere. One of the students, a young man majoring in chemistry, said, sir, you should get more class discussion. I went right off the wall and stormed out of the class. When I came back for the next class, they just sat there again. I don't know what to do. Meng Dejing said it has something to do with the great respect they have for their teachers and the Confucian tradition of listening to those in authority. I told him I would give up a lot of respect for a little response."

Stan, nevertheless, liked Horace, and especially liked Martha, a saint in his opinion.

Now Martha was here without Horace. "Horace has been in the hospital for the past few days," Martha said, although she didn't seem particularly distressed by that fact. Stan was stunned and asked if he really went to a hospital here in Nanjing. He had read in one of his travel books that if anything serious happens you should immediately head for Hong Kong, which has world-class medical facilities.

"He hadn't been feeling well," Martha said, "so I took him to the infirmary here on campus. They said his blood pressure was dangerously high, and they sent him to the hospital, the big one down by the Sweeping Leaves Pavilion. They did some tests immediately and said his heart is very bad and he should not be moved. I'm going there now. Would you mind coming along?"

Stan agreed to go. He was concerned about Horace, but he also wanted to see the inside of a Chinese hospital. The hospital was about a mile away, through milling mobs, a perfect distance for a heart attack about to happen, On the way to the hospital Martha explained how Horace was admitted. She said they walked there, and then discovered they had to walk up a large hill to the hospital entrance because that's where the special building is for foreigners and high government officials. When they got there, they asked what they should do and were told to check in at the building at the bottom of the hill. So off they went, Horace huffing and puffing. Finally, back up to the top of the hill Horace was taken to his room, and that's where Stan and Martha found him when they arrived, sitting in his street clothes on the side of his bed, pale but grinning, eating his lunch, which consisted of rice and two hard boiled eggs.

Stan asked Horace if he knew that eggs are not good for either cholesterol or a heart condition. "Oh, sure," Horace said, "I've had eggs of some sort with every meal. I even told the doctor about eggs and cholesterol. He just smiled."

Horace's room was large but plain and fairly grungy with a strong antiseptic smell. It contained two single unmatched beds and a desk and chair with a dim lamp hanging from the wall over one of the beds. "It's a pretty dim light," Horace said, "but it does have a rheostat, so I can make it dimmer. Besides, you don't really want to see a lot of things in here." He pointed to the wall with its rusty stain about waist high and running down to the floor. "I think someone got upset about getting a transfusion." Martha laughed. Martha seemed to laugh at all of Horace's jokes.

While we were there, several people came in, including a nurse with medicine, and Dr. Wu, a young woman doctor who spoke English. She examined Horace carefully. Horace said everyone at the hospital was pleasant, even solicitous. He also said he thought they were quite competent, even though he still had no idea why he was there or what they were doing to him. "They have me up to forty pills a day now," he said. The small card at the end of the bed said something in Chinese behind his name, but no one had translated it for him. Everyone told him he was doing well. He told them if he is doing so well why is he in the hospital taking up to forty pills a day. "Ho, ho," they laughed, "that American is really funny."

The next day Horace checked himself out of the hospital and began to make arrangements for his return to Canada. He said he felt fine and that he suspected they were keeping him there just to get the money, although he confessed that he had no idea where the money was coming from since he had not received any sort of bill.

CHAPTER TWENTY-THREE

When Martha and Stan got back from the hospital, Stan went up to see Meng Dejin about the trip to Pearl Buck's home. After his conversation with Annie, he was even more eager to finish his assignment and leave. The next day found Stan, Meng Dejin, and their driver bouncing over potholed and rutted roads in a shock-less van on their way to Zhenjiang. Despite the teeth-rattling trip, Stan enjoyed talking with Meng Dejin about Pearl Buck since all Stan knew was the book she wrote about China called <u>The Good Earth</u> and that she had won the Nobel Prize for Literature, much to the dismay of John Steinbeck. Meng Dejin on the other hand knew everything about Pearl Buck.

"Her parents were both missionaries here in China," Meng Dejin said, "and she was born and grew up here, up where we're going. Zhenjiang is really quite an interesting place in itself. I think you'll enjoy visiting the city." Stan said he was sure he would enjoy visiting the city, although he never could get used to Chinese academics who spoke better English than he did. "Tell me more about Pearl Buck," he said.

"She and her mother were alone a lot here because her father spent so much of his time in the countryside, trying to convert the peasants to Christianity." Meng Dejin added that he didn't think he was very successful. "Pearl Buck grew up with the Chinese language; in fact, it was really her first language. Her mother had to teach her English. The family had some frightening times here during the Boxer Rebellion when they feared for their lives and fled to Shanghai. They returned, however, and Pearl lived here until she went away to college, to Randolph-Macon Women's College in Virginia. I visited her school a few years ago. I was a guest there because I had done some work on her. I enjoyed my stay there very much. Pearl then married an agricultural economist named Buck. Her name had been Sydenstricker. I'm not sure if that's how it's pronounced. They told me at Randolph-Macon, but I forget. Anyway they were not happy together, although they remained married for eighteen years. That all came later, after she and her family had left Zhenjiang."

Stan tried to concentrate on what Meng Dejin was saying, but he was distracted by both the ride and his fascination with the rice paddies along the road and the Chinese with their traditional pointy hats. Just like the pictures, Stan said to himself. I feel like I'm in a travelogue.

Finally, they arrived at the outskirts of Zhenjiang and slowly pushed their way through the streets congested with buses, taxis, horse-drawn carts, bicycles, mostly bicycles, and untold thousands and thousands of people, many spilling out onto the street because there was no more room on the sidewalks.

"Here we are," Meng Dejin said as the driver pulled up beside an uncharacteristically open space, a small grassy area, a low hill, mound really, surrounded by a deteriorating metal fence, not the solid kind but the kind made up of narrow, curling bars, familiar to Stan because the fence looked exactly like the sort he saw often in the older towns of Ohio. Here it was definitely out of place, as was the house itself, a wooden, clap-boarded, two-story house right out of the American Midwest. It, along with the fence, was well-worn and in desperate need of upkeep.

Meng Dejin insisted they go inside so he could show Stan what the local government planned to do with the structure. The rooms were bare and also in need of paint. "This was Pearl Buck's bedroom," he said and admired how large and open it was. Stan realized that several Chinese families could live comfortably in this spacious house. In Nanjing he had seen much smaller structures, no more than three rooms, housing three generations of a family, six or seven people easily, and he recalled visiting a student's room at the university and finding eight students living in a room no bigger than a dorm room for two at his college back in the States.

Meng Dejin explained how the government planned to renovate the building and refurbish it with period pieces so that visitors could see how Pearl Buck lived when she grew up. He seemed to have visions of multitudes of Chinese paying money to walk through the rooms once inhabited by this Nobel Prize winner, but all Stan could think of was the disdain with which Pearl Buck had been dismissed by one of the graduate students he had met at Nanjing University. "What did she know about peasants?" the student had said, "All those romantic notions about sticking your hands in the dirt. Her books are fantasy." He had said nothing to Meng Dejin about that conversation.

While Meng Dejin talked with a man apparently acting as some sort of curator/janitor, Stan roamed the building, looking for a suitable place to deposit his ashes. He found no place because the interior, although devoid of any furniture, was also devoid of any dirt or refuse. His ashes, or rather his advisor's ashes, would clearly be swept away, and Stan could not allow for such an ignominious end to Professor Schumer after coming half-way around the world to perform his duties.

While Meng Dijin chatted with the janitor, Stan told him he would be outside, that he should take his time, that he was in no hurry. Once outside he wandered over the grounds, the grass uneven, uncut, and interspersed with areas of dirt of varying sizes, much like he found at the university, much like he found most places he had visited in China. He also found a large tree, a plane tree it appeared from the whitened, scaling bark. Perhaps it had been planted by Pearl Buck's father, he thought. At least he knew it must be old enough to have been here when Pearl Buck lived in the house. This is it. This is the place.

He thought initially he might climb the tree and allow the ashes to float down through the limbs, but he dismissed that as too romantic and, especially, too dangerous. He could just see himself following the ashes and landing with less elegance. What would the Chinese neighbors think? Instead, he took the plastic bag from his pocket and gently scattered the ashes at the base of the tree. They blended in perfectly with the soil. He did not even have to stir the ashes around.

The return trip was just as bone-rattling as the trip there, but Stan didn't care. He had completed his mission, and could now think of Russia, of St. Petersburg, of Annie. And so, two days later, after a hurried phone call to Kyoto in which he arranged to meet Annie in Moscow – Moscow! – he left China. If I can survive China, he thought, as the plane lifted into the sky above Shanghai, I can survive anything, and then he realized he had said that before, often. He also realized that China had been for him an amazing experience, more interesting, more enjoyable, and more accessible than he had ever thought possible. Were these locations just getting easier to deal with or was he changing somehow? He was not sure of the answer, but he had his suspicions.

PART SEVEN RUSSIA

CHAPTER TWENTY-FOUR

"Shoosh."

The guard inside the mausoleum made it clear he would not tolerate talking, even a low whisper, here in this place made sacred by the body of Lenin. Stan and Annie were not talking in a low whisper; they were giggling.

They had just entered the mausoleum out of the bright sunlight of Red Square and found themselves in the darkened, dangerously so, interior. Annie had not seen the one step down as they entered and stumbled before Stan could catch her hand. "It's a trap for capitalists," she said, laughing quietly. Stan laughed in return.

"Shoosh."

Suitably reprimanded, Stan and Annie walked around the black sarcophagus, following the black-clad women in front of them, and found themselves staring at what passes for the body of Lenin enclosed in glass, dressed in a black suit, with head slightly raised.

"I've seen better dummies in Tokyo department stores," Annie whispered.

"I've seen better preserved specimens in our biology department," Stan added.

"Shoosh." And this shoosh sounded like the final one this guard was going to utter.

Lenin was placed here shortly after his death back in the 1920's. Over the years it's been "fixed up," Annie's phrase, many times until today it's not quite clear just how much if any of the original Lenin remains. His face is pale, of course, and discolored by the yellow-hued light that hangs over the sarcophagus. He looks even deader than dead, Stan thought and dared not look at Annie. He was sure she was thinking the same thing. As they stood there staring at this relic from early in the last century, Stan peeked around and saw two other people, heavy grandmother types, babushkas, coming up behind them with complete and respectful silence, heads bowed and hands folded before them. Stan wondered if they were praying. He looked at Annie and motioned toward the exit; she nodded, and they both, slowly and reverentially, made their way out of this house of wax and into the cold November air.

Only the day before Stan had waited at the Moscow airport for Annie's plane to touch down. The airport was seedy, barren-looking, a stark leftover from the spartan Soviet days. Finally, she came out from customs, dragging a large suitcase on wheels, looking around, at first not seeing Stan. Stan called to her, "Annie!" and waved. She waved back and hurried toward him. Now what do I do, Stan thought. A hug? A kiss on the cheek? A handshake? As he was ruling out the handshake, Annie put her arms around him, pressing her cheek against his. She stepped back and said how good it was to see him again. He said it was good to see her. "How have you been?" she said. "Fine," he said. Now what, he thought. He took her suitcase from her, and she held his hand as they walked out of the airport and got a cab to the Intourist Hotel, just off Red Square, where Stan had reserved a single room, daring for him. He also chose double beds, however, just to be on the safe side. He needn't have bothered. Annie was as open and honest as ever, and he relaxed into her enthusiasm, despite the cramped room, sparse furnishings, and yellowing lace curtains. "Okay?" he asked. "Okay," she said.

"I can't believe I'm here," she said the next morning as they lay in the single, rumpled bed and discussed what they wanted to see first. Stan wondered if she meant here in Moscow or here with him. Annie smiled at him, looked into his eyes, and said, "Both." She then laughed and added, "Let's do Lenin first. I hear it's a hoot."

Now, back in the dullness of Red Square they faced another choice. They could either walk across the square opposite the Kremlin to the large department store known as GUM or go down to the far end of the square to St. Basel's Cathedral. Stan suggested they go to the department store since he thought Annie might want to do that. He was wrong. She wanted to go to St. Basil's, perhaps because she thought he might like to do that but more likely, Stan realized, because that's what she wanted to see. It was only two o'clock in the afternoon, but already the sun was beginning to set.

"I have a friend in Japan who said I have to see St. Basil's," she said. "She calls it St. Bagel's." From then on, this hallowed spot of Russian Christianity, this hymn to Orthodox iconography, was known to the two of them as St. Bagel's.

It deserved better. Its nine towers, each a different onion-domed design, swirled around the edge of the square, colors ranging from pink to green to yellow to red, all muted and all seeming to twist in the light wind blowing across it.

"I particularly like this cathedral," Annie said, "because it was named after a fool."

"Really?"

"Yeah. St. Basil was known as the Holy Fool."

"How do you know that?" Stan was clearly impressed.

"Stan, your guide book will tell you that."

"Oh."

"He was also known as Basil the Blessed. I suppose the two go together. You know, fools and being blessed. Blessed fools. There's a long tradition of that in Christianity."

"So, is that in my guide book too?"

"No, I just made that up." Annie laughed again and added, "But it might be true. It's possible, isn't it? Blessed fools?"

"I suppose so," Stan said, and wondered what she would make up next.

As spacious as the outside is, the interior is surprisingly small, even intimate, as Stan and Annie discovered when they entered. Corridors meander throughout, and even the main chapel itself looks too small to accommodate any sizeable group of worshippers.

Annie pointed to the walls. "Look, Stan. The paint on the walls is even more muted than the outside. I love this place. Outside it looks like a movie set from some 1930's exotic musical. Inside, it's . . . functional, down-to-earth. I don't know. It just seems to work somehow. What do you think?"

Stan looked again at the interior, turning slowly, taking in the details. "I see," he said. "It does work, doesn't it? I mean, it's solid somehow, comfortable. The colors are right, even if they're the result of centuries of fading. Now, here in Moscow, after the austerity of the Soviets, it's almost like it's coming out again, being reborn somehow, back to what it was originally intended for." Stan surprised himself.

"I think you're right, Stan," Annie said and leaned her shoulder against his arm. "It does feel right here," she said, and then added softly, almost too softly for Stan to hear, "Reborn. I like that."

That evening Stan suggested they might like to have dinner at one of the small restaurants not frequented by tourists. The previous evening they had eaten at the hotel restaurant, a sorry meal of stringy meat and over-cooked vegetables. They were ready for some local food, maybe a big dish of borscht, Annie suggested only half seriously. Wrapped in heavy coats they walked through the dingy streets of what looked every bit like a dying city, grey, dirty, the people dour and looking away. Only the young seemed sociable, perhaps because many of them were walking the streets, cans of beer in hand. It was not a promising sight, Stan thought, as he felt Annie link her arm in his. Still it could be worse. He could be alone.

After a half hour or so Stan saw what looked like a restaurant sign but with no sign of a restaurant. When they went over closer to the sign, they looked down a pair of steps and into a cellar where they saw what could be a restaurant. A few steps down to the entrance, they examined a menu on the door, in Russian.

"Good sign," Annie said, rubbing her hands. "That's the good news. The bad news is we won't have any idea what we're eating."

"I'm up for the adventure," Stan said as they tentatively opened the door and peered in. A man wearing a white apron motioned them in and showed them to a table. The restaurant was larger than they expected; in fact, it had several rooms laid end to end, and it also had a number of customers. None, Stan thought, looked anything like tourists. He wondered if Annie and he did.

"We do look out of place here, don't we?" Annie said.

"Story of my life," Stan said. They both laughed and decided to stay.

Fortunately, the waiter could at least pronounce the names of some of the food in English. "Borscht," he said and pointed to the appropriate entry on the menu. "Two," Stan said and held up two fingers. The waiter smiled. This is easy, Stan thought. Until the soup came, they had a chance to prepare for the main course; however, they could have had an eternity and still not have been ready. When the waiter returned with the soup, he pointed to several items on the menu and said, "Meat. Meat. Meat." Annie suggested they each take a different meat and see what happens. They did, and shortly after were rewarded with two delicious meals of beef and pork. "I think we got lucky," Annie said. "I know I did," Stan said and smiled at Annie. She reached over and squeezed his hand.

Later that night, after they had returned from their dinner, the desk clerk at their hotel warned them not to go walking in certain parts of the city, one apparently being where they had just eaten. "Lucky again, " Annie said.

After another night of sharing that single bed, Annie woke first and nudged Stan awake. She propped herself on one elbow. "So, tour guide, what do you have planned for today?"

Stan, still groggy, put his arm around her waist and drew her even closer. "You know," he said, "I've always wanted to see the ballet, and I hear they have a pretty good one here."

"You've never been to a ballet?"

"No," Stan said, "Not much chance of that in Carlow."

"Well, if there's any place that's perfect for your first ballet, this is it. Let's see if the concierge can get us tickets for tonight at the Bolshoi."

That evening, thanks to an outrageous amount of money, Stan and Annie sat waiting for the curtain to go up on "Swan Lake." The Bolshoi theater was built in the 1820's, so its white columns and balanced exterior reflect the Neo-Classical fashion of that time, but Stan was most impressed with the interior. He counted seven gilded tiers with red velvet chairs. From any distance the impression was of wealth and class. When Stan looked at his own seat, however, he saw the plush was matted and beginning to fade.

"Not what it used to be," he said to Annie.

"No money," she answered, "Ever since the Soviets were kicked out, the government has less and less money to spend on things like this. The Soviets supported anything that made them look good to the rest of the world. Ballet, gymnasts, cosmonauts. Whatever it took. Now maintenance costs alone are killers. Don't even ask about their nuclear weapons."

And then the theater darkened, the curtain opened, and Russia was world-class once again. Stan was sure he would have to strain to show how much he enjoyed ballet, but he immediately gave himself up to the music, the movement, the spectacle as effortlessly as the dancers glided across the stage. And when the curtain finally came down on the dying swan, Stan realized he had tears in his eyes. He tried to turn from Annie, but she saw.

"You really did like this, didn't you?" she asked. Stan nodded.

They followed the crowd out the large door, past the white columns shining in the spotlights, and into the area called Theatre Square. They walked the few blocks back to their hotel, but decided not to go in. Instead, despite the dropping temperatures, they walked the short distance back to Red Square to see what it looks like at night. They were not disappointed. Lights shone on the massive red walls of the Kremlin to their right and on St. Basil's at the other end of the vast open expanse of the square. The large white structure in front of the Kremlin that houses Lenin also gleamed, and Stan remembered, could visualize even, the Soviet dignitaries standing on top of the tomb as row after row of Red soldiers, armament, and especially large missiles went by every May 1. They were now gone but not the vague, softened terror he felt. He had known the Soviets and their threat ever since he was a small child, and now here he was. Hard to believe.

"What are you thinking?" Annie asked, looking up at Stan, her brown felt hat pulled down to her eyes.

"What? Oh, nothing really. Just how we all feared this place, and now here we are after watching 'Swan Lake' at the Bolshoi. I was just thinking it's hard to believe."

"It is," Annie said, "but then so's a lot of other things, especially here in Russia. What are the odds we would be here together now, at this moment, in this place?"

After a few more days of sightseeing among intermittent snow squalls, Stan and Annie began to pack for their flight to St. Petersburg. Since they had to return to Moscow to go their separate ways, they decided to return from St. Petersburg to Moscow by overnight train, one more night together.

"So do you have the ashes?" Annie asked as she tried to stuff some more dirty laundry into her bag. "I'll have to get this stuff laundered in St. Petersburg," she said.

"Yeah, I have them," Stan said, "I've pretty much decided to sprinkle them over Dostoevsky's grave in St. Petersburg. I remember he talked a lot about Dostoevsky. He's buried in a cemetery close to where we'll be staying." Stan stuffed his own clothes in his suitcase, and then added, "I made the arrangements. I hope you like the place."

"I'll like it," Annie said, " as long as it's not some expensive fancy hotel with plenty of space and plenty of hot water." Stan smiled.

Annie asked Stan if he had been giving any thought to St. Petersburg since it's supposed to be a beautiful city, the place Peter the Great built as his window into the West just about 200 years ago. It had recently regained its old name. During the Soviet period it was known as Leningrad, she said.

"Such is fame," Stan said and then added, "Yeah. I've thought about it some."

Stan continued packing, eager to get to St. Petersburg but reluctant at the same time since this would mean he and Annie would have to part again. He also felt both reluctance and anticipation because of his life-long fascination with World War II and particularly with the event known as the Siege of Leningrad, that 900 day period in 1941-44 when Germany pummeled Leningrad with bombs and mortars and blockaded the city into starvation. One in every four people there died as a result of Hitler's hatred for the city. He had vowed to level it.

"What are you thinking, Stan," Annie asked.

"What?" Stan was brought back by the question. "Oh, nothing. Just thinking."

"C'mon, you don't just think. You think about something, of something."

Stan began to push his extra pair of shoes into his bag, already full. "I was thinking," he said. "I was thinking of the Siege of Leningrad. I first read about it when I was a kid, and I've never gotten over the idea of people starving in the streets, boiling wall paper to make soup. That sort of thing. All those people died because one man wanted to conquer the world."

"Lots of people died in the war," Annie said.

"I know, but I became almost obsessed with Leningrad. I studied it in college and read everything I could about it. I never forgot it. That's another thing I remember about Dr. Schumer. We had some long talks about the Siege. For some reason he was interested in it also. I don't think it was an obsession, but he seemed really interested."

"So, we're going to do some siege touring while in St. Petersburg?

"I hope you don't mind, but I do want to visit the cemetery where they buried the dead in these huge common graves, and I'd like to see the hotel where Hitler said he would celebrate the total destruction of the city. He even sent out engraved invitations. We can do other things as well."

"Thanks. There is a little something like the Hermitage there that might warrant a visit. And, since you're so captivated, we might take in a ballet at the Mariinsky. They say it's even better than the Bolshoi."

"Can't wait," Stan said, and he meant it.

CHAPTER TWENTY-FIVE

The flight to St. Petersburg was uneventful, except that Annie held Stan's hand so tight he was afraid of gangrene.

"Annie, I thought you were the brave one."

"Brave, maybe, but not stupid. These Russian-built airplanes go down pretty regularly, and the bolts flopping up and down in the wing out there don't exactly instill confidence."

Stan realized that Annie had a point. The plane, a notorious Ilyushin, was bouncing furiously all through the hour-long flight; several people had gotten sick, and all showed signs of terminal terror. The flight attendants even stopped going up and down the aisle and strapped themselves into their jump seats. Finally, the flight ended with a thump, snapping Stan's head back. Aeoroflot strikes one last time, he thought.

"We made it," he said, "May I now have my circulation back?" He laughed.

Annie did not laugh. "Sorry. I guess I overreacted. We are going back by train, aren't we?"

It was mid-afternoon when a long taxi ride brought them to their hotel. The Moskva Hotel is another relic from the Soviet days. Huge, sprawling along the Neva River, the Moskva stands as a monolithic block of concrete with an interior to match, each room itself a tiny block of concrete.

"I like it," Annie said. "It's the real Russia, the Russia that once was."

"And still is," Stan added, looking around at the dreary, beige bed cover, the wooden night stand, the tiny television set on a small platform hanging halfway up the wall.

"Look," said Annie, "We each get three hangers." She was looking at the small alcove that served as a closet.

"Sorry," Stan said. "It looked better on the internet."

Annie laughed and gave Stan a kiss. "Don't worry," she said, "We won't spend much time here, and when we do the lights will be off so you won't need to look at this."

Stan said if they waited just a few more minutes it might be dark outside, but Annie suggested they take a walk. Stan wondered if this is what married life is like. He liked it. He liked the way they were beginning to take each other for granted. Why not take a walk?

Stan and Annie stood outside the hotel, beside the entrance to the Metro station, men and women in dull clothes milling around, buying food from the several stalls located next to the station. It was just as cold in St. Petersburg as it had been in Moscow.

"So which direction do we walk?" Stan asked, already beginning to feel the cold seep into his bones.

"The Hermitage."

Stan pointed out that the Hermitage was located at the other end of Nevksy Prospekt several miles away. "It will take hours just to get there," he said. "And besides," he said, "the place is huge." He pointed out that, according to his guide book, the Hermitage has five main buildings and 1057 rooms. "Maybe we should wait until we have a full day to devote to it. Annie agreed, reluctantly, and asked Stan what he wanted to do.

Stan confessed he would really like to visit the cemetery where Dostoyevsky is buried. He said he knows it's getting dark and a cemetery is no place to visit at night, but this is that one thing he wanted to do. He suggested they make their visit now, while it's not quite dark and then walk along Nevsky Prospekt. He thought they might look for an interesting place to have dinner while walking.

Stan and Annie crossed the busy Nevsky Prospeckt and walked quickly to the Alexander Nevsky Monastery's grounds where the Tikhvin cemetery is located. Stan paid the entrance fee over Annie's objections. "They actually charge you to go into a cemetery? Fifty rubles. What is that? About two dollars. What if your mother is buried there and you promised to visit her every day? It could wipe out your pension." Stan laughed and assured her that no one has been buried there in many years. No mother's sons are still living.

The cemetery looks like any other cemetery with its weathered and varied tombstones, monuments, and busts, and its grounds not particularly well-kept, weeds sprouting from the stones in the walkways, grass long and sparse. The difference is that it holds the remains of some of Russia's creative geniuses.

"It's humbling to think," Stan said to Annie as they strolled leisurely along the narrow path, "that we're only a couple feet from people like Rimsky-Korsakov, Mussorgsky, Borodin, and Glinka." Stan was surreptitiously glancing at his guide book. "And look, Annie, over there. Against the wall. That's a bust of Tchaikovsky. Didn't he write something called "Swan Lake?"

Annie rolled her eyes. "Give a man a guide book," she said, "and you give him the world." Finally, after peering for a while at the bust and wandering a bit more, she asked Stan where Dostoevsky is buried. "Or more precisely," she said, "Where does your guide book say he is buried?"

Stan held the guide book before him and read formally, "Following the wall back along the path you come to the grave of Dostoevsky." Then he added, "That must be his grave over there."

The grave of Dostoevsky is marked by a stone monument with the bust of the author mounted on to its front and a cross on its top. The grave area itself is surrounded by a small, black iron fence. Stan and Annie stood before it silently. Stan could utter only the word, "Amazing."

"So," Annie said finally, "Are you going to sprinkle the ashes?"

Stan thought for a moment and then told Annie that he would rather wait until later, explaining that they can easily come back since it's so close to the hotel. "And besides," he said, "Now that I'm here, I don't really feel right about doing it. I just have a feeling that I should do it somewhere else."

Once outside the cemetery and once again on Nevsky Prospekt Annie took Stan's hand as they walked down the wide street. Stan knew that all the interesting buildings and most of the activity were at the far end of the street, down near the Hermitage, the Admiralty, and the Church of the Savior on the Blood. This stretch of Nevsky Prospekt has its share of people on the street, its small shops, and its crazy traffic with lots of taxis, buses, and especially the trolley buses that insist that everything and everybody keep out of their way. Stan enjoyed the frantic mish-mash of people and was sure Annie did too. Occasionally, they peeked in the window of a small restaurant and looked at the menu, some of which had English translations, and discussed which ones might be worthy of a visit later on.

After an hour of meandering Stan said he was getting hungry. "I know it's ridiculously early to eat in Moscow, but I do tend to get hungry about 6:00 every evening, and besides we've had a long day." Annie agreed, saying that she believed her stomach had recovered from the flight. "I don't know why, but I now think that after that flight the rest of my life is just icing on the cake, icing I never expected to see, let alone taste." She looked at Stan. "It tastes good," she said.

Earlier in their walk they had seen a small restaurant down a few steps in the basement of a building that did not seem to have any discernible purpose.

It could have been apartments or an office building or storage – they couldn't tell – but Stan had insisted that this is where they should eat. "After that great meal in Moscow, I'm now sort of partial to basement restaurants," he said, and then added with a little flourish, "and let's eat the rest of our dinners only in basement restaurants." Annie suggested they hold off on any such rash decisions until after this meal.

It turned out that Stan was right. Although they were the only ones in the tiny restaurant, the meal itself was hot, well-prepared, and perfectly presented by several young waitresses, who smiled and spoke a bit of English. The only disconcerting aspect of the evening was the trio of men who stood in the entranceway and watched them eat. They said nothing and never approached Annie and Stan. They seemed more interested in watching the waitresses perform their duties; nevertheless, Stan and Annie were a bit nervous with their presence. "Pimps?" Annie asked under her breath. "Russian Mafia," Stan replied equally softly. "I've read about them. They use restaurants as a front for money laundering." Annie looked at Stan to see if he were serious and then said, "Wow. This is exciting. You really know how to enliven an evening, Stan. Imagine that. Mafia." "Shhh," Stan said, "Let's wait until we're out of here to make fun of them."

Later that evening, about 11:00 back at their hotel, Stan asked Annie if it were now dark enough for her. "Sufficiently," she said. Stan decided he loved St. Petersburg.

The next few days were filled with wonderful wandering, first through the Hermitage.

"That's one down, and 1056 to go," Stan said, only half in jest. "This place is huge."

"It's overwhelming," Annie agreed. "Just think, this one room is filled with Van Goghs." Annie had insisted they go straight to the top floor of the Winter Palace, one of the buildings comprising the Hermitage. She couldn't wait to see the Van Goghs. "I love his work," she said. "The sophisticated primitivism, it includes everything of art and nature."

Stan looked at the paintings through Annie's eyes and began to see what she saw.

"C'mon," Annie said, "Let's try to make a dent in those remaining 1056 rooms." She was clearly thrilled to be there. Stan was thrilled to be there with her. They spent the day wandering among the adoring crowds, Annie pointing out the chiaroscuro of Rembrandt, the subtle use of lighting in Vermeer, the rustic sophistication of British landscapes, the shimmering flickering waters of the Impressionists, and the fractured new realities of the Cubists. By the end of the day Stan was totally exhausted, and Annie was totally invigorated. "I could do this forever," she said, and Stan believed her.

After leaving the Hermitage they sat by the river, shivering and enjoying gin and tonics in a can. Stan said he had never seen this before, gin and tonics already mixed. "What a great idea. Someone should market this in the States," he said. Annie laughed and said that's more enthusiasm than he showed for the early Russian icons. Stan replied that he liked the modern Russian icons better, these cans of gin and tonic.

"So, Stan, what did you really think?

"Of the Hermitage?"

"Yes, what were your thoughts?

Stan thought for a moment and then said, "I know you want me to say I was completely taken away by the art work, and I was, but to be perfectly truthful with you, I thought of other things."

"What?"

"Well, you know that the Hermitage was hit by German bombs."

"Oh, the Siege." Annie turned to look across the water at the Peter and Paul Fortress.

"Yes. And I was thinking how the people at the Hermitage, including the Curator himself, worked furiously to pack up and send away much of the collection and what they couldn't send away on all those railroad cars, they hid and even buried in the ground. And all the time they were doing this they were starving, literally starving. Tens of thousands of people died of exposure during the winter, some of bombs, but most of starvation, especially the children. And while all this was happening to them, they tried to save this art. I find that effort overwhelming, and I see it as real evidence of the value of art to the human spirit. I don't know if that makes any sense, but that's what I mostly thought about today. Sorry."

"Stan," Annie looked at him, into his eyes, "I don't know what to say." She leaned over and kissed him lightly on the lips. Stan looked around, embarrassed. "Don't worry," she said, "I see the Russians doing this all the time." That night they made tender, silent love.

The next morning they took a ride on the canals of St. Petersburg, a pleasant respite from the previous day's miles of walking, and had lunch at the Hotel Europa's restaurant, a cavernous, white-walled, chandeliered homage to good taste in all senses of the word.

"I could live like this," Annie said as she looked around the busy restaurant. Stan mumbled agreement but looked forward to getting back into the jumbled streets of the city, pickpockets and all. Earlier as they had been walking over to the Hotel Europa, an old lady had stopped them and pointed to a group of boys across the street. "Thieves," she said in English and motioned to her pockets. Stan put his hands in his own pockets and then felt ashamed that he thought she might be setting them up.

"Now off to St. Bagel's north," Annie said. They had both been looking forward to visiting the Church of our Savior on the Precious Blood located on a canal down near the Hermitage. Stan said that according to the description in his guide book, it out-St. Bagel's St. Bagel's. As they rounded a curve on the canal, the church, also known as the Church of the Resurrection, hove into view like a psychedelic ship made up of thousands of pieces. "Wow," Annie said, "the Beatles would have loved this." The onion domes seemed too many to count, spiraling almost out of control, the façade featuring numerous arches over entrances and windows, each made up of different colored small blocks, and, as with St. Basil's, colored in blues and reds and oranges and yellows, and, of course, the shining gilt of the largest dome, dominant but off-center, which also serves as the bell tower. Stan and Annie just stood there beside the canal and stared.

"I'm almost afraid to go in," Annie said, adding, "It has to be a let-down." It was anything but a let-down as, once inside, they inspected the thousands of tiles making up the elaborate mosaic icons lining the walls. "My God," Annie said as they stood in the center of the church, "Look at this floor. It's pink marble. I've never seen anything like it."

Stan mentioned that they've done an amazing job of restoring the church. Annie said, "Restored? Oh, this was damaged during the siege as well?" Stan nodded his head and silently surveyed the scene.

After that Stan decided it might be a good time to visit the Astoria Hotel, the one where Hitler had planned to host his victory banquet after bringing Leningrad to its knees. He knew it was just a short walk; at least that's what it looked like on the map. Half an hour later they were standing before the Astoria Hotel, Annie blowing in her hands, gazing at its imposing grey stone façade, its six stories arranged with predictable regularity but without the Soviet bulkiness. The hotel had been built just before the Russian Revolution.

Annie asked Stan if he would like to go inside. "No," he said, "It's now a four-star hotel, so it's probably nothing like it was then. I just wanted to see it as the symbol of Hitler's defeat. It's still standing, and he's gone So much for the Third Reich's lasting a thousand years." They did look briefly into St. Isaac's Cathedral just across the square from the hotel, but by now they were both exhausted. "This touring is tough work," Annie said.

When they left the Cathedral, Annie said she didn't think she could walk all the way back to the hotel. Stan said he was sure he couldn't and suggested they get a taxi. "Actually," Annie said, " I want to try the Metro system. It worked pretty well in Moscow, so let's give it a try here." They walked over to Nevsky Prospekt and found the entrance to the Metro, which they knew would take them right to their hotel, and pushed their way through the narrow door with dozens of other people. The escalator ride down into the bowels of the Metro was the longest either had ever seen. "They said the Metro was made this deep so it could double as a bomb shelter," Stan said. "During the Cold War the residents were told to go here in case of an atomic attack from us Americans."

Finally, they reached the bottom, and, after getting the necessary tokens, checked the map of the Metro system. "Four stops," Stan said. "I can't understand any of this Russian, so we'll have to count carefully." Annie agreed. They went to the appropriate platform and waited for their train. Soon it appeared and soon the doors of the Metro opened to the train, which then opened its doors. They followed the flow into the train. Stan began to tell Annie about the bus in Shanghai that had been so full he was not able to tell when to get out. "Shh," Annie said, "I'm counting." At the fourth stop, they pushed and shoved their way to the platform with hundreds of other people, pushed and shoved their way to the escalator, and, finally, found themselves being pushed and shoved toward an exit door that was far too small for the crowd approaching it. With no choice on their part they were rushed toward the exit, squeezed into it, and expelled from it with the violence of a cannon ball. Stan thought again of the bus in Shanghai.

After another day of visiting sites, shrines, and museums, Stan told Annie he had one more place he wanted to go, the Piskaryovka Cemetery. He told her it's pretty far out of town, but he was sure they could take public transportation or even rent a taxi for a couple of hours. Annie opted for the taxi. She also asked if this is the cemetery he had told her about earlier, the one that had to do with the Siege. Stan admitted it did, explaining that this is where tens of thousands of victims of the Siege were buried in mass graves. "They died in such vast numbers," he said, "that nobody had the time or energy to bury them properly. They just dumped them in these huge holes they dug once the ground thawed out enough." Annie said it must have been pretty horrible, Stan said, yes, apparently so. He told Annie she needn't go, that he could do this alone, but she insisted on going with him. Stan thought she might be worried about him, about what was beginning to look like an obsession. He thought maybe it was.

CHAPTER TWENTY-SIX

The taxi dropped them off at the entrance to the cemetery and waited, the driver immediately sliding down in his seat and closing his eyes. He had a guaranteed fee for the afternoon and looked to Stan like he was without a worry.

Annie squeezed Stan's arm. "Are you sure you're ready for this, Stan?"

Stan took a deep breath, looked up and around. He exhaled. "Yes, I think so. Let's go in."

Immediately inside the entrance they saw the eternal flame and then the two pavilions that house the many photographs of the German atrocities and their effects on the citizens of Leningrad. "We'll keep that for later," he told Annie. "Let's just walk."

They walked slowly up the central pathway, passing people walking equally slowly toward them. Acre after acre of slightly raised mounds signaled the mass graves, each marked with the time period of their burials. No one spoke above a whisper. Stan realized this is sacred ground to the people of Russia. He also realized, for some reason he did not fully understand, it was sacred ground to him as well. Annie said nothing as they walked slowly through the cemetery.

When they reached the end of the path, they saw before them a large statue of a woman. "Mother Russia," Stan said to Annie. Annie nodded. The statue of a grieving woman holds in her outstretched hands a wreath of oak leaves, the Russian symbol of glory. Stan and Annie stood outside a group of Russian women, dressed in black, all old as far as Stan could tell. He thought they might be relatives, children perhaps, of those unknown victims of the Siege of Leningrad. How could people do this, he thought. Why? And yet he knew something like it was at that very moment happening in several places around the world, perhaps many places.

As they walked back the path, Stan motioned to an empty wrought-iron bench beside the path. They sat. Over the next ten minutes or so they said nothing to each other. Stan stared at the mounds of mass graves. Annie held his hand and stared at the ground, glancing at him from time to time. Finally, she asked him if he was ready to leave.

"No," Stan said, "I have something to do first." He reached in his pocket and brought out his little plastic bag of ashes. "My last one," he said, "and I'm going to deposit it here." Annie asked about his decision to deposit the ashes over Dostoevsky's grave. Stan shook his head. "No, this meant a lot to Dr. Schumer as well. I think if he could have gone through what I've gone through here, he would agree. I want at least part of him to share this place with these people. Nobody knows who they are, and nobody knows he's here. It seems right, somehow."

Stan walked over to one of the mounds and knelt before it. No one would know what he was doing, he thought. He hoped he looked enough like an ordinary mourner that he would not arouse suspicion. He opened the bag and slowly spread the ashes on the ground.

When he returned to Annie, he said, "Now let's look at the pavilions."

The pavilions were actually museums containing mostly photographs, graphic accounts of the terrible hardships and suffering endured by the people of Leningrad. Stan looked closely at the piles of shrunken bodies waiting to be carted off to the cemetery, at the frozen streets, at the people slumped on the sidewalks, at the bombed out shells of houses, at the utter stillness of each scene, lifeless, desolate. He also read some of the translated diary and letter fragments written by the people as they were suffering. One said simply, "Grandmother died this morning." Another: "All are dead."

And here we are, Stan thought, more than half a century later, enjoying a fine November day in a beautiful if somewhat shabby city filled with people going about their business and their pleasures. "I guess I just don't understand," Stan said to no one in particular. "Don't understand what?" Annie asked. "Oh, nothing," Stan said and took Annie's hand. They walked out of the pavilion, back to the taxi, and back to their hotel. During the taxi ride it suddenly hit Stan that they would soon have to go back to their separate lives, he to his home in Ohio and Annie to her students in Kyoto.

That night they were scheduled to take the overnight train to Moscow and then immediately go out to the airport for their flight. Back at the hotel they quickly threw the rest of their laundry into their suitcases and went out for a final dinner, back to the first restaurant, the one run by the Mafia.

As they sat sipping the last of the wine, Annie said, "Should we talk?"

Stan knew what she meant but said about what anyway.

"This has been a very special time for me, Stan. Will I see you again? Or will I have to wait for another telephone call out of the blue?"

Stan laughed slightly, nervously. "Do you want me to?" he asked.

"Stan, don't do that. Let's be open and honest. I don't know you that well. In fact, I think I know you less now than I did when we first met on that boat ride to Penang. But there is something here." Stan began to speak, but Annie interrupted him. "No, let me finish. I enjoy being with you, and I think you feel the same." Stan did not respond. "Well, Stan, please say something, anything. You're the only person I ever met who has trouble responding to me. Please, say something."

Stan looked at Annie and said, "I love you."

Annie was silenced. "That, sir," she said, "is quite a response. Do you know what that means? Love, I mean."

"I think so. I can't imagine the rest of my life without you," Stan paused and then added, "But to be honest I also can't imagine my living in Japan or you living in Ohio."

Annie smiled and said, "That's not a problem. How about neutral ground?"

Stan nodded, still confused, not knowing exactly why he said he loved her except that he knew he meant it.

"Look, Stan. Why don't we go back to our homes, you to Ohio and me to Japan, and think about this, see how it goes, how we feel with some perspective. You're pretty much inexperienced with this marriage thing." Stan recoiled slightly at the word; Annie saw it but continued, "And I'm overly experienced with it. It's a lot to ask."

"You're right," Stan said. "We should get out to the train station. The train leaves at midnight, but we should be there early since we know nothing about the station and everything will probably be in Russian."

The taxi dropped them off in front of the Moscow Station. It was beginning to snow, lightly. The station is built in the Neo-Classical style seen in so much of St. Petersburg architecture. The front has large dark entrances between tall white pillars, and the building is capped off with a rounded black roof.

Stan paid the taxi driver, and they went through one of the entrances into the first large hall of the station. It was darkened in part because the sun had set long ago and in part because of the grime on the windows. Since only a few people were standing and sitting in this section, they went through another door into the next room,

Here they saw a smaller room full of people, apparently waiting for their trains, huddled in groups, families mostly, their luggage an assortment of canvas bags and cardboard boxes wrapped with brown twine. The people stood along the walls or sat on the floor or on the one bench along the wall facing them, occupied by four elderly, overweight women, babushkas again. Stan and Annie walked to the end of a small bench. Annie sat and Stan stood beside her.

"Do you think we should find out which track our train is on," Annie asked. Stan did not respond. Annie became more insistent. "Stan, let's at least look around."

At that point, a couple approached them with a child of five or six years of age. They stood before Stan and Annie, pointed at the child, and then the man pointed at his watch. The woman said something in Russian, and the two of them left, the child standing quietly before Stan and Annie, looking at them with large, brown eyes, reflecting a sadness Stan had seen elsewhere in St. Petersburg, had seen elsewhere in old photographs of Leningrad.

"What's this all about?" Annie said, "They just walked away from this kid. Just like that."

Stan was puzzled, and frightened. "Maybe they just want us to watch her until they get back. Maybe they've just gone to check on their tickets or something."

"I don't know, Stan. They seemed to go around the corner there, and that's the way out of the station. I don't know what's going on here."

"I don't know either," Stan said, "but I'm sure they'll be back. Maybe we should keep an eye on the kid for a while and see what happens."

"Our train leaves in an hour," Annie said, "and we don't even know which track it's on. What if we miss the train? What about our flights in Moscow?"

"But they said they would be back," he said to her.

"Said? Stan, they said something in Russian. How do you know what they said?"

"I know," he said as he shifted from one foot to the other and looked around the station. It was dark. Soot from the smoke, he thought. It looks like pictures of old London stations before they were gentrified. No gentrification here. He had noticed often over the past few days how all the buildings in St. Petersburg, once apparently beautiful, at least to his developing Neo-Classical tastes, were now bordering on seedy, if not seedy: paint flaking, stone crumbling, signs of pollution everywhere. And here he and Annie were, in this crowded station with depressing families huddled together and single individuals standing apart, at least as much apart as they could manage. No one seemed to know anyone else. Even the family members were not talking with each other. They just sat there, waiting until an announcement was made, and then some of them got up, gathered their bags, and pushed their way through the crowd and out the door, toward the trains. And the girl stood before them.

"You know, Stan," Annie said, "We don't even know what these announcements are saying. They might be telling us which track we're supposed to go to."

She said she wanted to go to the tracks. "At least we can try to match numbers."

But he insisted he stay there, with the child. "These people left the child here," he said, "They asked us to take care of her until they get back. I heard the father say something about tickets. In English. At least he said tickets in English. I'm sure they just went to get some tickets and will be back in a few minutes."

He looked at the child. She was dressed no worse than the other travelers, perhaps even a little better. She wore a grey dress that went to her ankles, a padded black coat to her waist, a knitted woolen hat, and boots. She also had a scarf around her neck, which she needed because it was cold in the station, unheated.

"Stan."

Stan did not respond. He was looking at the girl's eyes. They were brown, large, and very sad. He thought of depth. He thought of himself as a child. Was he really like her? Sad. Alone. She seemed to look into his own childhood. What does she see? He saw his father walking out on them when he was her age and remembered how confused he was, and then, later, angry. His father had a suitcase and wore a long grey coat and a hat. He never even turned around to say goodbye. Later his mother also left to go to a hospital, but she never came back either Stan was raised by his grandmother, a fact he tried to hide from the other kids. She died when he was in his first year of college. He realized then he had loved her. I turned out okay, he thought. It all worked out, finally. Not so bad.

"Stan!" He turned to Annie. "I'm worried about the girl too," she said, "but this is really none of our business. I'm going out to the tracks. I want to find our track. If you want to stay here, you can. It's okay. I'll be okay."

He looked anxiously at the door to the waiting room, the door through which the parents had disappeared. Just my luck, he thought. Annie is angry, and this kid is staring at me. She thinks she knows me. She thinks I'll help her. Well, she's wrong. I'll give her parents ten more minutes to get back here. She's nothing to me. If they don't show up, too bad. No one helped me.

Stan stood there, looking around, wondering what the other people were thinking. Did they see the trick played on him? Did they wonder how he would get out of this one? Were they laughing behind their sad facade? Did they even care? After a few minutes, Annie returned. "I found the number for our track," she said. "In fact, I found three tracks that have our number. I'm really confused. I think we should try to find someone who speaks English."

Stan looked again at the child. He wanted to help, but what could he do?. "Stay here," he said to Annie. "I'll go outside and look around. Maybe I can find the taxi driver who brought us here. He speaks some English. We have time."

He walked out of the waiting room and through the large first room, which was still nearly deserted. When he left the building he saw it was snowing much harder. He thought about it for a moment, wondered what was going on, but then continued out the door, only mildly concerned. Once outside he found the sidewalk covered with at least a half foot of snow, much of it trodden down by endless walking. In half an hour, he thought. How is that possible? He looked around for taxis but saw none. In fact, he saw no vehicles, except for several horse-drawn wagons, and a few people. As Stan walked out onto Nevsky Prospekt, he felt the cold bore into his bones and saw more snow piled higher against the buildings across the street. He picked up a torn, faded pamphlet. The script was Cyrillic, but the Nazi swastika was clear. He stared at it, not knowing what to think, and then threw it behind a pile of snow. He looked around, trying to find something familiar, anything. The city was even darker than it had been just a few minutes earlier. And then he noticed that the street lights were not lit. They were in fact not the same street lights. A single bulb hung from the middle of a metal circle. He suddenly realized the truth of his situation. This is not St. Petersburg. This is Leningrad, in Nazi darkness. His throat tightened. He had to get back.

Suddenly he felt a tug at his sleeve and looked down to see a woman in worn clothing, what he took for a long dress and several layers of sweaters, looking up at him. Her face was lined, almost black, her cheekbones protruding, and she was pleading, both hands extended. He looked at her but didn't recognize her. He had seen nothing like her in St. Petersburg, nothing this ragged, this shriveled, nothing this hopeless. Confused, he backed away only to stumble over something covered with snow. When he looked at it, he saw the body of an old man, eyes open, staring, snow clinging to his beard and eyebrows. Stan looked back at the station but could barely make out its black outline in the heavy snow. I must find a taxi, he thought. As he began to cross the street, Stan saw, through the falling snow, piles of corpses lying along the far sidewalk, some covered with blankets, others simply piled there, almost naked, their useable clothing gone. Why doesn't someone take them away? Disoriented, still wanting to find a taxi,

Stan turned back to his side of the street, the station side, and saw beside him another woman — he could not tell her age — propped against an iron fence. He knelt and looked into her face, transfixed by her eyes. Look at me, he thought. And then he shouted, "Look at me!" Her eyes stared, but they never focused on him. He lowered his head and murmured, "What do you want from me? How can I help you?" But her eyes remained staring at a spot well beyond him.

Stan stood and wiped the sweat from his face. It must be below zero, he thought. As he backed away from the woman, he bumped into another woman, this one holding the hand of a child, a girl Stan thought. The woman was in her twenties, perhaps much older, the girl five or six. Frozen to the spot, unable to move, Stan stared at the woman, who put out a hand and then motioned toward the girl. Although he could not understand anything she said, he knew she was asking him for help. At that point a man passed them on the street pulling a sled, which contained a thing wrapped in a white sheet. The woman began to cry, pointing to the sled and then at the girl. She fell to her knees and grasped the girl tightly to her, crying and looking at Stan. Her eyes were sunken and black, her hands only bones and veins. The girl was motionless, passive, but she too looked at Stan, with large brown eyes. He stared at her. "You don't understand," he said quietly. "No one helped me." She looked into his eyes. And then he shouted into the snow, "No one helped me!"

Stan stood, verging on panic. What does she want? Where am I? He knew he was in St. Petersburg, just outside the Moscow station, but nothing looked familiar. He wanted to return to the waiting room, to see Annie, to get on the train to Moscow, but he couldn't leave the girl. She needed help; they all needed help, but he didn't know how to help them. He offered her money, dollars, but she looked at the bills, brushed them aside and pointed to her mouth. I don't have that, he thought. My God, what can I do? They're all starving. More sleds went by, pulled by skeletons, heads down, rags reaching to the snow, the sleds carrying still more bodies, some wrapped in old clothing, some wrapped in blankets, but many wrapped in white sheets, the ever-present white sheets, tucked neatly into the outlines of the bodies, revealing the adults, even the women, but mostly the children, their smallness clear, their vulnerability visible.

Suddenly, Stan looked up and saw a sign. It was in Russian but he knew what it said. He had seen it in a book, this very sign on this building. The building could collapse, he thought. It says the building could collapse from the bombs. The German bombs. And then he heard again the squeaking of the sleds on the ice, a squeaking that tore into his memory, a squeaking that carried the dead through the streets of Leningrad. Why doesn't someone stop the bombs, he thought. Why doesn't someone do something? Where are the British? Where are the Americans? The city is dying. He dropped to his knees in the snow.

When he finally looked up, he saw her eyes again, the sad, brown eyes of the girl staring at him. Is she already dead, he thought. Am I too late? Are we all too late?

Torn by the sight of death he had only read about, Stan ran back to the station, tripping and stumbling in the snow, almost falling into still one more horse-drawn wagon piled high with still more corpses, the driver not even look-ing at him, hunched over and silent, like a penitent statue. He pushed through a group of old men and women huddled in front of the station entrance and into the deserted ticket area. All the counters were closed. He stood in the middle of the room and turned around, not knowing what to expect, and then stopped to stare back at the entrance. The door was partly open, but he could see only darkness.

Frightened by what he might find, he walked over to the waiting room door and looked in. He saw people, crowds of people, the same people he had left just a short time before. Some were carrying luggage to trains; others were just waiting, apparently in no hurry. Still others, also waiting, walked slowly to no-where in particular.

"Stan! Stan! What is it? What's wrong?" Stan looked up and saw Annie, panicked. "My God, Stan. What happened? You look like you've seen — Are you sure you're all right?"

Stan was not sure. He wasn't even sure where he was. He stared at the room, not blinking, his mouth open, and ran his hand through his hair. He then looked at his hand.

Something had happened, and he didn't know what. He felt confused, frightened, but he also felt oppression and guilt.

"I'm — I'm okay," he half murmured. "It's just that — . I was outside — ."

It's okay," Annie said. "I found someone who speaks English. We can go now. I know where to go." She pulled at his sleeve. "Get your suitcase," she said.

"Yes," he said and reached down for his suitcase, but as he did so he looked again into the sad, brown eyes of the young girl. They stared back at him, into him. He could see that she was asking for help. He knew that. She didn't move, her face remained expressionless, but her eyes were large and brown, and sad.

"I don't know what to do," Stan said to the girl. "What do you want from me? What do you want?" He knelt on one knee before her and took one of her hands.

Annie looked at Stan and the girl, rubbed her hands down her slacks, and said, "Stan, we need to go now. Someone will take care of her. There's nothing you can do."

Still looking at the child, holding her hand, Stan said to Annie, "You don't understand. I must do something."

Annie looked at the door. People were moving toward the trains. She looked around the room and then back at Stan, who was again looking at the girl.

"Stan, I don't know what's happened here, but we have to leave," she said softly. "The train is leaving. Come with me."

Stan turned from the girl to Annie and said simply, "Why does this happen? I wish I could help."

"I know, Stan. I know."

Stan said nothing after that, and once on board the train he collapsed in the narrow bed of the compartment he shared with Annie.

He was wakened at six the next morning by a knock on the door. He rolled over and saw Annie, already awake. "Hi," he said.

"Hi," Annie said. "Sleep well?"

Stan assured her he had, although the night was filled with disturbing images..

"Some night, huh?" Annie said.

"Yeah, sorry about that. I don't know what happened. It seemed so real. The Siege. That little girl. It was —"

"No need to explain," Annie assured him. "It's okay. It was a rough time. You really care, don't you?"

Soon the train was slowing down, about to slide into the St. Petersburg Station in Moscow, an exact replica of the one in St. Petersburg. Stan hoped that was the only parallel.

After a taxi ride through the morning traffic of Moscow, Stan and Annie stood in line for an hour before being allowed past security and into the ticketing area, where they stood for another hour waiting for the ticket counter to open. While Stan had waited for Annie to arrive from Tokyo, he had been told by several people to get to the airport early, several hours early in fact, or they could miss their flight. Now, since there was no place to sit, he stood with Annie in the bottled-up swell of hopeful passengers. It was no place for intimate conversation.

Finally, the counter opened and they were soon through another security stop and into the main terminal waiting room where they could finally get some coffee and rolls and find a seat. They still had an hour before boarding.

As they sipped their coffee Stan apologized for all the waiting. "We could have had a proper breakfast somewhere before coming to the station. I just didn't know."

Annie assured him that he took the right precautions. "Our time here went fast," she said." "Too fast," Stan said. "Yes, it did," Annie said. They chatted about the times they had, about what they liked in St. Petersburg. About why they liked St. Petersburg over Moscow. About their preference for basement restaurants. They laughed again at the Russian Mafia watching them eat, and they laughed about Lenin's tomb. They talked and laughed about everything except themselves.

Finally, as if they had run out of things to talk about, they sat quietly side by side.

"You know, Stan," Annie said at last, "This has all happened too quickly, and now we're going back to our separate lives and we might never know if this could work."

Stan shifted in his chair and without looking at Annie said, "I know."

More silence.

Stan broke the silence. "So what should we do?"

Annie took a deep breath. "Let's keep in contact. Let's write to each other. We can talk on the telephone."

"We can e-mail."

"No," Annie said, "Don't do that. It's too easy, too facile. We need a test. We need to make an effort. If one stops writing, that will tell us something."

"Okay."

"We're both English teachers, in our own way, so writing should be easy. We can get to know each other that way, and if we like what we hear we can keep on writing. We'll see what develops."

Stan turned to Annie and said, "I know what developed. For me anyway." Annie smiled. Stan continued, "But you're right. I'm not very experienced with this sort of thing, so I should step back. I don't want to, but I will. I'll write."

It was time for Annie to board; the call came in English as well as Russian. They stood and embraced. Stan walked Annie to the gate and handed her the carry-on.

Annie gave Stan a brief kiss and quickly walked down the tunnel to the plane. Halfway there, she stopped, turned, and mouthed the word, "Write." Stan nodded as she turned and disappeared around the corner. He then walked to the window and watched the plane until it taxied away. Stan sat for a while looking out at the planes moving in and out of the gating area.

Realizing he would be unable to tell which plane was Annie's, he turned to go to his gate, where he would shortly leave for London and then, seven hours later, home.

PART EIGHT OHIO

CHAPTER TWENTY-SEVEN

Stan sat in the commuter plane, halfway between New York and Cleveland. Almost home, he thought. Annie was on his mind all the way, but so were all the people at Carlow: Rodney, the Medievalist, and Tom, the theorist. They could have their own little domains. Dean Deane. He could have his silly name. Dr. Kinsella, now forever known as Priscilla. She held no fear, nor any emotions whatsoever for Stan. A sad creature in a way, Stan thought, isolated in her own little world, her power circumscribed by those few people she could intimidate, a small group now no longer including Stan.

Stan thought of Maria and wondered what he would say to her, and then realized that she has long since probably forgotten all about him. He had not thought of her very much since he had met Annie, but he knew he liked her and looked forward to seeing her again, talking with her, a good friend he hoped. He knew that Maria would always be a part of him, a much bigger part than she knew, or ever would know, a bridge in a way, more accurately the beginning of a bridge, a bridge that, miraculously, circled the globe.

And, of course, the ashes. Dr. Schumer was now at rest, here, and there, and there. Stan wondered if Dr. Schumer had had any idea what he would do for Stan. Did he know about Stan's life, about what it had become? Was it just pure luck that Stan had been chosen? Was it, somehow, Fate? Stan rejected the latter possibility in his usual commonsensical way. Luck, then, he thought. How fortunate. He would never have traveled as he had. He would never have visited the places he had visited. He would never have changed as he had. He would never have met Annie. Pure luck, Stan thought. Good luck.

As he floated freely in his thoughts, he heard a strange beeping sound coming from the seat next to him. When he had entered the plane, he was surprised to be sitting next to a young boy, perhaps ten or eleven, alone. Stan had assumed the boy's parents were somewhere else on the plane, last minute additions who could not sit together. If his parents were on the plane, they had not checked on their son, so far as Stan knew.

Stan asked the boy what he was playing with and was told PlayStation 2. He said this without looking up and without removing his rapidly moving fingers from the small electronic instrument. At one point the boy stopped and without looking up at Stan said, "You wanna try it?" Stan declined politely.

"You're pretty good at that," Stan said.

"Yeah."

"You play that a lot?"

"Yeah."

Stan was intrigued that the boy had so little to say. He was also challenged by it.

"So," Stan said, "Where are your parents?"

"Euclid. That's in Ohio."

"I know," Stan said, "So who are you traveling with?"

"Nobody."

"Nobody? Aren't you a little bit young to be traveling by yourself?"

"No, I do it all the time. My grandparents put me on the plane in New York. My parents pick me up in Cleveland. They even have one of the flight ladies put me on the plane and take me off. They don't really need to do that. I know what to do. I'm eleven. But I guess they have to do it or something."

So you travel all by yourself?"

"Yeah."

"And you play with the Play Station?"

"Yeah."

"So how's school going?"

"Good."

"You know —" Stan sensed this conversation was going nowhere, so he tried a new approach. "What's your name?"

"Danny."

"So, Danny, my name's Stan. I'm a teacher."

"You are? What grade do you teach? I'm in fifth grade."

"I teach in a college."

"Really? What's your college teacher's name?"

Stan was taken back by the question and then realized what Danny meant. "Oh, you mean — Pickering. Dr. Pickering? Is that what you mean?"

"Yeah."

At least I was a college teacher until I retired."

"So you're not a teacher, really."

"I guess not."

Stan was getting desperate for something to discuss, anything. Usually Stan just ignored kids. But this one was interesting, independent in a way, confident, at ease with himself, especially for an eleven-year-old.

Danny continued playing with his Play Station. "Do you have any kids," he asked Stan. Stan thought about his old response about not knowing of any but decided against it and simply said no.

Stan then asked, "Do you have a girl friend?"

"Yeah," Danny said, "Two."

Stan was impressed. "How do you manage two girl friends?"

"I don't talk to them?"

"You just ignore them?"

"Yeah."

Stan was now more than impressed; he was intrigued, perhaps because he was in total ignorance of what constituted the world of an eleven-year-old boy. "Then why have two girl friends, or even one, if you ignore them?"

"I don't know. It's fun."

"Oh." Stan was no closer to understanding what was in Danny's mind. He decided to give up, especially now that they were beginning their descent into Cleveland. Twenty minutes, Stan thought, and then a two hour bus ride. Home. What would that bring? Talking with an eleven-year-old is easy compared to conversations in Carlow.

"You have a girl friend?" Danny asked, still furiously working the PlayStation 2. He was obviously a master of multi-tasking.

Stan suddenly returned from Carlow.

"Me?"

"Yeah."

"Well, I don't know. I'm sort of old for a girl friend." Stan was trying to figure out how to respond to Danny, and then he realized responding to Danny would be easy. How would he answer that question to himself?

"Anybody can have a girl friend," Danny said, again without looking up.

"Oh, right. I suppose I do. She's not just a girl friend. Maybe more. I don't know. Do you miss your girl friends when you're in New York?"

"No."

Stan paused for a moment before responding. "Then maybe she is more than my girl friend." He was thinking about Annie in a new way. What would his life be without her? He misses her now. What will he feel six months from now? Twenty years from now? He saw clearly in his mind what it would be like to have her with him, to share meal after meal, to learn about her likes and dislikes, to know her past intimately, to sit in a darkened movie house with her.

Danny was back in his own world as the plane neared the airfield. Now it was no more than twenty feet to touchdown. Ten. Five. Stan felt the bump of the wheels on the tarmac. Danny closed his Play Station and looked out the window. Then he turned to Stan and looked at him for the first time.

"When I get home, the first thing I'm gonna do is call my grandparents and tell them I got home okay. What's the first thing you're gonna do?

Stan thought for a moment before responding. "I don't know."

"Will you phone someone?"

"Maybe," Stan said.

By the time Stan was out of the airport in Cleveland, it was well into the evening and more than twenty hours since he had awakened, but he wanted to get back home, so he took a taxi to the bus station and waited for the bus that went through Carlow. He knew he would arrive late at night, but even with his luggage, he could walk to his house from the bus stop.

And then he was home. This strange place. He thought he should call Annie to let her know he arrived safely, but he also knew it was the middle of the day in Japan and she would be in class, so he decided to rest a bit, until morning, and then call her. He slept for twelve hours, and by then it was the middle of the night in Japan, so again he thought he really should not call her. He would wake her up. He was sure she would understand. So he unpacked his luggage, made himself some coffee and sat in his kitchen, thinking hundreds of thoughts, all at the same time. Whom to see? What to say? Where to start? What to do?

Late in the afternoon, Stan decided to go over to the campus and walk around a bit. He figured by now everyone would be off campus, back to their homes or wherever they go when classes are finished and office hours end. He was wrong. He heard a voice call him. "Hey, Stan. I didn't know you were back. How's it going?" It was Tom Osgood. The theorist. Just what I need my first hours back, Stan thought, and then said to himself, at least he's not Priscilla.

"Hi, Tom. Yeah, Good. Good to be back." Now why did I say that, Stan thought.

"I heard you were traveling. Nobody seemed to know where."

"Yeah, traveling."

"So why didn't you keep in contact?"

"Busy, I guess."

Tom continued talking. Stan tried to get away. "Say, did you hear about the English Department party at Priscilla's house? It's starting about now. End of semester, you know."

"No, I hadn't heard. Actually, I've just got back. Flew in yesterday, from Russia. Still a little groggy."

"Russia. What were you doing in Russia? It's winter there, isn't it?"

"Almost. I was just sightseeing."

"So anyway, you're invited to the party."

"I don't think so. First I heard about it."

"Yeah, I just invited you. You spent a good part of your life in this department. The least we can do is spring for an invitation. Priscilla won't mind. She invites everybody, even some non-English Department people. Besides, everyone will want to see you again. Find out what you've been doing. Of course, you're going to have to be a lot more talkative than you are now. Any great adventures?"

"You've no idea," Stan said.

And so, a short time later, Stan found himself, after a few drinks and the occasional hello, in conversation with Priscilla Kinsella, Chair of the English Department and the person who made it easy for Stan to accept Professor Schumer's generous offer to sprinkle his ashes around the world.

"Good to see you, Stan. You look well."

"I am, Priscilla," Stan said, and then realized this was the first time he had called her by her first name. "Thank you," he added with a smile, swirling his drink a bit.

"Good trip?" she asked. Priscilla shifted her weight from one foot to another. This won't take long, Stan thought.

"Good," Stan said and looked around to see if anyone new had arrived.

Priscilla spoke as though duty called. "Things are pretty much the same around here. People finishing up the semester. Papers, finals, that sort of thing. I know this is a bit early for a Christmas party, but as you know we finish up early around here. Academics can always use a party. At least that's my take on academics. Do you agree?"

"Yeah."

Stan could tell that Priscilla was trying hard to be civil, but he was pleased with her discomfort. She tried a new tack. "I hear you did some traveling."

"Some."

"So where did you go?

"Around."

"Around where?"

"Around the world." Stan enjoyed the game.

Priscilla persisted. Stan had no idea why.

"Really," she said, "Where did you go? I'm interested. I've done some traveling. I like to hear about other people's traveling. Did you get to England?"

"Yeah," Stan replied, again reluctantly, but then he began to warm up. "London. Cambridge. Places. I visited where Rupert Brooke and Virginia Woolf swam naked. Together."

"Really." For the first time Priscilla seemed interested. "Where else?"

"Greece, Syria, Malaysia, China, Russia."

"My. You did get around."

"You might say that," Stan said, and then added, "You ever see the Great Wall?"

"No."

"How about Greece?"

"Yes," Priscilla brightened up. "I attended a conference there once, in Athens. I forget the topic."

"How about the island of Skyros? Rupert Brooke is buried there."

"No, I didn't know that." By now Priscilla was beginning to look around for a way out. Her interest had peaked.

Stan continued, thinking she's not going to get off so easily. "Penang is a beautiful island off the Malaysian coast. I spent some time there. Ever been there? No? Didn't think so. How about Damascus? No." Moscow? You must have been to Moscow? No? Then you've probably never been to St. Petersburg either. Amazing places. You should really go there sometime.

Priscilla excused herself, explaining that she should look after her other guests. "You shouldn't try to monopolize me, Stan," she said.

Stan refreshed his drink and looked around the room, cautiously. Rodney Sweeney was over in a corner by himself. Stan could not face a lecture on Medieval tapestry. And then he saw Maria, the only person he hoped would be at the party but didn't really expect to be there. He knew the chances were small since she was not in the English Department, but he had noticed several other non-English types there, especially from the library. He assumed Priscilla wanted to be on the good side of librarians. Most English types do. And there she was, all alone, sitting in an alcove, obviously feeling out of place. Stan walked over and stood for a moment. Maria was somewhere else.

"Hi."

Maria turned and looked up. "Stan? My God, you're back. How have you been? Where have you been?"

"It's good to see you too."

"I heard you were off on some sort of secret mission."

"No, it wasn't secret. Just helping someone out. I just didn't tell anyone."

"CIA?" Maria laughed. She looked up at Stan and smiled. "You know, Stan. We have to stop meeting like this."

"I know we should," Stan said, and then added, "But it's kind of fun, isn't it?"

He sat down beside her, but looked straight ahead.

"How's your husband?

"Fine, Stan. Thanks for asking. We're doing well, really well"

"Happy?'

"Yeah. We're happy."

Stan looked at Maria, into her eyes.

"That makes me happy, too."

Maria smiled. "You've met someone," she said. It was not a question.

"How —" Stan shook his head and said. "Women are amazing."

"You did. Right? I can tell."

"How can you tell?"

"I don't know. The look. Something. The demeanor. I can just tell. Am I right?"

"Maybe. Maybe not."

"You've changed."

"It doesn't always take a woman to change you."

"True. But in your case it did."

Stan tried to change the subject. "Travel does it too," he said.

"Really? So tell me where you've been."

"All over."

"All over where?"

"All over the world. Literally. England, Greece, Syria, Malaysia, China, Russia.

"Interesting," Maria said and then brightened. "So which was the lucky country?"

"The lucky country?"

"Yeah. Where you met her?"

"Jesus, Maria. Don't you want to know about me?"

"Yeah. Sure. You and her. I know. I can tell. Stan?

"What?"

"You're blushing."

Stan thought, God, I hate it when a woman does that to me.

"So what's she like?"

"I don't know." He knew it was out now. She had tricked him. He was glad.

"You don't know? Is she pretty?"

"Pretty? I guess so. I really hadn't thought about it. She's bright, intelligent I mean. She's funny, witty. She's a teacher, English teacher. In Japan."

"Is she Japanese?"

"No, she's just teaching there. She loves it, loves Japan."

"Too bad."

"She's divorced. Has a son."

"'So how did you meet?"

"On a boat. Going from the Malaysian mainland to the island of Penang."

"That's so romantic, Stan."

"Not really. We got drenched."

Maria was on a mission.

"Have you been to Japan?" she asked.

"No," Stan said.

"You will," she said, "Trust me. I can tell these things."

Stan relaxed and told Maria about Penang, about their meeting on the boat, in the rain, about the funicular railroad, about their exploring the island togeth-er, and then about Russia, especially about St. Petersburg. She laughed at the description of Lenin's tomb and cried a bit with Stan when he told her about the girl in the train station, telling him he had done all he could. But she was most interested in hearing about Annie. As Stan talked about Annie to Maria, he came to see Annie in the context of his own life, and he liked what he saw. She was part of it.

All too soon, at least for Stan, Maria said she really had to go. She told Stan that her husband was working late, and she had promised she would be home by the time he got home. "Actually," she said, "I didn't tell him that; I just want to be there. I guess I told myself."

Stan said he understood. He watched her walk over to Priscilla and thank her for the evening, and then as she walked out the door, she turned and gave Stan a small wave. He smiled.

Later that evening, about ten o'clock, Stan called Annie, hoping that she would still be home.

"Hi," he said, "It's Stan."

"Stan. I know it's you. I've been waiting for your call. Is everything okay?'

"Everything's fine. Sorry I didn't call earlier. This time thing has me all confused, and I crashed for twelve hours when I got here. It was the middle of the day your time. And then when I woke up, it was the middle of the night your time."

"That would have been fine, Stan You can wake me up any time."

Stan hesitated. "Annie?"

"Yes, Stan?"

He didn't know what to say. "How is Japan?"

"Japan? Japan is just fine." Annie laughed and then said, "Stan, you are so – Stan. Don't change, okay?"

Stan did not know what she was talking about, but said, "Okay."

He then took a deep breath and tried not to shake or at least not let his voice shake. He knew for the first time in his life what he wanted.

"Annie?"

"Yes, Stan."

"I'm coming to Japan."

"You are? When?"

"Tomorrow."

Author Biography

Arthur L. Ford is Professor Emeritus of English and Playwright-in-Residence at Lebanon Valley College in Annville, Pennsylvania. While at Lebanon Valley College he taught a variety of courses, serving as department chair for eighteen years. He also taught as a Fulbright lecturer in American Literature at Damascus University, Syria, and at Nanjing University, China.

Later in his career he was appointed Dean of International Programs at the college and was charged with recruiting international students and setting up study abroad programs. Retired since 2001 he and his wife, Mary Ellen, continue to travel.

In addition to the usual academic publications, Dr. Ford has published his own poetry, plays, and short fiction. He is the author of a non-fiction book, <u>Cinderella and the Seven Dwarfs: The Lebanon Valley College's 1952-53 Basketball Team's Improbable Run to the NCAA Sweet Sixteen</u>, and the novel, <u>Shunned</u>.

Made in the USA
Lexington, KY
24 July 2010